TROUBLE IN TOMBSTONE

Richard S. Wheeler

A SIGNET BOOK

SIGNET
Published by New American Library, a division of
Penguin Group (USA) Inc., 375 Hudson Street,
New York, New York 10014, USA
Penguin Group (Canada), 10 Alcorn Avenue, Toronto,
Ontario M4V 3B2, Canada (a division of Pearson Penguin Canada Inc.)
Penguin Books Ltd., 80 Strand, London WC2R 0RL, England
Penguin Ireland, 25 St. Stephen's Green, Dublin 2,
Ireland (a division of Penguin Books Ltd.)
Penguin Group (Australia), 250 Camberwell Road, Camberwell, Victoria 3124,
Australia (a division of Pearson Australia Group Pty. Ltd.)
Penguin Books India Pvt. Ltd., 11 Community Centre, Panchsheel Park,
New Delhi - 110 017, India
Penguin Group (NZ), Cnr Airborne and Rosedale Roads, Albany,
Auckland 1310, New Zealand (a division of Pearson New Zealand Ltd.)
Penguin Books (South Africa) (Pty.) Ltd., 24 Sturdee Avenue,
Rosebank, Johannesburg 2196, South Africa

Penguin Books Ltd., Registered Offices:
80 Strand, London WC2R 0RL, England

Published by Signet, an imprint of New American Library,
a division of Penguin Group (USA) Inc.

First Printing, December 2004
10 9 8 7 6 5 4 3 2 1

Copyright © Richard S. Wheeler, 2004
All rights reserved

 REGISTERED TRADEMARK—MARCA REGISTRADA

Printed in the United States of America

Chapter 1

I still think that I was spared a violent death because God made me an instrument of justice. It's a cast of mind I fell into during that fleeting moment in my life when I lived in Tombstone, Arizona Territory. It's hard to get shut of a mystical feeling like that, and it still yanks me awake sometimes. *Why am I alive?* And then I gaze out the bedroom window upon a peaceful night, and think that forty years hasn't changed me much.

As I look back, I often wonder how that damned trouble began down there in Tombstone. I've spent my life reliving those months, trying to make sense of it all. How did it start? Was it when I discovered that Billy Clanton had stolen my racehorse, and I confiscated it? He didn't like that and squinted at me with eyes measuring me for a coffin.

Maybe it was simpler than that: trouble found me and my brothers when we pinned on the badges we wore. From the moment we took oaths of office and served as peace officers, we faced troubles that spiraled out of control, murdered and wounded my family, and grievously damaged my reputation. Before it was over, Morgan lay cold in his grave, wounded once and then murdered; Virgil was maimed, wounded once in the street fight, and then taken to death's door by assassins in the dark of Tombstone.

While I escaped a score of bullets that seared by, my reputation as an honorable man lay in tatters. That was the brawl I didn't know how to fight, and the one I lost. I bore those knife scars ever after, but no one sees them.

I am old now, and I sometimes conjure up the past, hoping that maybe I'll have some new perspective on those Arizona times. Tombstone made me a notorious person, so that is where I travel in my mind's eye these days. How the hell did it happen?

I never was much for telling my story, although I tried it a few times. I'm not fancy with words. I am so much a private man that I never succeeded. But I keep mulling these things in my mind, and I don't suppose I'll ever make them known. What I really think about Tombstone is going to die with me, and that's the way I want it.

The only sense I can make of Tombstone was that trouble was there, waiting for us, even before the Earps rolled into town from the territorial capital, Prescott, where Virgil had been doing some lawing.

Tombstone lay in an arid hinterland along the Mexican border, a land thinly populated by a few Apaches off their reservation, a scatter of Mexican farmers in the river valleys, and a number of renegades. There were some isolated ranches and a few mining camps, but mostly it was empty and dry. There was not much to recommend the place except the silver that lay thick and deep in veins that outcropped there.

What I didn't know then, and was slow to grasp, was that Southeast Arizona Territory had become a paradise for badmen, who could live exempt from law and all the ordinary rules of God and man. The new mining camps needed beef; how simple it was to slide across the border, lift Mexican cattle from the big ranchos south of the line, rebrand them in mountain hideaways, and hawk them cheap to butchers in Tombstone, Contention, Charleston, and other towns. It beat working at an honest job for a living.

But something much more important than ordinary banditry was infecting that place. That crowd had a certain attitude I had never come across before and have not seen since. Yes, I'm talking about a cast of mind among those outlaws. You may not think something like that is important, but I do. That attitude is why poor Morgan lies in his grave, and I've been thinking about it for years. If I ever explained all that to a reporter, he'd think I'm senile, slap his notebook closed, and abandon the interview. So I keep it to myself and the idea will die with me.

It was as if they were the lords of that corner of the world. I remember when my brother Virgil, the deputy U.S. marshal, was asked by a certain army lieutenant named Hurst to help track down some stolen army mules, and these were eventually located on the McLaury ranch, where some ranch hands were in the process of changing the US brand into a D8 right before his eyes.

Here's the amazing thing. The rustlers were so incensed that the army was actually after them for merely stealing a few mules that Hurst backed off after extracting the promise that the rustlers would return the livestock. They weren't returned, of course, and then Lieutenant Hurst rolled into action, accusing the McLaurys and Pony Deal and others of stealing the critters, and sending Virgil after them.

Virgil told me that a little later the enraged McLaury boys actually stopped him on the street and threatened to kill him if he went after them for stealing some damned old army mules. *You'll have a fight if you do,* they told him. Imagine saying that to a United States marshal. It was as if *they* were the affronted parties. That's the attitude I'm talking about.

Virgil shrugged it off, but he shouldn't have, as events would prove. That was when I began to fathom that this place, Southern Arizona, was different from any other I had known. It was as if we were living in the heart of an outlaw kingdom; it was they, not us, who were the government. In Dodge City, Kansas, not even the wildest cowboys up from Texas imagined that they were exempt from law and order.

Little did I know then that, with one exception, those who tried to preserve peace and property in that area were marked men. That exception was the sheriff, John Behan, who was minting money by carefully not noticing the rustling and robbing throughout his county. But that came later. When the McLaurys first threatened Virgil, Behan wasn't sheriff.

I remember the lies. There were more lies spun in Cochise County, Arizona Territory, in the space of two years, than in the rest of the entire world, and most of them involved me. I have not overcome those lies— maybe never will—and they have governed what people think of me all of my days. That still bothers me, even four decades later. I knew plenty about lawing but not much about lies before all this began. Words are bullets, but that didn't dawn on me at first.

Before I was done with Arizona, I had been accused of robbing stagecoaches, shooting men with their hands in the air, pursuing a private vendetta, and violating laws of all sorts. I'm a quiet man, not given to gabbing the way Sheriff John Behan was, so I didn't really know how to deal with his insinuations, his cheerful clap on the back, his smiles and good humor. He was a politician.

I'm not a politician, and that explains how I got into trouble. My brothers aren't politicians either. We don't glad-hand people on the streets, except maybe Morgan did once in a while. I keep to myself, keep my life private, and live as quietly as I could. At least I did until this Tombstone business changed everything. I would just as soon not talk at all, but now that notoriety has caught up with me I will talk to some fool reporter, mostly to keep him from spreading any more lies.

My purposes have always been simple. I want to get ahead. I am the only Earp brother with a business instinct. It was I who suggested we roll down there to that arid corner of the world, because I saw profit in it. We know mining and cattle towns, and know how men with our skills can get ahead. So I rounded up Morgan and his wife, Louisa, persuaded Virgil and his wife, Allie, and told Mattie we were heading for the new mining camp. It didn't take much to persuade Jim and Bessie, either.

Before we started, Virgil got himself appointed a deputy United States marshal by Crawley Dake up there in Prescott, and soon enough I got myself a deputy sheriff job for Pima County, having a little experience in that field. We made some private arrangements too. I worked for Wells Fargo, mostly as their eyes and ears. I was a company detective, but also a shotgun messenger. Morgan rode shotgun on Wells Fargo coaches that carried bullion out of Tombstone and cash payroll in, and sometimes I did also. That was how the Earp brothers got along.

There were other ways of making money in a new camp, and we plunged in, picking up some good silver claims and buying town lots, a surefire way to get ahead. They would all skyrocket if the silver didn't play out, and we would all profit. The camp was hardly more than a shack town before Jim was tending bar at Vogan's, I was running a faro game, Morgan was guarding the stagecoaches, and Virgil was doing all sorts of police work and handling federal crimes.

We purchased three shotgun houses side by side and moved in, making a sort of Earp corner out of Fremont and First streets. I am strong on family ties: it was a plentiful convenience to have so many brothers and their wives at hand. In time, Virgil became city marshal as well as a federal one, and all that while, Tombstone enjoyed perfect tranquillity. He, like me, moved hard and fast to stop peace breakers in their tracks, and it seemed to work. It certainly worked in Dodge City while I was policing there. The idea that Tombstone ate a man for breakfast is nothing but the scribbling of crackpots. There was little bloodshed at any time we were lawmen, except for our hoedown with the McLaurys and Clantons. That peace was largely Virgil's doing.

But even as we settled in, bought mining claims, tended bar, or ran a faro game, things were changing. We hardly noticed, except that Tombstone suddenly was a wooden town, no longer a canvas one. And some of the resorts were fancied up to attract that class of men who habituate them. There were miners everywhere, about 650 in a town of four thousand, most of them working in the Toughnut or the Contention or the Lucky Cuss, and the rest of the town consisted of carpenters and teamsters, butchers and merchants, and their wives and families. Ordinary good folks. There were two satellite towns, Contention and Charleston, located on the San Pedro River, and in each place mills processed ore and employed another few hundred men.

Tombstone lay in an arid valley, water was scarce and cost a nickel a pail, but the nights were especially fine, cool, and pleasant most of the year, with a bright black sky above. If the days were hot much of the year, the evenings were splendid, and that was when those who lived in that happy camp got together in saloons to enjoy some good company.

There was plenty of cheap beef around, and maybe I should have thought more about where it was coming from, but I didn't at first. Southern Arizona had plenty of fine grama grass, and there were enough ranches to supply a mining camp with all the beef it could consume, and that was all I thought about it. How little I knew. Out there, in those vast and empty spaces, things were changing too.

It was no trick at all for a bunch of rustlers to slip into Mexico, round up a herd of skinny corriente cattle, drive it north, alter the brands in a mountain camp, or drive it to the Clanton or the McLaury ranches, and let them fence the beef for low prices around the mines. No one much cared. It was Mexican beef, after all, and that didn't bother the miners none. What we didn't fathom at first was that all this grassland and desert and dry mountain country was an outlaw empire, and only a certain sort of man was welcome out there, least of all a man with a badge. Once we left the safety of the city, we were entering a forbidding and dangerous world, where any traveler might be halted, robbed, shot, and left for the vultures.

It didn't happen all at once. There seems to have been an outlaw telegraph, a way of putting word out to the wild ones from all over the West: down on the Arizona border, a man could make an easy living and be safe from the law. There never was a single organized gang, as far as I could tell. Just a loose-knit bunch of men without scruples who saw the work and wealth of others as something to be plucked. They picked on the Mexican herds first, but inevitably their successes led to other things, such as picking on Wells Fargo, the company with the perilous task of transporting the wealth of the mines to safety, and carrying money and securities into Tombstone.

They called themselves Cowboys, but they really weren't, and what they did would dishonor honest drovers, the real cowboys who raised and mothered and fathered their beeves and lived an altogether different sort of life from these outlaws who had borrowed the name.

I suppose it was Wells Fargo that finally drew us into the maelstrom, killed and wounded my brothers, and ended up turning the new Cochise County into the bloodiest ground ever seen in the West. They needed shotgun messengers. By 1880 the mines of Tombstone were producing nearly 2.5 million dollars of silver a year. By 1881 they were producing five million of silver. They did even better in 1882, the last year I was there. All that bullion had to be transported to the Southern Pacific Railroad, which was building east from Tucson during that period and had established a stop at Benson, north of Tombstone.

Wells Fargo had the task of carrying all that silver safely, and that is why the company needed shotgun messengers, men like my brothers and me, who knew how to deal with bandits.

A host of big outfits were churning out profits and handing out payroll: the Grand Central Company, the Contention Company, the Vizina, the Toughnut, the Boston and Arizona Smelting and Reduction Company. Wealth was riding on the leather thoroughbraces of the stagecoaches, and that is where the trouble would come. And it did come.

Chapter 2

Who knows what kindles a fire? Maybe it all began that chill evening in the spring of 1881 when I hiked home after closing my game at the Oriental. It wasn't late. There had been little trade that Wednesday night. I hadn't won enough to pay the rent.

I opened my door and stepped into a house colder than a hanging judge. Mattie hadn't tended the stove. I made my way through the shadowed parlor and the dark kitchen, with its dead range to the bedroom in back, and found the untended coal-oil lamp lit and smoking and Mattie sprawled on the bed, all red gingham, disheveled, and half buttoned. She had been to the Chinaman again. Her eyes were as large and black as stovepipes, her lips as loose as a whore's.

She focused briefly, smiled, and sighed. "Want some, hon?" she asked me.

Before I could reply, she began tugging her skirts upward, baring a smooth white calf.

"Five is all, honey," she said, her words as unformed as her loose mouth.

She meant she would charge me only five dollars.

I stared.

"No," I said. Not like that. Never like that.

She pouted. "Suit yourself," she mumbled, and tugged her skirt and petticoat higher, baring corduroyed knees and ribbed white thighs. She was not yet thirty.

I had found her in my sister-in-law's Kansas City

parlor house. I don't know where Bessie picked her up. Mattie was young, halfway pretty, and not used up, not yet anyway. I don't think she had seen her seventeenth birthday. I liked the looks of her and told her I'd take her away. All she had to do was cook and ply her skills whenever I wanted her. Skills she had, fine furious hands and lips and loins that sent me bucking like a two-barreled shotgun.

So I used her and kept her, and found out she'd been born with another name, Celia Ann, and she'd run away very young from a hard and abusive father, and ended up living the life that stray girls fall into. There was not much that was different about it. Thousands of girls end up like that. Her past didn't concern me. The Earps all prefer real women, not stiff and proper females full of manners and prohibitions and legs clamped tight together. Some deacon's daughter would be at the bottom of my list.

So I didn't mind her past. I did mind her future. My brothers and I have always found women wherever they were to be found. Jim hooked up with a boisterous madam named Bessie. Virgil hooked up with an Irish spitfire named Allie, who had a sharp tongue and opinions for all occasions. Morgan pulled Louisa out of a bawdy house, and she exuded musk and animal magnetism. There were moments when I envied my wilder brother. What did it matter? There wasn't a wedding license among the whole lot of us, and we never gave preachers a thought.

Mattie was staring at me, waiting for me to start unbuttoning, professionally licking her lips, leering at me in the squalid light of the lamp. The sweet acrid tang of the opium hung in the air.

It was cold there. I felt my body sag.

"No," I said. "Not like that."

Mattie looked wounded.

Not tonight, not with a woman who wasn't all there, wasn't with me. I didn't ask much, but I did want a woman who would be with me, sharing the trip. I didn't drink, not then. Later I did, and still do. But not then, when I didn't want anything to numb my senses or befuddle my mind. She wouldn't even remember it in the morning.

So I quit her. A two-dollar slut on Allen Street would have brought me more cheer. Mattie had raided the grocery money I gave her, and now I would have to fill her purse again. It was always like that, more and more now. The hell with Mattie.

I didn't even want to be in that cold house, if that little shotgun arrangement could be called a house.

I turned down the wick. Tomorrow she would scrub the smoke-coated chimney. In spite of her vices, she kept a neat house.

"Go to hell," she mumbled.

She got that right, anyway. I walked through black rooms into a lighter starlit night, where a sliver of moon lit my path. My loins ached.

I thought maybe it was time to ease her out. All she had to do was be there, call me Wyatt, but more and more she was off in some other world, and when I wanted her she was gone somewhere.

The night was cold and quiet, and the high desert air drew the stars close to the earth. Tombstone never slept, and I drifted through darkness, wary of the foot-pads who haunted the shadows, until I hit the glowing streets where yellow lamplight spilled from glass-paned doors. I didn't know what time it was. Mid-night, maybe. Time never mattered in Tombstone. There was always a shift coming out of the mines, or another about to drop into the pit, and always prey for gamblers and whores and saloonkeepers. I heard the rattle of a piano as I passed the Eagle Brewery.

I drifted toward the Oriental, the fancy cream-enameled, frosted-glass joint whose restaurant and bar were run by big-nosed Milt Joyce, who was no friend of mine, but what did it matter? I had a piece of the gam-bling concession in the back, and could have reopened my game if I felt like it. I didn't. I was thinking about being alone, all alone, because Mattie wasn't company and my brothers were in bed. At the bar I ordered a sar-saparilla. Joyce surveyed me from behind the bar, look-ing for reasons to nurture his annoyance. He charged me the price of a whiskey.

"Special price for Earps," he said.

I drifted, drink in hand, to a cushioned booth and waited. Its occupant studied me and nodded, so I sat down. I did not introduce myself. She knew who I was. We had been eyeing each other for weeks. Maybe she had been waiting for me, the dark beauty who sat across from me with a glass of red claret before her. Young, hardly out of her teens, an actress with the *H.M.S. Pinafore* company that starred Pauline Markham, the toast of Prescott, Tucson, and Tomb-stone.

I knew the type. Alone. We had been circling each other, looking for the right moment. I had checked into her situation a little. She had lived with Smiling John Behan, proprietor of the Dexter Livery Stable, now deputy sheriff of Pima County. She had no visible means of support, but actresses somehow manage, either vertically or horizontally. A lone woman in a saloon after midnight.

"Mrs. John Behan," I said.

"Not now," she replied.

"Then what?"

"Chanteuse on occasion."

"I prefer to know a woman by her real name."

She smiled. "Josie Marcus."

"The former Mrs. Behan, then."

"There are about three Mrs. Behans, depending on who he's laying at the moment. I was dumb enough to think it would last. He has a hell of a smile, and he touches you on the shoulder and arm like you're his long-lost sister. And he has magical fingers that do nice little things."

That was a fine, outstanding confession, and I admired it. This one had shared Behan's bed and board for a while. She was an actress, featured in a recent production out of San Francisco; he, a stagedoor johnny. Their arrangement hadn't lasted long.

Behan was really a politician, smiling, glad-handing, backslapping, and cold-eyed, but not many saw the calculating eyes. He had a way with women. For that matter, he had a way with most everyone. It was a gift of his, being everyone's pal. And it paid off. He had his choice of women, and now he was sucking the tax dollars of the new Cochise County into his own pocket. I was waiting to see if I would get a cut. We had made a deal: I would not oppose him for sheriff of the new county, and he would name me his undersheriff. I'd handle the law enforcement; he'd handle the tax collections and get to keep ten percent.

So I didn't run for sheriff. I figured it would work out better, me being undersheriff. Behan was a Democrat; Governor Fremont was of the other persuasion, but the territorial legislature was Democrat too, and so was the new county. I had thought undersheriff would be a good deal for a Republican like me. But now the days ticked by, and I was not yet an undersheriff, and I was beginning to see Smiling John in a truer light. I am dumb about some things, but I need to learn a lesson only once.

And now, sitting across from me, was his former lover.

That was how I first saw her: a chance to stick it to Johnny Behan. But my eyes were telling me other things. She was a hell of a girl, this Josie, with delicious curves and creamy flesh. There was an adventuresome quality about her; a timid woman would not be sipping claret alone in a saloon at midnight. There are some women born for just one thing, who exude only one thing, and this young lady knew it and used it, but she was also prim, and I couldn't fathom how a woman could be so openly sensuous and prim at the same time. It was a hell of a thing, sitting across a table from her, wanting to tear that table out by its roots.

"You're Wyatt," she said, in a voice that rang of French horns. "Johnny talks about you."

"What does he say?"

"You're an old pal of his."

I smiled.

"That you've got a wife."

I nodded.

"That you never drink. Or do anything."

I lifted the glass. "Sarsaparilla," I said.

"Or anything." There was a question in her sultry voice.

I didn't answer. I don't talk much. She had one of those complexions, smooth and creamy, that women envy. But that wasn't it. There was something coiled up in her, some sort of tigress inside. I am poor with words. I can't describe it. I only knew that I dared not touch her, because if I did, I wouldn't stop touching her. Now, with decades behind me, I still marvel that any woman could shoot such electricity through my body.

"Does your wife like sarsaparilla too?"

I didn't reply. Not her business. She was butting into areas where she didn't belong. I was too naive to see the mockery in her question. Mattie was a mechanic; I had never known any woman other than a mechanic of the art of love. But she was a very good mechanic, and had learned her skills well.

But I was about to learn more. Josie knew it; I knew it.

And so did Behan, who wandered in, studied the denizens of the Oriental's posh saloon, and drifted straight toward us.

"Wyatt, Josie," he said, that affable smile on his face.

He knew how to read people and situations better than I did. It was something I never learned.

"Have a drink?" I said.

"No, I'm just keeping the lid on," he said. An odd statement.

I nodded. "Keep that old lid on," I said.

He smiled, drifted off, but not before he gave Josie a cold, assessing gaze. He didn't like the sight of us in a booth at the Oriental after midnight, the two of us several blocks from my bed and my wife.

I sensed that something had passed between us, and in that, at least, I was right. From that moment on, Sheriff Behan would look for ways to make life miserable for the Earps. But I didn't see it that way then—quite the opposite. I was thinking, as he studied us, that this man who might cross me would find the Earps more than he wanted to handle.

Josie finished her wine. "Well?" she asked.

"I'll see you outside," I said.

And thus the transaction was done, without hesitation, without probing, without remorse. It was as calculated as a stock market purchase, or would have been but for the heat of the moment. I stared, seeing straight through the fabric of her costly dress, seeing the ivory of her flesh. Her lips parted slightly. She looked at me, soft-eyed as a doe. I downed my sarsaparilla and slipped outside, drifting out of yellow lamplight spilling from the doors. She found me a couple of minutes later, in the quiet, cold dark, tucked an arm into mine, and led me I knew not where. It turned out to be a one-room cottage at the rear of a house lot on Fremont.

"I don't do this," she said. "I'm not like that. You understand?"

"You're broke and a long way from home."

She didn't reply, but in that moment a transaction had been completed.

She let me in and turned to light the lamp, but I could not wait that long. I grabbed her.

"You'll take care of me, Wyatt?"

"Buck the tiger and see," I said.

"I'm game," she said. I never saw such a knowing smile on a woman.

It wasn't like making love to Mattie. Josie was all there, adventuring.

Life was never the same after that. And now, decades later, our adventuring is still what holds us together.

Chapter 3

Or was it Holliday? Sometimes, when I look back, I think the trouble began the day that Doc stepped off of the Benson stage. If Doc had never come to Tombstone, none of it would have happened. I tell myself that, but I don't really believe it. Doc may have been the lightning rod, and maybe he collected trouble around him, but trouble would have come to the Earps whether or not Doc was dealing cards in Tombstone in 1880 and 1881.

Because of Doc's friendship, my reputation was all but ruined. There are plenty of old-timers in Tombstone to this day who think my brothers and I were stagecoach robbers along with Holliday, and we played a flush hand in the famous holdup of the Benson stage that resulted in the death of the jehu, Bud Philpott, and a passenger. I never knew how to fight lies like that, which were spread by the whole crowd of cowboys and their paper, the *Nugget*.

Maybe someday the historians will sort it out. When they do, they might get around to clearing my name. I never was able to do it myself, and the whole thing rots me and will keep right on rotting until I die, and it'll rot my ghost after I'm laid to rest. They'll find that Wells Fargo put its utmost faith in me before and after that robbery, and that should quiet some of my critics. In all the years I worked for them, the company was as faithful as a deacon's wife. I don't know why I care so much about my reputation, but I do.

Doc was about as opposite from me as a man can get. The Earps were and are yeoman farming stock, plainspoken and strong for the Union and the North during the war. Doc, well, he was different from any sort I'd ever known.

He came from a prominent Southern family, professional and merchant people who owned land and buildings and good names. But that doesn't describe them very well. They were Georgia gentlefolk, and Doc was a Southern gentleman born and bred. They fought for the South, and the family fortunes were gravely damaged by war and defeat and William Tecumseh Sherman's brutal march through Georgia. But I've never heard a bitter word from Doc about that war.

Doc was born with a cleft pallet, which had been repaired by surgery when he was a little fellow, and that affected his speech a bit so that he spoke not as a Southerner, not as anything a man had ever heard before. There were a few things he couldn't pronounce and his sharp, velvety voice would glide past those. Maybe that was one of those things that set him apart. But whatever it was, he was always different from those of us more humbly bred. Put him in a saloon or a gambling parlor with the rest, and he would be as visible as Beau Brummel, and somehow solitary, so ordinary people eyed him and invented stories about him and supposed things about him that weren't at all true.

In fact he was usually gentle, and had the courtesy of a true Southern man. He knew horses and firearms; all men of his station knew them and had been immersed in such things from childhood. They call it a cavalier tradition, but I wouldn't know anything about that, being from Illinois and Iowa originally. All I knew was that he drifted west after practicing dentistry a while. He suffered from consumption, which had ruined his trade. Who wants a dentist coughing up blood while he pokes around your incisors?

Sometimes, during the late-night lulls, when the gambling fraternity was idling at the green baize, waiting for the last lone player to wander in, or the rain to quit, or the next shift to boil out of the mines, we would talk a little. He would ease back in his lacquered chair at the poker table and reminisce. That was when I discovered he was, above all, lonely.

"You know, Wyatt, when you get the goddamned news that you're doomed, that changes everything. It isn't just an early death and a wasting disease you're wrestling with. That's the easy part, the nearness of death. It's . . . broken friendships, broken loves. Broken engagements."

Doc was staring at something within that I could not see, but it was sad.

"I hadn't thought of it, Doc."

"Who'd marry a man whose lungs were dying faster than the rest of him?"

"Was there someone?"

He studied the dregs in his whiskey glass. "There was. Her name was Melanie, and she was my cousin." He eyed me sharply. "Consumption tore us apart. Now she's fixing to become a nun."

"A nun?"

"A warm, brown-haired, yearning, and sweet woman. She's begun her novitiate and soon she'll be Sister Melanie. I had already received my sentence: to live out my days without a wife."

"I thought your family was Presbyterian," I said.

"The Hollidays were wounded by war and we're all seeking solace wherever it might be found," he said softly. He was as close to tears as I had ever seen him.

So there he was, a lonely man set apart. He never again spoke of Melanie, at least not to me. But in that fleeting moment, I learned what consumption had cost him.

As I look back now on Doc, after these many years, I know that he was the loneliest of men, cut off from all normal society by the fatal disease that made him the man outside the window glass looking in upon someone's happy family gathered around the hearth. I understand Doc better now than I did while he lived.

Doc was unique, and like all different people, gossip engulfed him. He may have been a Southerner, but those Cowboys, nearly the whole lot of them bitter ex-Confederates, hated him worse than they did the Yankees and Republicans running Arizona Territory. And it wasn't just because he was my friend, either.

Doc started ripples wherever he set foot. Let him start up a game in a saloon and trouble would follow. Let him deal some poker, and there would be those trying to test him, push him. I often think that Doc's greatest virtue was patience. He had a temper but it took a lot to set him off, and I am amazed by the number who tried, right to the end of his life.

I had watched him deal and knew how he played. He was the soul of politeness, that soft Southern civility that welcomed players, smoothed down ruffled feathers, invited cheerful talk. But he was also an experienced man who knew the perversity of those he rubbed shoulders with, and Doc was a man with no illusions. He was usually heeled, as much as any town's constables would permit, with a nickel-plated revolver snugged in a shoulder holster, and he was not loath to use it.

As for his reputation, it was greatly exaggerated. The notion that he had killed dozens of men was simply nonsense. He had been in a scrape or two, mostly with someone who was cheating.

He was not alone in Tombstone. Sharing his quarters above Fly's Photo Gallery was a fiery and weepy woman named Kate Elder, also known as Big-Nosed Kate, his concubine. She had a scarlet reputation. They made a pair: a volcanic gambler and a volcanic whore, but little did the world understand that they were both gently born and spotted that quality in each other, and hated it in each other too.

Mary Kate Harony was the daughter of a Hungarian doctor living in Iowa, but was soon orphaned and placed in the care of a guardian. It must have been a bad time for her; by age sixteen she had escaped and slipped down the Mississippi. By the time I met her, she was one of Bessie Earp's girls in Wichita. By the time Doc met her, she was plying her trade in Fort Griffin.

She and Doc hit it off, and they lived together now and then, the rest of their lives. That is, when they weren't fighting. As long as they treated each other coldly, they got along; the moment she turned tender, or he turned gentle, they fought like banshees. They were both afraid to be discovered caring about the other. She had no use for me, and the feeling was mutual. She was nothing more than a case of giant powder with a short fuse.

Doc had a temper, and it could boil up at odd moments, turning the suave and civilized gambler into a menace in a split second. He was supposedly a killer, but I never saw much of that. I always thought he liked people to think it because the reputation kept his poker games peaceable. Maybe he killed or stabbed one or two; they say he killed Ed Bailey at Fort Griffin, after warning Bailey to quit tampering with the cards. But he never was the depraved multiple killer that dime novelists and assorted journalists made him out to be.

Back when we were floating around Texas we got to visiting some, and I told him about Dodge City, a place where he could pursue his vocation without being harassed by the law, as he was in Texas. People have made much of our friendship, reading things into it that never existed.

Some people wonder why a lawman, like me, could befriend a notorious badman, like Doc. But the fact is, he wasn't a badman. He lived his life honorably, was no crook, and made his usual living playing poker or running a faro game. He was good at both, and scarcely needed to make a living by dishonorable means, especially because he could replenish his bank after a streak of bad luck simply by yanking molars. Dentists were in short supply in those frontier towns, and he had all the trade he wanted, consumptive or not.

But he didn't want the trade. What he wanted was a shiny, stiff deck of cards, or some dice, and some players who were half as skilled as he was. Given an evening or two spent in that fashion, he would be primed with all the cash he and Kate ever needed.

It's an odd thing about reputations. The world didn't see him the way I saw him. Garish headlines, gossip, saloon talk—all painted him as a badman. And the only thing that ever supported that notion was his occasional volcanic outbursts, which usually sent saloon patrons scrambling out of the range of that nickel-plated, ivory-gripped revolver nestled at his breast.

Neither Virgil nor I had serious trouble with him as we patrolled Tombstone. Once Virgil separated Doc from a two-bit tinhorn who was threatening to exterminate him. The reality was that Doc was our ally. In any hoedown, he was ready to back us up, and once in Dodge he did just that when I was trying to disarm a boozy cowboy who got the drop on me. He may have saved my life. I accepted and enjoyed his friendship, not least because Doc was honorable. I saw no reason to distance myself from his company, even if his occasional rages brought him to the brink of murder.

Little did I know when Doc and Kate first rented rooms in Tombstone the sort of trouble it would lead to: not bullets, but words. That's always been my weakness. Some people a lot smarter with words use them as weapons, and they're as deadly as a lead pill.

If Doc had a reputation as a badman, and Wyatt was Doc's friend, that made Wyatt a badman too. That was the logic of it, and the case was so compelling, at least the way the *Nugget* dished it up during the trouble, that people believed it. A gambler reputed to lay many a man in his grave comes to town; a lawman is his friend; suddenly the lawman's guilty of robbing stagecoaches and siphoning off the very gold that he's been paid by Wells Fargo to protect.

But I'm ahead of my story. When Doc arrived, I welcomed him. He and Luke Short and Bat Masterson were all friends of the Earps, hard men who could be counted on to help enforce the law if the Cowboys and rustlers and badmen sailed out of control. And it happened, down the road a few months, that trouble came,

but by then Bat and Luke had decamped, and there
was only Doc for an ally.

"Wyatt, what's the best place to set up my game?"
he asked, just as soon as he'd taken rooms at Fly's.

"Oriental. It's a few cuts above anything else in
town. It draws the trade. But it's also no place for anyone friendly with Virgil or me."

Doc cocked a blond eyebrow and grinned. He was
waiting for an explanation.

"Milt Joyce, he runs the saloon part of it. He's no
friend of the Earp brothers. He's a Democrat who sides
with the Cowboys."

"Well, hell, Wyatt, I'm a Democrat and I side with
the devil. But the only good thing about Cowboys is
their ache to get rid of their pay at my game."

That was Doc.

I spent the next few hours running through the politics of Tombstone, and who the Cowboys were and
how they made their living. Getting a pay envelope
every week wasn't one of those ways.

Doc thought it was funny. I'm a solemn sort, slow
with words, and when I try to make a case the ideas I'm
trying to express go skittering off, but Doc just stood
there beside me at the Eagle Brewery, sipping whiskey
while I worked on a sarsaparilla, and I made no headway at all.

"You'll see," I finally glowered.

Doc just laughed.

"Wyatt," he said, "I'll even side with Republicans
and carpetbaggers if I have to."

He drank to that. Much later, many years later, his
wit haunted me.

Chapter 4

By the time 1881 was half over, I had formed a good idea of John Behan and decided to run against him in the next election. Behan was a slippery character with a glib word for everything, and a way of shifting the blame whenever people wondered whether the new Cochise County had a real sheriff. He was a Democrat in a heavily Democrat new county; it would be uphill for me. But I wanted the job and needed the money. And I soon had a score to settle with the sonofabitch.

The sheriff served as tax collector and kept ten percent for his efforts, and that meant that Behan was pocketing a fortune. He wasn't interested in enforcing the law, which is part of the reason he was so popular. Everyone but me called him Johnny; I never did. He had an infectious smile, a clap of the hand on the shoulder for every pal, and a way of turning everything into a quip or a joke. I wasn't smart enough to grasp that these things were weapons, and Behan was getting exactly what he wanted out of Cochise County.

I wanted that office, and not just because it would fill my pockets, either. He had welshed on our deal; I should have been undersheriff, but that went to his pal and ally Harry Woods, editor of the *Nugget*. No one welshes on me and walks away, and I knew I would run against Behan, any way and every way, until I whipped him.

I suppose the feeling was mutual, especially since I began keeping Josie. She had been, for a while, "Mrs.

John Behan," until she wearied of his wandering
pecker, and then she was mine and only mine. I offered
her a living, and told her that if I paid her rent, she
would be all mine. She had tried to survive with an occasional discreet liaison, an actress in between jobs, and
I wanted her to cut that out. She leapt at the chance, not
liking what she was becoming.

I was tired of Mattie—tired of her melancholia and
her opium, tired of a drab house that had no happiness
in it. My brothers never said a word about Josephine,
but they knew. They had seen too much of Mattie to
question me. So I left Mattie alone in her stupor and
whiled away my time with a little cupcake who was
fast company. It was purely commercial: I had bought
a lively woman. And it was revenge. I paraded her in
front of Behan, made sure Josie was with me every
night. I made no bones about it, and if John Behan
didn't like it, all the better.

Odd how it worked out. I bought Josie and used her,
and next I knew, we were spending a lifetime together,
and she's a fierce and loyal wife. I was lucky. I had
snared an actress and put her in a love nest. But of all
that I say nothing now. The prying public doesn't need
to know anything about it.

All this was afoot while I was taking the measure of
the new sheriff and his stable of deputies. Among them
were little Dave Neagle, a tough and honest lawman as
far as I could tell, toothy Billy Breakenridge, an excitable and porky fellow without much judgment, and
Frank Stilwell, a hard and cynical mustang whose loyalties to the Cowboys were well known.

It was Deputy Stilwell who interested me the most.
Why the hell had Behan given him a badge? Probably

because the Cowboys demanded it. Or more likely, a Clanton or a McLaury, or maybe Ringo or Brocius, had cut a deal with Behan. They wanted one of their own in the county sheriff's office. Still, I wasn't ready to call Behan himself a crook—not until later. Venal, on the take, yes. But eventually I realized smooth Johnny was pig swill.

Josie was more than willing to talk about her former lover, and in language that tickled my fancy. Josephine Marcus was one hell of a woman then and now. I didn't really understand Behan until she made the man plain to me.

"Wyatt," she said over some claret at Vogan's, "you think too much. Johnny is simple. He wants more of everything, has no scruples about getting it, and he's got small balls. That's all there is to the man."

She eyed me levelly. "I rang his fire bells. He'd never had a real woman before. Not like me, anyway."

I had never heard a woman talk like that before.

She smiled seductively. "And when he found out what little Josephine Marcus could do for him, was he satisfied? No. There must be other women who'd drive him even wilder, so he started roaming. He propositioned every madam on Allen Street for starters. God, Wyatt, that's how he is.

"I thought I was Mrs. John Behan, but the better I was at doing that, the more he wanted. He didn't know a thing about women until he met me. Then he learned. And after that, he found them, and they serviced him, and I was nothing but Johnny's castoff. That's Johnny Behan. If he gets a good lay, he looks for ten better, and he doesn't care how he gets them."

She was smiling and licking her lush lips and I

wanted to hush her up, talking like that. I'd never known a woman like that, and eventually Josie and I could talk privately about anything, and read each other's moods so well we didn't need to talk at all. By God, she was a man's woman.

She's not like that now. Her mouth's full of sawdust whenever anyone asks how we got hooked up, and she's chasing after respectability, and whenever I bring up the past, she pretends not to remember, and she's working on me to tell the world about a romantic courtship that never happened. I laugh and pat her sagging behind. But I'm not like I was back then, either.

So John Behan was simple: he wanted more, and didn't care how he got it, and that's all there was to him. I never forgot that. Josie had a way of cutting through to the heart of things. Some people can be explained in one sentence. He wanted to be sheriff, offered his rival Wyatt Earp a deal, and then welshed on it. John was as simple as could be. You didn't need to know anything more about him.

The very day he was appointed by Governor Fremont to be sheriff of the new county, I had a chance to see him in action or, rather, in inaction. Virgil had ridden out toward Charleston, exercising my hot-blooded horse, Dick Naylor, when he came across Constable McKelvey of Charleston, driving a wagon pell-mell toward Tombstone. In the wagon was a prisoner, a tinhorn named Johnny O'Rourke, or better, Johnny Behind the Deuce, a basic sort of rattlesnake.

Virgil swiftly learned that the tinhorn had ambushed and murdered a popular mining engineer named Schneider for no good reason at all, possibly an imagined slight, but probably because he and Schneider had some falling out at cards. Boiling along behind the wagon was a lynch mob of enraged miners, plainly intending to string up the tinhorn on the spot. Schneider was a well-liked and honored man.

Virgil, lawman that he is, had no use for lynchings. Swiftly he settled the tinhorn behind him on my racehorse, and made time for Tombstone, where he summoned me from the Wells Fargo office and then deposited the miserable killer in Vogan's Bowling Alley and Saloon, where Jim was keeping bar and had some artillery handy. City Marshal Ben Sippy swiftly showed up with a few armed men, but in the meantime a howling mob of miners had filled the street, all of them summoning the courage to rush Vogan's and grab the tinhorn. I arrived with a shotgun borrowed from Wells Fargo. Across the street, doing nothing and obviously afraid, was John Behan, the famous law-and-order man, still a Pima County deputy, though unknown to us his appointment as sheriff of the new county had been made that very day.

We were seconds from a lynching, and even though U.S. deputy marshal Virgil had no jurisdiction and I had no badge at all (having resigned as a Pima County deputy sheriff in November), the pair of us couldn't stomach a lynching. The killer deserved his day in court. That's what law and order are all about. The crowd had grown ominous and there were plenty of revolvers and some hemp in sight. The crowd had bloomed into a large mob that choked Allen Street, stopping traffic just as it would soon stop O'Rourke's throat.

I took a deep breath. There wasn't time to think things through. I pushed out of Vogan's and confronted the seething crowd, looking for someone I knew. It turned out to be Dick Gird, assayer, partner in the Lucky Cuss and other great Tombstone mines, a leading man.

"Get out of the way, Earp," someone yelled.

"Well, Dick, nice mob you've got here."

"Let us through, Earp."

"Don't be a fool, Dick."

I pointed the shotgun squarely at his chest. The effect was visible. He hesitated, peered up those black bores promising instant death, and sagged a little.

The miners didn't like the thought of their boss dying for this, and they knew I'd shoot if they rushed me. They knew I would stop the lynching with both barrels even if I fell a moment later. A few seconds passed and then the heat faded away. No one advanced a step, though there were enough of them to overwhelm me and the few guns behind me, and take their quarry.

"All right, then," I said. "He'll be tried proper, according to the law."

They didn't move. Then Gird, eyeing those black bores, simply gestured, a wave of his hand, and the crowd began to disintegrate. It had been close.

He nodded curtly, wheeled into the crowd, passed to the rear, and vanished from my sight.

I stared at Behan. He had lounged across the street, doing nothing. He had not attempted to protect the prisoner. He had not risked his precious hide. He had not made any enemies. He had not tried to protect legal process. Yet this was the man who that very day would become the sheriff of the new Cochise County.

Behan turned away as the mob disintegrated.

We ran the prisoner over to the jail, while Constable McKelvey preferred charges, and then we took turns guarding the tinhorn, with no help from Behan, until the mob drifted back to Charleston. Johnny O'Rourke would have his day in court.

The next day the papers referred to the brave officers of the law who had stopped the lynching. They made no mention of me, nor did I much care. I have never paid attention to words, though it strikes me now that I should have. All my life, I didn't pay attention to the things people say, and now in my old age, I realize how dumb that was.

Chapter 5

All these years, I never doubted that the thing that put the match to the fuse was a stagecoach robbery upon the Ides of March of 1881. After that, things whirled out of control, and when it was over, one of my brothers had been murdered, another gravely wounded, and I was regarded as an outlaw and desperado in the very town and county and territory where I had been a lawman.

I was running my faro game at the Oriental that cold night when shouts and alarms boiled up from Allen Street.

Virgil popped in and signaled. At once I closed my game, taking the sixty-dollar loss. When I reached the street, he already had Morg with him, and both were armed.

"Benson stage robbed," Virgil said. "Philpott's dead. Passenger named Roerig dying. Bob Paul chased 'em off."

"Paul? He would."

"Two loads of buckshot."

Paul was the giant lawman who was awaiting the result of an election recount to determine whether he would be the sheriff of Pima County. Meanwhile he was fetching a living as a security man for the stagecoach outfit.

"How many?" I asked.

"Four to eight. We don't know. Paul didn't pause

long enough to count. The wire from Benson didn't say a lot."

"Posse?"

"Behan's organizing one. He wants us."

That surprised me.

"I told him I want Bat and he agreed. Marshall Williams is coming to represent the company. Behan turned down the rest."

"You letting Behan run it?" I asked.

"For the moment. But I'm deputizing you."

That was all I needed to know. Virgil, as a United States marshal, could mount his own posse anytime. There was U.S. mail on that coach.

If I had known then what I know now about Marshall Williams, I wouldn't have let him anywhere near that posse. But he was coming, and we welcomed the help, and the presence of the Wells Fargo agent would be valuable.

The Wells Fargo stagecoach en route to Benson, the railroad junction thirty miles north, had been waylaid not far north of Tombstone. The coach was carrying a heavy load of specie worth $26,000, but the robbers never got it. Bob Paul, the shotgun messenger, had emptied both barrels at the bandits and then took over, driving the coach to safety, leaving Philpott dead on the road behind, and carrying the dying passenger with him.

Mattie had bread and a slab of cheese ready by the time I got my gear together, and I stuffed them in my saddlebag. She was sober, for a change, but morose as usual. We didn't touch; we didn't say goodbye. I didn't thank her, and I suppose I should have. Her lips twisted as she saw me gather gear in the lamplight. I nodded and closed the door behind me.

When I returned to Allen Street, I found most of the posse waiting in the deep dark in front of the Eagle Brewery, including Bat Masterson, a compact and deadly man. He had a rifle in his saddle scabbard. He was an old army scout, gifted at smoking out a faint trail, and I didn't doubt that he would point the posse in the right direction as soon as we had some daylight.

"Wyatt?" he said.

"We need you," I replied.

"Whose posse is this? Yours, Virgil?"

"No, it's Behan's," Virgil said.

"I just want to know who's paying me," Bat said. "I like money." He rode over to the sheriff. "Masterson here."

They shook across horses' withers. "Earp wanted you along, and that's all right with me," Behan said. "I hear you're a good tracker. I'm running the show this time."

"Maybe we'll be lucky," Bat said. He was not one to underestimate the cunning and skills of the outlaws of Cochise County.

It all fit into a pattern. When the Mexican government posted Federales along the border to curb the rustling of Mexican beeves, the wild bunch turned to other pastures, including American ranchers and now the stagecoaches, which were easy pickings unless a shotgun messenger was aboard. Mexican beef was no longer easy to pluck up. I knew at once we'd be seeing plenty of coach robberies. The Cowboys were averse to work, robbery was easy, and there was plenty of traffic on the roads to Tombstone.

We rode quietly into a cold night with a sawed-off moon to light the way. The horses snorted, shivered, and picked up the pace. I felt saddle leather hammer my ass. For once Behan was doing some law enforcement rather than just lining his pockets. He had little choice: if he stayed home in the comfortable saloons of Tombstone this time around, he would hear about it at the next election. From me.

He acted as if he were the Top Tortilla, but Virgil was making the decisions. I don't suppose that Behan liked that, but he was smart enough to keep his yap shut and let a hard professional lawman lead that posse into the cold night.

We didn't get far when we ran into Bob Paul, who was riding back to Tombstone on a borrowed saddle horse. Behind him, slung over a packhorse, was the body of Philpott. I took one look at that shadowed load and felt bad. Everyone knew the cheerful and cool Bud Philpott, as good a man as ever put his fingers around the lines.

"There's one of the best men in the county," Virgil said. "By God, I plan to get to the bottom of this."

Marshall Williams dismounted, walked over to the body, which was tied crosswise over a saddle, and studied it.

"My God," he said. "Not much left of his face, is there?"

"A good driver's alive and happy one moment, dead the next," Morgan said. "It could've been me."

"Passenger named Roerig's dead too," Paul said. "I left him at Benson, wired his family for instructions."

"Tell us about the robbers."

"Several. They wore strange masks that looked like beards. They meant business and fired back the moment we began running. That's when we lost Bud. He tumbled forward off the coach."

"Any you know?"

Paul stared into the darkness. "Not a one."

"What direction did they go?"

"I don't know."

"They didn't chase you?"

"I think I put a ball or two into some."

"Where was this?" Behan asked.

"Three, maybe four, miles north of here. You'll read the sign in this moonlight. A brushy hollow where the road dips and then pulls up. Plenty of cover for ambushers."

"What happened after that?" I asked.

"I had a team out of control. I got hold of the lines, slowed them to a trot and kept on going. I left Philpott on the road—not any choice about that. Came back here as soon as I could wire you from Benson and get a horse."

"You did the right thing," Behan said.

Paul studied the sheriff, nodded—a momentary truce.

"Anything we should be looking for? Unusual hat?" I asked.

Paul shook his head.

"Tall, short, fat, dark, light?" I asked.

Paul just shrugged.

"Southerns? Northerns?"

"No, just a shout or two."

"Black boots, light boots?" I persisted.

"Dusty boots," he said. "Wyatt, I couldn't even tell you the voice if I heard it again."

"You had your hands full," I said. "We'll look for

wounded men, blood on the ground, and several horses."

"I wish I could do better."

"Bob, you saved a coach and twenty-six thousand dollars and some passengers."

"Speaking of that, I asked them for their impressions of the robbery. There might be some clues there. But they saw less then I did, cooped up in there."

I had a small, dark notion come to mind. "You were riding shotgun and Philpott was driving?"

"Just as you say, Wyatt."

"You hadn't switched positions, had you?"

"No . . ."

"This wasn't an effort to settle an election with a bullet, was it?"

"Oh, Wyatt," Behan broke in. "That's a fool question."

"Is it?" I asked.

Bob Paul considered it. "No, that shot was intended for the jehu. They wanted a wreck."

"Just thought I'd ask. Were they Cowboys?"

Paul smiled, his teeth white in the moonlight. "They weren't the mine supervisors," he said.

"Don't jump to conclusions," Behan said. But every other man in the posse already had.

We left Paul and rode quietly north, the smell of resinous desert shrubs caught on the night breeze. The spot was easy to find even in the dark of night. There were plenty of boot prints but nothing distinct. Fresh manure where the horses had been kept. No blood that we could see. There were two trails, one leading to a deserted cabin we all knew about. It showed evidence of the wait beforehand, and was littered with yellow-back dime novels.

There was little else of consequence to get out of the place. It had been a spot to while away the time while the gang waited. Then I spotted a yellowback that had been torn apart. Most of its pages were missing, everything from twenty-seven onward. I kept it. Cowboys like to have a little paper along to wipe their butts or start a fire. I would be looking for those missing pages.

Masterson led us out into the night, along a trail only he could see. There was no one like him for tracking.

"Three, four horses," he said. "Maybe three ridden and a spare. Not a large bunch."

"I don't know how you can tell that. I can hardly see the ground."

Bat turned and grinned. There was something in a Masterson smile you couldn't explain: warmth and chill all at once, serious gray eyes and a welcome on the lips, friendliness and deadliness. No man was better at reading how things happened, at reading other men.

Masterson nodded, and his gaze rested lightly on Behan, who had imperceptibly fallen to the rear of the posse. There was something about it that Bat was reading. Something about it that I was reading too. Maybe John Behan was not eager to catch the bandits. Maybe Behan knew them, knew how they voted and what taxes they anted up—taxes, if that was the word, that made them immune to sheriff's posses.

Virgil caught Bat's silent meanings, and nodded. Morgan was oblivious to that, but he was keeping a sharp eye out for ambush. Even as the posse rode through the night, its purposes had divided.

Chapter 6

Masterson led us straight into Len Redfield's hard-scrabble outfit after three days of tracking. From the hill where we paused, the pearly dawn light revealed a rough-built cabin, no smoke from the chimney pipe, a low adobe barn, and some mesquite pole corrals, all located around a spring shadowed by a big cotton-wood, and a grama-grass meadow grazed down to stubble. Two saddle-stained horses stood side by side in the pen, nose to butt.

Bat was a bulldog; he would burn the image of a hoofprint into his brain and then would follow it to hell and back, across rock, water, hardpan, fields of grama grass, and cactus forests. We had Bob Paul with us now, the man who might remember a voice or a gesture.

The farther we got from Tombstone, the less John Behan liked it, but he was trapped by events. There was no way he could quit the search and win reelection, not with me, his political rival, on a hot trail. That wasn't the only reason he kept to himself: this trail would probably lead straight to one of his cronies. But I had no proof of that. There was a lot going on in Cochise County that eluded me. His deputy, Billy Breakenridge, had joined the posse, and his under-sheriff, Harry Woods, too, and the three had ridden close together, a knot of horsemen often fifty yards apart from the rest of us.

Redfield was one of the Cowboys; like the McLaurys he operated a small ranch that was little more than a holding operation for stolen and rebranded beeves. I couldn't prove it; I didn't need to prove it. We rode in not long after first light, with Behan suddenly leading, well ahead of the rest of us, and some of us knew why. But Morgan didn't head for the ranch house like the rest of us. He angled off toward the outbuildings and corrals, and there he cornered someone who was hastily sneaking into the barn.

"Wyatt," he yelled.

I rode over there to assist. I saw the pair of sweated horses in that pen and Morgan leveling his six-gun on a whiskered young man who reluctantly kept his arms in the air. The fellow was well armed, with a brace of six-guns drooping from skinny hips.

"I don't know what you want me for," the man said. "I was just going out to milk the cow."

Morgan eyed the man's artillery and laughed.

"Slowly unbuckle," I said. "Take a care how you do it . . . if you intend to stay alive."

Whiskers saw my leveled revolver, and eyed Morgan's, and slowly, ever so slowly, unbuckled and let his belt and holsters slide into the dry manure. I motioned him toward the farmhouse.

"Name?"

"I'm just traveling through."

"Traveling Through won't do for a name. I want a name or I'll pound it out of you. When I'm done, you won't even be able to pronounce it."

"Luther King."

We reached the others. I was less interested in King than I was in Behan, who had shrunk into himself. Harry Woods was eyeing the man with frank curiosity.

"This is Mr. King. He was heading for the barn to

milk the cow. He wore a pair of shooters to do the job right," Morgan said.

"Keep him from the Redfields," I said to Behan, eyeing the ranchers who were approaching now, tucking shirts into jeans. "I want to get their stories separately."

Behan nodded, and rode toward the Redfields. But he didn't stop them and a moment later the ranchers and King were palavering. Behan had let it happen. Had wanted it to happen.

I motioned to Morgan, who pulled King away from the Redfields and spun him toward us.

"Who rode the other horse?" Virgil asked.

"What other horse?" King asked.

I laid a barrel over Mr. King's cranium. He howled and clutched his head.

"Name them all," I said, "or we'll help you remember."

"Remember what?"

"Those horses," Bat said, "were at the robbery of the Benson stage. And now they are here. And you were on one."

King mopped his bleeding temple with a bandanna.

"Who were you with?" Virgil asked.

Behan said, "Let's take him to Tombstone. I'll question him there."

I grabbed King by his dirty shirt and pulled him toward me, twisting the fabric, until he was inches away. "Talk," I said, "unless you want another headache." Then I let go suddenly. He staggered, righted himself.

"All I did was hold the horses!"

That was what we were waiting for.

King was holding his head. Blood oozed into matted hair and dripped down his cheek.

"Who?"

"You'll leave me alone?"

"Who?" I lifted my revolver.

He cringed, stared at all of us, but his gaze lingered on Behan.

"I was dragged into it. You know, it was sort of a joke. All I did was hold."

I dropped the barrel again, but he dodged and it smacked his shoulder. I kicked as he dodged, caught him in the shin. He howled.

"Bill Leonard, Jim Crane, and Harry Head."

"Who else?"

"No one else!"

I kicked, caught the shin again.

"Enough, Wyatt," Behan said.

"Where are they?"

"We split."

"Where are they?" I lifted my barrel. "Two horses in that corral, both fresh ridden."

"How should I know?"

"Where will you meet them?"

"I don't know!"

I kicked him again, exact same place. He howled, and hopped around.

"Who shot the jehu and the passenger?" Virgil asked.

"I don't know!"

I lifted my revolver.

"Leave him alone. He's hurt," Len Redfield said.

"He'll hurt more in about two seconds," I replied.

"All I done was hold the horses."

I turned to Bob Paul. "You know Crane and Head and Leonard?"

"By God, I'd like to see them, Wyatt. I got some idea of them, even in the dark."

"Then come along with us. We'll send King back with Behan."

"All right, Johnny, you and your outfit take King back and lock him up good," Virgil said.

Behan stared at Harry Woods and nodded. Why didn't I trust the man?

We had missed Hank Redfield's move. He had slipped off. Next I knew, the rancher was galloping out on a fresh horse. We watched him go, knowing our mounts, jaded after three hard days, wouldn't keep up.

I turned to Len Redfield. "Well, now we know," I said. "That makes Hank a wanted man, don't it? Obstructing justice? Aiding and abetting?"

Redfield glared but said nothing.

"Sort of puts a handle on you too, don't it?" I added. "You run with the churchgoing crowd, I guess. Probably a deacon. You been full-immersion baptized?"

"If you're done here, get off my place."

I smiled suddenly and clapped him on the back. "Well, you can go milk the cow and take up all your stock-growing and fencing and branding your increase, and all those peaceable law-abiding things you do."

I saw fires of rage burst in his eyes, but he clamped his tongue tight.

Behan had manacled King and collected the holster belt. "You keep him tight as a tick, John," I said. "He's evidence."

Behan nodded. A half dozen of us had heard King name names.

"Long ride to Tombstone," Behan said.

"Longer the ride, the more you can charge the

county," Morgan said. Behan missed my brother's meaning. Or maybe he didn't.

We watched John Behan, Harry Woods, and Billy Breakenridge start back, with King riding in front of them, his wrists manacled. I watched them ride into the sweet quiet of an Arizona morning, and knew beforehand that things wouldn't go as planned. John Behan would find ways to thwart us. Or maybe it would be Harry Woods, editor of the *Nugget*, friend of all stockmen except those who possessed their own cattle. But I didn't know what or when or how. I would soon learn.

"Taking any odds?" Morgan asked.

Virgil and I knew what Morgan was driving at, but it eluded the rest.

"Fifty-fifty," I said.

Morgan laughed.

Virgil swore in Bob Paul, and suddenly we were a United States marshal's posse: the Earp brothers, Fred Dodge, Marshall Williams, Bob Paul, and Bat Masterson, who sat his horse eyeing us sardonically.

"You want to follow Hank?" Bat asked.

It was Virgil's call. He nodded.

"Good as any," I said. "Hank wasn't headed for a poker hand in Charleston."

We watered and grained our horses, courtesy of Len Redfield, who glowered at us but had the sense to shut up. I knew that about five minutes after we topped the hill, Len would be saddling up to ride in another direction.

"Enjoyed your hospitality," I said. "King was some strange milkman, though, all got up with revolvers. I guess he was going to shoot a few holes in the bag and put a tin cup under the fountain."

Morgan was smirking.

"We'll see who laughs last," Redfield said.

I took him seriously even if Morgan didn't. It was the way he said it; the way Frank McLaury had said it; the way the Clantons had said it. With murder in their eyes.

We rode hard through that March, through cold and heat, dry and wet, across greasewood flats, grama meadows, paloverde draws, and over piney slopes. The country kept its secrets. We drifted east, toward New Mexico Territory, the sign growing dimmer even to Bat's trained eye, but we uncovered nothing. Leonard, Head, and Crane had split up, and where Redfield was we didn't know either. We lived off the land, having left with few provisions, and the best Virgil could do was give chits to ranchers for meals, for grain, for the few horses we could trade.

Arizona is a vast and empty wild, sweetly beautiful from almost any prospect, some of it covered with waving grama grass, green in the spring sun. It's also a mysterious land, where armies can vanish, where mirages can lure a traveler, where fantasies and delusions heap up in men's minds.

We were worn down to bone.

Bob Paul's horse died one night—it just lay down and didn't get up. Our mounts were done in. When we got to a place on the Southern Pacific, with the creosoted ties smelling strong in the sun, Virgil telegraphed Behan to meet us with fresh mounts and provisions, and named the springs. John never showed. No one else did either. Bat and I walked toward Tombstone for help. Bob Paul, on a fresh saddler, along with Virgil and Morgan, continued the chase.

Jim Hume, chief detective for Wells Fargo, arrived

from San Francisco and posted a three-hundred-dollar reward for each bandit. I didn't think the three hundred would tempt anyone. But Hume considered the robbery crucial, and was determined to bring matters to a conclusion. Solve this, put the bandits away for ten years, and we'd put a damper on stagecoach robbery in the county. He was right to think it, even if Wells Fargo wasn't putting up enough reward money to tempt a shoeshine boy.

After I got back to Tombstone, I kept a wary eye on John Behan's lockup, knowing there were a few dozen Cowboys in town who'd like to spring King. The Cowboy wasn't talking; he whiled away his time exuding good cheer. He sat smugly in his iron cage, seemed to be expecting something, spit when I peered through the bars. I worried about a jailbreak, especially a massive one, in which a few dozen of the noble savages congregated around Behan's little office and overwhelmed the guards.

But my speculations were wrong. When I look back now, as an old man, I can see that young Wyatt never got a handle on the politics, and never even understood what Tombstone politicians were up to, or how taxes and votes and party politics were more important than justice, honor, or law and order.

John Behan had appointed Harry Woods undersheriff, casually ditching his agreement with me that if I would not run for sheriff against him, he'd make me undersheriff and leave the law enforcement to me while he collected taxes.

And that was only the beginning. Behan began running his jail as if it were the Ritz, where a man like King could check in—and check out.

Chapter 7

Luther King walked out. He climbed onto a saddled nag conveniently waiting in the alley just outside the jail, and took off. The new undersheriff, Harry Woods, was in charge. His paper, the *Nugget*, blamed it on a momentary lapse of security, really nobody's fault, least of all Undersheriff Woods'.

An attorney, Harry Jones, was there when it happened, drawing up a bill of sale for King's horse, which the prisoner was selling to Behan's livery stable partner, John Dunbar. An interesting transaction, I thought. Jones was so disgusted by the obvious collusion he became an active partisan of mine ever after. It came as no surprise that the milkman pistolero was never seen again in those parts and Behan failed to recapture him.

So there it was: Undersheriff Harry Woods, an Alabaman, young, blond, well-schooled and a literary crackerjack, was a part of the ring, perfectly willing to let the prisoner escape and then blandly explain it in his partisan rag as a momentary lapse. The sheer effrontery of it was breathtaking.

The news of that escape didn't sit well in Tombstone, where people were enraged by the stagecoach robbery, the death of two people, and now Woods' probable membership in the Ten Percent Ring, as John Clum, editor of the *Epitaph*, was calling Behan's upright bunch. Talk of vigilantes hung in the air, something I wanted to discourage. Tombstone had been a peaceful place. The murders of a Wells Fargo jehu and a passenger had changed everything, and citizens were cleaning their revolvers.

Virgil and Morgan along with Fred Dodge and Marshall Williams were still out, while Behan had formed a new posse and gone out again, both posses drifting ever eastward toward New Mexico, following the faintest rumor of the workers of iniquity. I stayed in town, filling in for Virgil while he hounded the stagecoach robbers on federal mail-robbery grounds.

Virgil and his yeomen rode their horses half to death, starved themselves, picked up few whispers, very nearly died of thirst, and finally dragged back to Tombstone without capturing anyone. Leonard, Crane, and Head had vanished from the face of the earth, along with Luther King. Behan's new posse didn't do any better, and I suspected it didn't want to do any better, even though it had some members who were not closely tied to the Cowboys, the elegant shootist and bon vivant Buckskin Frank Leslie among them. The great Southwestern desert had swallowed them all.

I understand lawing but I don't understand politics. That is how I was blindsided once again, this time by men who have that cleverness about them that has always eluded me. In this case, it was the *Nugget* editor and new undersheriff, Harry Woods, who engineered a campaign to turn the tables and hang the Earps. Or maybe it was the *Nugget*'s top writer, a bright newcomer named Richard Rule, who did it. Between them, they could spin words into lies so plausible that the whole county believed them. And I was too slow to grasp what was happening.

Next thing I knew, there were rumors all over Tombstone, like little lizards in the noonday sun, that Doc

Holliday had engineered the holdup of the Benson stagecoach. Worse, that Holliday was either a frontman for ourselves, the Earps, or that my brothers and I were the real robbers and were going through an elaborate charade, chasing Leonard, Head, and Crane all over the countryside to conceal our criminal conduct. The *Nugget* was pumping the rumors.

In short, the whole story had been turned on its head into a cockamamie yarn. I first heard it from Milt Joyce, who summoned me to his bar rail and told me with relish he'd heard that Holliday had masterminded the holdup, the Cowboys had nothing to do with it, and Behan could prove it.

I found Doc immersed in a poker game at the Eagle Brewery and nodded to him. He folded, pocketed his winnings, which I noticed were substantial, and met me outside in the chill of the night. I peered around automatically, not wanting eavesdroppers to siphon off our palaver.

"The air's so clear it's going to cure me unless I'm careful," he said. "I'd better get back in where I can cough away."

"Doc, I'm hearing rumors."

He laughed, that faint heaving of his chest that usually ended in a wheeze.

"So am I," he said. "They're saying I got my dental training at the Philadelphia School of Holdups." He was mocking. "Extract a molar, extract a strongbox—what's the difference?"

The idea that Doc, a frail and urbane Southern aristocrat, would take to sticking up stagecoaches was absurd, but I didn't say so. I wanted to hear what he had to say. Doc was a skilled gambler, rarely in financial straits, and when he was, he hung out his shingle, pulled a few incisors, and was back in business again. He had more than a faro bank; he had a profession. He was entirely capable of swindling at cards, but as far as I knew, didn't do it, probably because he didn't have to. He was also a lifelong loner, and the thought of him plotting a holdup with some ruffians he wouldn't pass the time of day with was ludicrous.

"Where were you that night, Doc?"

He eyed me as if I were his Judas, but I wanted to get it straight. "I rode to Charleston that afternoon and took my layout with me. Change of scene. It's been slower than hell here. I can't even make a living on paydays.

"They're saying I rode out of the livery barn with a long weapon. Actually, it was my black faro layout case, with the oilcloth, chips, cards, and faro box. I was back here by six thirty or so. I was right here in Tombstone that night, at the Oriental, liberating chumps from their cash. Ask around. There were fifty people who saw me."

"Where'd this rumor start?"

"Wyatt, it's because they all love me here and want to improve my reputation. I am honored. No longer am I a class-B badman, but now a grade-A bandit. But just in case you're not seeing the details, it's you they're after: the Earp brothers. I'm just the stalking horse. You've graduated from lawmen to a gang: the Earp Gang. They shine their badges by day, rob by night. And I'm your mascot."

I wasn't quite following him, but Doc often talked over my head.

"Plenty of people in this town are thinking you did it, Doc."

"Wyatt, like all true Southern gentlemen, I'm lazy. Holdups are a deal of work. The very thought of planning one exhausts me. Organizing distinguished citizens like Bill Leonard, whom I know slightly, and his gentlemen colleagues sounds like sheer toil. I prefer to sit on my skinny ass and deal and watch Republicans squint at their aces and deuces. I don't even get tired doing that, and it's safer by far than risking a blast from a shotgun messenger. Now does that satisfy you?"

"No, I don't understand this."

"It's simple, Wyatt. Leonard, Crane, and Head didn't do it. You Earp boys and I did it, double-crossing Wells Fargo, siphoning off the loot, killing Bud Philpott and that Roerig fellow. Nice shot, Wyatt. You nailed poor Philpott without even trying, and left me to shoot passengers riding on top. Too bad old Paul fired at us."

He pulled out a cheroot and lit up, coughing cheerfully. "What should we do with that twenty-six grand, Wyatt? Since I organized it, I'll take my third and retire to the isle of Capri, and you can retire in San Bernardino."

"Damn it, Doc, be serious."

He sucked, the cheroot suddenly shedding orange light. "I am serious, Wyatt. If you don't see it, I damned well can't help you. Republicans are born without brains. It's a birth defect, being born Republican. It's the Earp brothers they're after."

He laughed nastily. I was ready to grab him by his spotless cravat and rattle his lungs a little.

"Why don't you answer the *Nugget*?" he asked. "Write them a little letter. The reply's obvious. The money *wasn't stolen*. Bob Paul ran that coach out of there and no one got that strongbox. The twenty-six thousand in bullion arrived safely in Benson. The attempt failed. Wells Fargo didn't lose a dime. The *Nugget's* accusing the Earps of piping off money that was never stolen."

"I never respond to accusations," I said. "People can think whatever they want. I don't care."

"Suit yourself, Wyatt. You're one stiff sonofabitch."

"Watch your back," I said.

"I'm heeled," he replied, his swift gambler's intuition about six yards ahead of me.

I nodded. We were through. Doc headed back to a game, any game, where he could smile lazily at the rubes, ruin his lungs, and clean up the jackpots.

I stood there on Allen Street, trying to make sense of things. Now, decades later, I have a better idea of it, but young Earp, there in Tombstone, was slower than a buffalo bull to grasp what was afoot.

Why would the Cowboy crowd and the Behan bunch and their mouthpiece try to pin that holdup on us? Everyone knew me and my brothers. Everyone knew our record as peace officers in Dodge and in other cowtowns. So what good was it to start rumors like that? I consoled myself with the notion that rumors were harmless, and that any damned fool could separate the facts from the lies about the Earps, about Holliday for that matter, whose actual record was so clean he could run for office himself.

I didn't really know about lies, not then.

I met Josephine for a late supper at the Cosmopolitan, and must have been in a dour mood.

"I don't know what's wrong with you, but I'll help you get over it," she said, cheerfully.

"Things I don't understand," I said, munching on a

bread stick while we awaited oysters packed in ice all the way from San Francisco.

She sat there smiling, sipping wine, flirting with me, as she did every night I was in town, the actress within her putting an edge on everything she did, so sometimes she was seducing me with her eyes, scolding me with her ruby lips, sympathizing with me by stroking my arm, or sometimes my leg, playing footsies, and commenting ribaldly on everyone who walked into that great crossroads restaurant.

"You mean Doc," she said. "He's a bad boy, but he didn't do it."

"Where'd you hear it?"

"Billy Breakenridge is a blabbermouth."

"Why are they saying it?"

"Wyatt, you're so blockheaded sometimes."

There it was, again, and I was beginning to think that I was born without brains, like all the rest of the Republicans.

"Johnny could be king of the county but for you. You and your brothers," she added. "But now he's in trouble. The Cowboys robbed that coach, and he's the friend of the Cowboys. So he's started a few rumors about you, or maybe Harry the Whore did, and nobody even remembers where Behan fits into the puzzle."

"He's a sworn lawman, Josie. Whatever else he is, and whatever his politics, he has to uphold the law."

She laughed, and not at all kindly. "Wyatt, sometimes I wonder about you," she said.

The oysters arrived, and she began slithering them down her little white throat with her lucious lips, and I watched her and didn't care about anything else.

Chapter 8

Virgil suddenly found himself city marshal again. His rival, slippery Ben Sippy, had taken a vacation and not returned, leaving debts all over town and some city money not accounted for. The city council swiftly appointed Virg.

So we had two badges in the family and Virgil had another income. And so did the rest of us; Virgil appointed us special deputies whenever the occasion arose, and we earned a little drinking money.

But I was the Earp brother with ambition: I wanted a piece of everything. We had some promising mining claims, some city lots, and our games to keep us afloat. Morgan regularly rode shotgun for Wells Fargo, and I kept my hand in the detective business for that company, running tipsters and informants like a spymaster.

John Behan returned without the suspects, and growled that they were hiding out in Cloverdale, New Mexico, beyond his jurisdiction. But not beyond Virgil's. There had been heat on Behan to bring the stage robbers in but Behan was off the hook at least by his reckoning: his writ ran only in his county. If Leonard, Head, and Crane were going to face justice, it would be up to us to bring them in.

We held a council of war in the pool room at the rear of Hatch and Campbell's Saloon, a favorite corner of ours. We liked to wield our cue sticks while hashing things out; and this time Virgil was popping balls into pockets faster than any of us.

"We've got to lure them in," he was saying, as he lined up a corner shot. "The Cowboys own the county, but we own the town. We can't even ride out of here after 'em without a few spies reporting our every move. By the time we'd catch up with any of them, they'd be long gone."

"We can't count on Johnny. His business is squeezing taxes and women. It's up to us," Morgan said. "But when did that ever slow us down?"

I chalked my cue, thinking it over. "We're watched, all right," I said. "There's a hundred rustlers out there, and dozens of their watchdogs here, and they know of every traveler on every trail, and Behan likes it that way."

"Do you think he's actually in on it, the rustling and robbing, or does he just let it happen for a price?" Jim asked.

"I've been thinking on it," I said. "For a price, he lets it happen. It's all called taxes. He rides out to a place like Galeyville, and he says, 'Boys, you owe me taxes,' and they ante up a cut, and he lets them alone. Money's all he wants. Stay in office, coin money. Lots of money."

It was my turn, and I banked the eight ball into the left corner, and then cleaned up the table.

"Wait until the election," Morgan muttered. "We'll get some help from some new people in office. Like you." He loaded the balls onto the felt. "Wait until the next game," he added, eyeing me. He ached to whip me at everything, and especially billiards. For the life of him, he would beat me at billiards.

"We can't wait for the election," I said.

Virgil lined up the cue ball. "I agree. It's getting worse. Tombstone won't survive for long if they shut down the coaches, and the passage of people in and out of here. The mining companies won't stay open. They'll shut down and wait for the troubles to blow over. Same goes for Bisbee. There're four thousand people in Tombstone depending on the mines. Several million dollars of bullion is enough to tempt a hundred John Ringos and Pony Deals.

"The Cowboys outnumber us probably twenty to one, but we can call on a few good men. They have safe places, like the Clanton ranch or the McLaury ranch. They own the mountains, control the springs, have their own legal system, if you could call it that, that rewards or punishes their own. They've threatened the life of every one of us, not once but over and over, and Doc's life too. If we go after them out there, we're likely to end up in an arroyo."

Morg disagreed. "Virg, let's try some lightning strikes. We'll be everywhere. Slip in, hit hard, get out before they know what hit 'em."

I had thought of that, and didn't like it. Anytime an Earp posse left Tombstone, the Cowboys would know about it. I thought maybe to try some guile.

"Lure them in like Virg says," I argued. "I think I know how. Of all the two-faced bastards in that lot, Ike Clanton's the one we can turn. He's all wind, and all greed."

"So what does that get you?"

"There's twelve hundred bucks now on each of the robbers, mostly Wells Fargo money. They've upped the ante. Maybe Ike would like some cash. Let's say five or six thousand if we add something to the kitty."

"Lot of money," Morgan said. He jabbed and the cue ball caromed off three sides and then died in the middle of the table. He looked about ready to snap his cue in two.

"Ike's the one," I said. "He'd sell his mother to a whorehouse if it gained him something. But there's more. There's a ranch in Cloverdale owned by Bill Leonard where Ike's been running cattle. After the stagecoach robbery, when Leonard was on the lam, Ike jumped the ranch, put cattle on it, and now Leonard wants it back and Ike doesn't want to give it back. I got that from Breakenridge."

"Who seems to know a great deal," Jim said.

"I'll talk to Ike. I'll offer him the reward money. All he has to do is lure them close to here, and we'll take over."

"You think he'd do it?" Virgil asked.

"You got any other ideas?"

Virgil hadn't. He was a tough and good cop, but he left the details to the rest of us.

"You sure he's the one for this?" Jim asked.

"I think so. There's Brocius, but he's all wind and bluster. He's no double-crosser, either. Then there's Ringo," I said. Ringo was the only one I feared. He was smarter than I'd ever be, deadlier, quieter, more ruthless. Twisted and unpredictable. I could never guess what he had in mind, and that made him especially dangerous. Brocius was simply a bully, and I could deal with bullies. Ringo, that was another matter. I didn't want to deal with him. Years later, dime novelists were calling me fearless. Little did they know.

We went down the list. The McLaurys, Frank and Tom, were Cowboy loyalists and couldn't be enticed. They hated every Earp they had met. In a way, I respected both of them. Billy Clanton was a cipher. Pony

Deal wasn't around very much, and was little more than a corporal anyway. No, only Ike Clanton was rotten enough to betray a bunch of his friends, greedy enough to go for the bait, and esteemed enough among that rabble to be able to lure Head, Leonard, and Crane into the little scheme I was thinking about.

Morgan cleaned off the table and chortled. "You owe me a dollar," he said.

That was all the planning we did. If we couldn't get anywhere chasing Leonard, Head, and Crane all over Southeast Arizona and New Mexico, then we'd try luring them in. I would approach Ike Clanton as soon as I worked out something plausible.

"Don't talk. Don't tell Doc," Virgil said. He was far more wary of Doc than I.

"This is an Earp deal and it'll stay an Earp deal," I said.

"You lost," Morgan said. "I want a dollar."

I parked my cue and nodded.

There were things to think about. I bided my time, ran my faro game, bought and sold city lots, chased off some lot jumpers, and waited for Ike Clanton to show up in Tombstone. He never stayed away long. The Clanton ranch, on a spring the other side of Charleston, was a lonely stretch of country, and Ike and Billy found excuses to ride in every few days and lubricate their tonsils and privates.

Then I spotted him. He had his foot on the brass rail of the Eagle Brewery, and he was wearing his artillery.

"Best hang that up," I said, edging close.

"What if I don't?"

"Twenty-five dollars and court costs," I replied.

He tugged his scraggly little beard and nodded. Moments later the gun belt was hanging on a peg behind the lengthy bar.

"How's business?" I asked.

"What business?"

"Whatever business you're in."

"Bad," he said.

"You need some money."

He squinted at me suspiciously. "Your business ain't so good either," he said.

I shrugged. "Good enough. I'm running for sheriff in the fall."

Clanton wheezed as if something had gone down his windpipe.

"It won't be easy, John being so popular," I added.

"Earp, you don't stand no chance."

"Well, I want to talk to you about that. Improve my odds a little."

"Talk away."

"Not here." I studied a dozen customers. "We'll talk about some money. Lots of money."

He stared at me. I beckoned. He downed his pilsner, belched, and followed me into the night. There were too damned many people around.

"What the hell are you pulling, Earp?"

I smiled, and we walked to the alley behind the place. It was black and silent, except for the faint hubbub emanating from within.

"I want Leonard, Head, and Crane. That's how I'm going to get myself elected."

"So?"

"There's twelve hundred reward money on each. Mostly Wells Fargo cash. And I'll add a couple of grand if you reel them in."

"That's a lot of money. Hey, maybe it was Holliday. That's what I hear. Holliday was with 'em. That's what Johnny Behan's saying. How come there's no Wells Fargo money on him?"

"I want Leonard, Head, and Crane, the ones who were fingered by Luther King. He didn't finger Holliday, and he could have right there in front of six or eight witnesses. You bring them in to a place near here and tell me where and when. I'll capture them and get the credit, and I get to be sheriff. You get the Wells Fargo reward, plus my contribution. That's over five thousand."

"Wyatt, what do you take me for?"

"What do you have to lose? All I want is the credit. Behan soaks taxpayers. I collar robbers. I'll run for office on that and win. You can do it. Send out the word, Ike. Lure them in. You're a top dog, so howl a little. They'll listen. Just say something big's cooking. Maybe a payroll shipment you know about heading for Bisbee. Let's say twenty thousand in greenbacks en route to Bisbee, payroll money. Something like that. Coming from you, the King of the Cowboys, Ike Clanton, they'll think about it and like it. You've got a beef or two with Leonard, I hear. So there's nothing to lose. You don't owe that bunch a red cent. Bring them somewhere down there near your place and let me know where. That worth five thousand to you?"

Ike didn't reply. He was thinking about the trouble he could get into, and the fat pile of bills he could stuff under his tick, and how to settle a few old scores with Leonard.

He suddenly leaned close, and I smelled his foul breath. "This Wells Fargo reward—is it for alive only?"

"I think it's dead or alive. I'll wire San Francisco and find out."

Ike suddenly started walking. "I didn't hear any of this, and I didn't give you no answer, neither. If you talk, goddamn you."

I knew I had him.

"Suit yourself," I said. "I know how to keep my lips shut."

"I'll tell you my decision when you get an answer from Wells Fargo," he said. "Leonard's and Head's lives ain't worth a crap anyway."

"You up to it, Ike? You big enough to ride this one?"

"Goddamn you, Earp."

"You going to be around for a day or so?"

"Whether I am is not your business, Earp."

"I'll get an answer fast. It might take a few days."

"You damned well better. If the award's for capture only, I don't want no part of it. Someone, meaning you, would shoot 'em and I wouldn't get a nickel. I don't take kindly to gyps."

"I knew you'd see it my way, Ike."

"I never talked to you, and don't forget it."

"Sounds about right, Ike."

He started to piss in the alley, so I plunged back into the Eagle Brewery, and I knew he had taken the bait. If we couldn't catch Leonard, Head, and Crane, then maybe Ike would do it for us.

Chapter 9

I stopped by the Wells Fargo office on Allen Street and found Marshall Williams present and accounted for. When the fly-specked out-for-lunch sign hung on his door, one could often find him a few yards away, in Campbell and Hatch's, downing rye and chewing salty pretzels. But he did his job reasonably well, and seemed a loyal company man, or so I thought. Little did I then know how wrong I was.

"Marshall, wire San Francisco and find out whether the reward for Leonard, Head, and Crane is dead or alive."

"You going after them?"

"Just wire them. I want an answer fast."

"Wells Fargo can't offer a reward for a dead bandit. Murder isn't our business . . . or is it?"

"Just wire, and let me know."

"You're looking to get rich, I imagine."

He was grinning at me, the drooling red-haired bastard. He was already two or three whiskeys and seven pretzels into a fine morning.

"I'll be back tomorrow."

"Something's afoot," he said. "Wells Fargo's getting into the murder business."

I didn't reply. Actually, Ike Clanton had shown some rare intelligence wanting that information. Or maybe it was mere cunning. Three bullets could wipe out his Judas money if the company would reward only for the capture of the living. He wanted insurance.

I didn't wait until the next day as I had intended, but stormed Williams' stronghold late in the afternoon. He had a yellow flimsy in his tobacco-stained fingers.

"Dead or alive, it makes no difference," he said.

"I want the flimsy."

"Who ya gonna show it to, Wyatt? This is a private license to kill, I figure."

"Why don't you clean up this office? Those windows haven't been washed in six months," I said.

"They'll just get grimy again," he said.

I studied the telegram, which was from Jim Hume, chief of Wells Fargo security, tucked it into my vest pocket and stalked into the evening heat.

It was dead calm, and hot, and the city's latrines and piss holes all stank. Mesquite wood cook smoke drifted from miners' cottages. A dozen plugs tied to hitchrails lashed flies with their tails. An empty buckboard sagged before the Grand Hotel, its dray horse standing in a pile of green manure.

I found Ike Clanton hanging around the Eagle Brewery that evening waiting for word. He had Frank McLaury and Joe Hill sucking lager with him, and I started maneuvering to have a private talk with Ike.

"Want to see you soon," I said. "Out back."

"They're in," he replied. "Talk to all of us."

"I don't know about this," I said.

We trailed through the back door, into the alley.

I was surprised. Not so much by Hill, who could be bought for nickels, but by Frank McLaury, who couldn't. There were Cowboy politics here I didn't fathom—and plenty of chance to get myself into trouble. I didn't like it. Blabbermouth Ike was recruiting his

Cowboy pals. I figured the whole scheme would hit the *Nugget* within a day.

I backed out. "There's three of you. You don't need me. Why don't you just bring them in yourselves?" I asked.

Ike looked annoyed. "Our lives wouldn't be worth a snowball in hell if we did the job," he said. "You've got to do it. I'd gladly kill the three of them on the spot—they've crossed me—but I'd be signing my death warrant if I did."

I nodded, and handed Ike the yellow telegram. He handed it to McLaury and Hill.

McLaury hitched up his trousers. "That's what we needed to see, Earp. All right, Joe, you go get them."

Hill nodded. "I'll reel them in. Company payroll on the Bisbee coach," he said. "They'll bite. They didn't get anything from the Benson stage, so they'll be hungry. It'll take a few days."

"Let me know where and when," I said.

"I'll tell you when I feel like it, Earp. You better damn well have the money for us, and if you cross us . . . you'll end up in hell for sure. Now swear to me you won't tell a soul, not one soul, on your goddamn honor," Ike said.

"All right."

"Not even your brothers."

"There's going to be a point when they have to know. They'll be with me for the pinch."

Ike glared sullenly at wet clay, nodded, and turned away. McLaury and Hill silently followed. I went fishing for one Judas and found three. McLaury surprised me.

The deal was done. Or so I thought.

Fate intervened before I could pull it off. Whatever the Cowboy chess game going on in Cloverdale, New Mexico, it led to bloodshed. Two brothers named Haslett owned a ranch in the Animas Valley that was coveted by the outlaws, who intended to drive them off or kill them to get it. But the brothers got wind of the fate planned for them, and ambushed Billy Leonard and Harry Head, killing two of the three wanted men. Leonard, it turned out, was suffering two miserable holes in his belly from Bob Paul's shotgun blasts, in terrible pain, and didn't mind the dying.

But the Haslett boys didn't have time to collect their rewards from Wells Fargo. About twenty-five Cowboys executed them and a bystander for good measure. I supposed Jim Crane had a hand in it.

All this information arrived by mail a few days after the slaughter and was published in the *Epitaph*. I took it for a good indication of who ruled that rural country. It sure wasn't any bunch I wanted for neighbors, and it sure wasn't any branch of government.

Whatever the case, my deal with Ike now lay in the coffins of the dead stagecoach robbers and Ike didn't like the fact that the Earps knew his dirty little secret: he was a Judas. So were Frank McLaury and Joe Hill. It made me wonder how long Ike would survive in a crowd like that. It also made me wonder which of those three would squeal on the others. They were all guilty, and maybe that would keep them silent. But now it wasn't just Ike Clanton who was vulnerable; it was Frank McLaury. And one way to silence any talk was to kill the Earp brothers.

From the moment the deal fell through, Ike Clanton was looking for an excuse to kill every Earp he could shoot. That's how I figure it. He didn't trust us to be quiet, and knew that if someone like John Ringo or Bill Brocius got wind of his treachery, his life wasn't worth a nickel. But as usual, I didn't grasp that at first. Not until later, when Ike turned hysterical just a little while before that gunfight and I couldn't figure out what was eating him.

But maybe the real danger lay with Frank McLaury, a deadly man, good at hating and just as good at killing, whose secret betrayal of three Cowboys was now the secret of the Earp brothers.

That's clearer to me now than it was then. I didn't know back then how afraid they were, how they sweated each day in fear that I, or my brothers, would spill their secret to someone like Ringo. It accounts for much of what was to follow, including Ike's particular rage against Doc Holliday.

I thought Doc was pretty much clear of the dark winds whirling through Tombstone, but then he got himself into big trouble. All it took was a snarling match with his consort, Kate Elder. They pecked like fighting cocks between the moments when they wove their dreams so close that I thought they'd be partners for life. It was an odd thing, how hard they tried to hurt each other. She had a fling with Ringo, of all people, just to flaunt her independence, and that set Doc off. When Doc was in a mood, he was a lit fuse. But even then, he was on his best behavior because the Earps were policing Tombstone, and he was damned if he'd let us down.

She sure knew how to hurt Doc, and one night, after she had loaded up on mescal, she started blabbering. What she said galvanized the attention of everyone in the Oriental: Doc, she announced, had bragged to her about robbing the Benson stage. It didn't make any sense, but that didn't matter. In about two minutes, John Behan had corralled her, hauled her off to his coop, twisted her soft white arm, and gotten her to sign a statement implicating Doc in the holdup.

That was a hell of a thing. The damned mean-tempered firebrand had put Doc in the worst bind of his life, and not a word of it was true. Next I knew, Doc was sitting behind iron bars and I was raising bail. We got Doc out, but just for the hell of it, Kate got herself arrested for drunk and disorderly, and that cost her $12.50. That got her so mad that she was threatening mayhem against most everyone, got herself arrested again, spent the night in the hoosegow, and got out on a writ of habeas corpus. I had no use for the woman. She sobered up and recanted her accusation. There must have been some sharp words between her and Doc, because next I knew, she had vanished. I heard she had decamped for Globe, a new mining town north of Tombstone. But she wasn't gone long. I wished she'd get out of Tombstone and stay out, but that's not how thorny love works. Soon she was back, holding Doc in her ample arms.

Judge Wells Spicer didn't take long to toss the case against Doc out of court. He said he had "examined all the witnesses summoned by the prosecution and from their statements he was satisfied that there was not the slightest evidence to show the guilt of the defendant" and the evidence "did not even amount to a suspicion of the guilt of the defendant."

It was all nonsense, in other words. The complaint was withdrawn and the case dismissed. Behan had made a fool of himself, as far as I was concerned, taking a drunken woman's domestic spat seriously. But Behan had shown something about himself, once again, in all of that: he was a conniving son of a bitch looking for an angle, any angle.

Doc had swiftly been cleared, but now he faced the poisonous rumors that had been slithering around Tombstone for weeks, and there were plenty in town who thought he was guilty as hell, and no evidence to the contrary could dissuade them. Doc's reputation as a mean-tempered killer was doing him in. All of which was taking its toll on me and my brothers.

There were weird theories afoot: the Earps were involved in that holdup. Morgan was on board; we killed Philpott just to cover our ass. We knew there was specie on board and we were double-crossing our employer. Doc was in cahoots with his old friend Leonard. On and on, the blabbering of idiots.

These all defied logic, but people will believe anything. Why anyone believed Big-Nosed Kate's accusations is beyond me, but I have found out that the human race has its perverse, vicious, and obsessed people, and an obsessed man doesn't care about truth or justice or good or evil. He cares only about the thing obsessing him, and the widespread fear and loathing of Doc was reason enough.

I found Doc in the Oriental one night and took a moment to visit while we pissed in the alley out back.

"Doc, don't let it get you down. You've got the Earp brothers behind you all the way," I said.

He stared at me from the bright blue eyes. "The *Nugget*'s making hay. I'm your Achilles' heel." He laughed softly at his metaphor. "I'm a heeled heel, all right. If you want me to leave, I'll leave," he said.

"Stay."

"I better confess, Wyatt. I drove Kate out to Iron Springs, shot her, and fed her to the vultures," he said. "It was that or cut out her tongue. She's got the meanest tongue in Arizona. I did it for you, Wyatt. Buried the evidence. Who needs her? That's number one thousand seven hundred thirty corpses for Holliday. I have set two thousand as my goal."

That took me aback for a moment.

"I don't know, maybe that was one thousand seven hundred thirty-one."

"Damn it, Doc."

"Wyatt, Bat's gone back to Dodge, and Luke Short's quit this place, but Holliday's here, anytime you need me, anyplace, any way."

Chapter 10

I think the event that hardened my resolve to clean out that stable known as the Cochise County sheriff's office was the robbery of the Bisbee stage near Hereford on September 8. A couple of masked highwaymen halted the coach, liberated many hundreds of dollars from passengers and the jehu, Levy McDaniels, grabbed the United States mail, and vanished into the night.

The Sandy Bob stagecoach, as it was known, proceeded on to Bisbee and we didn't get word of the robbery until nine thirty the next morning. But even before we started after the robbers, we had a good idea who had done it. One of the holdup men had referred to valuables as "sugar," and we all knew that sheriff's deputy Frank Stilwell employed that term frequently.

What's more, McDaniels recognized him, despite his mask, and hastened to tell the world who did it. And Stilwell was nowhere to be found in Tombstone that morning or for that matter, the previous day.

This involved a mail robbery, so U.S. deputy marshal Virgil Earp deputized Morgan and me, along with Wells Fargo's private agent Fred Dodge.

"Anyone else?" Virgil asked.

"Let's keep the posse to ourselves," I said.

"No sheriff's deputies," Dodge said.

"They'll send someone," Virgil said.

And they did. We ended up in a sheriff's posse, but John Behan wasn't riding that day. He sent Breakenridge and Neagle instead. Once he heard about that word, "sugar," he knew this case would land right in his outhouse, and he would need to devise a way of shuffling the blame elsewhere. He was determined to duck and dodge, and he wanted no part of tracking down his own deputy. It wouldn't look good, not even in the *Nugget*, though I didn't doubt that the alchemist Harry Woods would find some way to turn lead into gold.

We rode through a furnace-blast morning, along flinty grades that chewed iron off horseshoes, and reached the site of the robbery in a couple of hours. I soon found some telltale evidence: a wide sharp-edged bootheel imprinted in the gritty clay, and the clear marks of an unshod horse, a rarity in that country.

We followed the getaway and eventually found that trademark bootheel imprinted in the dust again miles away. All we needed was to find who had recently put wide heels on his boots. And that proved easy enough; a Bisbee cobbler had nailed those very heels on boots belonging to Frank Stilwell. So we had our man, or so I thought.

"Got the order right here," the cobbler said, shoving the pulpy paper across the counter. "I done it free. He said deppity sheriffs, they don't pay."

I pocketed the order with Stilwell's name on it.

As luck would have it, within minutes Fred Dodge spotted Stilwell and Pete Spence right there in Bisbee, lounging in a livery, smiling like winners on election night. So we pinched them both and figured we had solved the case.

Stilwell often camped right across the street from us, staying in the house owned by Pete Spence, another hard case we'd been keeping an eye on. It figured that this pair of capitalists would go into business together. The sheriff's office solemnly brought robbery charges against Stilwell and Spence, and hauled them before the magistrate, Wells Spicer, for a preliminary hearing.

All the while, what really interested me was Johnny Behan, who was pretending the case didn't exist. The man didn't suspend his deputy from duty while the case was pending, didn't proclaim to either newspaper that he'd get to the bottom of this, didn't say that if Stilwell was guilty, Stilwell would be axed. None of that.

Instead, Behan busied himself rounding up some alibis for his deputy, and by the time it came to a head in Wells Spicer's court, there was a parade of stalwart citizens who blandly swore Stilwell and Spence were nowhere near the holdup site or Bisbee at the time of the robbery. Spicer dismissed the preliminary hearing, not finding the unique boot print or "sugar" evidence enough to bring the pair to trial.

Virgil and I steamed out of there, angry at Spicer, knowing that justice had not been done.

"It's not over," Virgil said.

I knew what he meant. He swiftly brought charges in federal court in Tucson for mail robbery.

I corralled Behan. "What are you going to do about Stilwell?" I asked.

"Do? Do what? He's innocent. Do you want me to cashier an innocent man?"

"Sorry, this wasn't a trial. It was a preliminary hearing, and there was no innocent verdict. All Spicer said was that there wasn't enough evidence to bring charges."

"Well, that means he's off the hook."

"No, he's not off the hook, John. The least you could

do is suspend Stilwell, start an investigation, get to the bottom of it. You might see how he's spending his money and how much he's spending. Stilwell pulled off that coach robbery. You know it. I know it. If you don't go after him, the voters'll have plenty to say about it."

He clapped me on the back. "Ah, Wyatt, old pal, you must not have slept well last night."

"If Stilwell robs another stage, John, I'm holding you accountable. And so will Clum and his *Epitaph*. And so will the people of this county."

Behan smiled lazily. "I'll take it under advisement, Wyatt," he said, tucking a toothpick between his incisors.

Then a dark thing happened, in broad daylight.

Frank McLaury stopped Morgan on the street. "You lay a hand on any McLaury, the way you did with Stilwell and Spence, and we'll kill all of you Earps," he said.

Morgan was astonished, and hastened to convey the warning to us. Once again, the Earps were threatened with murder if any of us interfered with the Cowboys or the way Behan was handling the sheriff's office. The whole thing was incredible: badmen openly threatening us with death for enforcing the law. There was that attitude again: keep your law to yourself. We own the world.

I had already put McLaury on my list of dangerous men, like Ringo and Brocius, who needed careful watching. He was looking for excuses and finding them, and working himself toward murder. There was only one way to deal with men itching to kill you: shoot first.

We did lay a hand on Stilwell and Spence a few weeks later when another coach was robbed and the evidence led straight toward John Behan's deputy once again. And once again the two sterling citizens wiggled free on the basis of well-planned alibis, and this time the Earps got another death threat from the Cowboys.

What a strange state of affairs. Let a lawman arrest certain Cowboys for a crime, and he would be threatened with murder. I reported it to Behan, who scoffed.

"Just talk, Wyatt."

"If it was you being threatened, would it be just talk?"

"No one's threatened me."

"That's right. No one's threatened you. What side are you on, John?"

"Don't get your feathers ruffled, Wyatt."

"All right. If you won't uphold law and order, we will. Any way we can. Any way. And anyone. We'll put outlaws behind bars. Including a sheriff's deputy."

Behan's patented cheer ebbed, and his eyes grew wary. "I've heard there's a secret organization, and you head it."

"Vigilantes? There's an organization all right, but I'm not a part of it, and any vigilante who violates the law is going to have to deal with us."

Behan smiled, suddenly. "A lot of businessmen are looking for ways to kill themselves," he said. "Wyatt, old friend, you just can't seem to mind your own business, can you? You don't have a badge. You could get into trouble."

I supposed that was a threat, but I let it pass.

I didn't like the way things were shaping up. There were now a couple hundred outlaws out in the county, congregating in places like Galeyville and Charleston, operating freely, hijacking cattle from both Arizona and Mexican ranches, and more and more frequently, robbing the stagecoaches or lone travelers on remote county roads, murdering rivals, running in deadly gangs.

We were almost alone. Bat Masterson had come and gone, called back to Dodge City in April to help his brother, Jim, who was in a jam there. I had counted on Bat, my old friend, a straight and honorable lawman and ally in any sort of trouble. Virgil had employed him to do some posse duty when we were chasing Leonard, Head, and Crane. Having Bat with us was like employing an army. The stocky old buffalo hunter and gambler could outthink and outshoot all the rest of us; he wore out a horse hunting down those three bandits.

Tough little Luke Short, another man we could count on, had pulled out after the jackpot he got into for plugging Charlie Storms in February. Storms, drunk and angry about a long losing streak, had been escorted to his rooms by Bat Masterson after threatening Short, who was dealing faro for me. But moments later, he appeared before the Oriental on Fifth and Allen, where Luke was taking the air, with the obvious intent to murder Short, but Short, a tough little Texan by birth, was swifter and a bullet to the heart, plus a few more, left Storms lying in his own blood before a horrified midday crowd.

It was ruled justifiable homicide, self-defense, and Luke was free. No one ever questioned the ruling as far as I know. But he decided Tombstone was not a healthy place to be, and caught the next stagecoach out. That left only ourselves, the three Earp brothers, who could fight, plus Jim, who couldn't do much because of his Civil War injury, and young Warren, who was in town doing guard work for the company. And of course Holliday, for whatever Holliday was worth. Maybe Doc was our ace.

Against us, loosely knotted into gangs, were the roughest bunches I had ever known. And they were well led by various of their fraternity. I didn't fear Brocius, who was more blowhard than anything else, but I did keep an eye out for John Ringo. I always figured it paid to respect my betters.

Ringo wandered into Tombstone now and then, an odd, lonely, mumbling man who seemed saddened by his outlaw fate. There was always a pool of darkness around him, as if he sucked light out of the air. It was as if he should have had a chair at some university as a professor of philosophy, rather than be engaged in cattle theft and murder and other mayhem. Maybe he was a little like Doc, well-bred and lamenting a hard fate. Even Behan treaded lightly around Ringo, smiling a lot, never disagreeing. Ringo was solitary, rarely in company yet somehow a chieftain of the Cowboys. I never quite understood how or why.

I knew what side Behan was on, and it often wasn't the side of law and order, safety and public peace.

I've had decades now to think this through, and it's become plain to me that John Behan's avarice lies at the bottom of almost everything that went wrong in Tombstone. He was the most important man in that whole drama that destroyed my family. Because of him, Morgan lies in his early grave, and Virgil is disabled, and my honor has been ruined.

If John Behan had been determined to rout the out-laws from Cochise County, things would have been different. If he had appointed a staff of tough deputies, instead of a politician like Harry Woods, an outlaw like Frank Stilwell, and an ignoramus like Billy Breaken-ridge, to ride herd on crime in the county, things would have been different.

If he had made his political base the law-abiding cit-izens of the county, instead of its outlaws, things would have been different.

If he had genuinely cooperated with the city consta-bles and the federal deputy marshal to stop crime in the county, things would have been different.

If he had been more interested in a peaceful and safe community, instead of enriching himself, things would have been different.

If he had simply and sternly enforced the law of the territory and county, things would have been different.

If he had not actively undermined the efforts of the Earps to bring criminals to heel, things would have been different.

If his cabal had not propagandized, lied, alibied, misled, and ultimately perjured themselves, things would have been different.

If he had had some strong and honorable deputies, a will to rid the county of its criminal class, a desire simply to serve the people, uphold the civil virtues and restraints that make a place safe and peaceful, and an eagerness to suppress crime, no matter what its origins, John Behan might be honored today.

Last I knew, he had become a prison warden in Yuma, having lost the confidence of the people of Arizona. It didn't much matter which side of the bars he was on: he paid for his venality the rest of his life.

I know now that I ended up a victim of John Behan, along with my living and dead brothers, my family, my friends, and a good portion of the people of Tombstone. Behan and his propagandist, Harry Woods, and the paper that whitewashed everything he did.

But I didn't hold that opinion back then. When all of that was happening day by day, I saw him as corrupt, venal, and casually opposed to justice and order. But he was likable, and his sheer affability blinded me to the truth: everything that went wrong during those days for me, for my family, for the town could be laid at the feet of the ring of politicians and newspapermen whom Sheriff John Behan had gathered around him.

Chapter 11

On August 13 more trouble erupted along the border, and it soon affected my brothers and me. In Guadalupe Canyon, just north of the line, Mexican Federales ambushed some rustlers led by Old Man Clanton, and slaughtered most of them.

Clanton and his gang of Cowboys had been south of the border shoplifting cattle, but this time the Mexican federal troops got wind of them and headed directly for the most likely crossing point, which was Guadalupe Canyon, a hundred miles east of Tombstone, and cut them off.

There, in the depths of the night, the Mexican troops pounced, snuffing five, including old Newman, the patriarch of the Clantons, and also, interestingly, Jim Crane, the stagecoach robber who had joined the party that very night. Two wounded men escaped, Harry Ernshaw and William Byers, but they lived to tell the tale, and it wasn't long before Tombstone absorbed all the details.

The ambush of Old Man Clanton climaxed a fierce border war that had sputtered all that summer. There had been a big fight earlier, when twenty-five of the Cowboy rustlers had invaded Sonora and run into Mexican posses and troops. And a half dozen incidents before that had heated up the border.

That spring, rustlers had attempted to drive several hundred beeves north from Fronteras, Sonora. They had been caught and exterminated by the Mexicans.

Sonora's governor, Luis Torres, mobilized death squads to patrol the border, and began penning letters to Arizona's territorial governor, John Fremont.

In July, a pack train was discovered in Skeleton Canyon, its mules wandering, its packs rifled, its owners nowhere in sight. Later in July, four Mexican traders with a pack train carrying silver bullion and merchandise were butchered north of the border and their goods liberated. In August, near Charleston, close to the Clanton ranch, robbers murdered three Mexican soldiers on their way home after buying supplies. Nothing was slowing the lawlessness and murder, least of all John Behan's snoring deputies.

Maybe some of Old Man Clanton's party weren't Cowboys at all, but it didn't matter: they knew what sort of company they were keeping. Ernshaw ran a dairy ranch, and the slaughtered Dick Gray was the son of Mike Gray, who ran the rapacious town lot company and diddled in politics. They may not have been bona fide Cowboys, but their fat fingers were sticky, and they paid the tariff for it. And they were all close to the Cowboys, even if not a part of them.

So the last of the Benson stagecoach bandits had departed from this mortal coil, and no reward money would ever be paid by Wells Fargo or anyone else. And there were those Judases, Ike Clanton and Frank McLaury and Joe Hill, robbed by fate of any chance of getting a plugged nickel out of it.

Worse, Ike's old man had perished. No wonder Ike went crazy in the next weeks. I date Ike's decision to kill us from the moment Byers and Ernshaw staggered in with the news that Ike's father, Newman Clanton, and Jim Crane, had croaked in a lonely and arid canyon a few yards north of the border. From that moment, there wasn't a dime of profit in being a snitch, but only endless fear that one or another Earp would start weaving tales.

There were the usual recriminations, accusations shotgunned across the border in both directions, but the reality was that Mexican sirloin was no longer an easy target for the rustlers. There were now armed pistoleros patrolling the line, and any Cowboy bent on rustling cattle out of Sonora would take his life in his hands.

"That's a half dozen outlaws we won't have to deal with," Morgan said over billiards at Hatch's. "Good riddance."

But Virgil, in a subdued mood, objected. "Any loss of life troubles me," he said. "That's why Wyatt and I've always preferred to buffalo a man or disarm him swiftly, before real bloodshed. I'm not rejoicing."

"Nor am I," I said.

"I'm a peace officer," Virgil said. "The term is worth some study."

But Morgan didn't see it that way. "It's a few less outlaws we have to deal with," he said, jabbing with his cue. Balls caromed in all directions. Hatch's billiard balls had been so abused no one could shoot accurately.

"Damn it," he said, waving his cue like a sword. "Why doesn't Hatch get some new balls?"

He laughed.

I understood Morgan's point and often had shared it. But Virgil was right. Virgil took his profession seriously, as a trust and an honor, and enforced the law in an evenhanded manner. He had even pinched me once when I lost my temper, and I had paid the damned fine.

What kind of man was this, for whom some things were sacred? I always had something to learn from Virgil about law enforcement, and I've kept that in mind all these years.

"Jim Crane's dead, and now Wells Fargo won't have to pay a nickel," I said. "Wonder how Ike feels about that."

Morgan grinned. "Watch out for Ike!"

"Ike must be feeling a little naked," Virgil said.

"We told him we wouldn't talk, and we won't," I said.

"That won't stop him from thinking we're blabbing everything to everyone," Morgan said. He jabbed again, showering balls across the table, and they were rolling every way except the pockets. He was playing petulantly.

"If I was Ike," Virgil said, "I'd be worrying about the Earps, I'd be upset because we know something dirty about him, something that could get him executed by Brocius or maybe Ringo or Pony Deal, and I'd be thinking of ways to shut us up. Think what's going through Ike's mind. Every time he sees Ringo, he's wondering whether Ringo knows, and whether there's going to be an execution."

I thought I'd drop the six ball, but it hovered on the lip of the corner pocket and then rolled off. I stood, disgusted. I was playing badly too. Maybe Bob Hatch should get new billiard balls.

"Newman Clanton was no more honest than his boys, but he was a prudent man," Virgil continued, relentlessly. "He was always careful, and when he cracked the whip, Ike and Fin and Billy knuckled under. I've seen him haul his drunken boys out of

Tombstone before they could get into worse trouble. Now he's absent. And so is the only voice of caution in that outfit. Here's Ike, out there on his ranch, nothing holding him back now, scared shitless we're going to squeal on him. There's no old man around to slow him down. I say he's the one to watch out for. He was always a blowhard, and now he's going to be crazy too."

I thought there was something in it, but Frank McLaury was the one I worried about, the one whose pill I could almost feel as it hit me. He was the hater too. I felt a chill run through me whenever I thought of him, and the hot fires blazing behind those rattler eyes of his.

"Ike hasn't threatened our lives," I said, quietly. "Frank has. Several times."

My brothers didn't respond to that, not until the eight ball, last on the table, dropped. It clicked against the others resting in the corner pocket. People in the alley stared at us through the ornate glass doors but left us alone. When the Earps were playing billiards at Hatch's, no one bothered us.

"I'm tired of this game," I said, racking my cue stick.

I hit the dark street, feeling like a target. I didn't much care what Virgil or Morgan thought. I thought that Frank would start the trouble. Ike would only drink himself into a stupor.

But in a way I was wrong. Ike might not have been the most dangerous to any of us, but he was the one who inched his way into trouble and dragged the rest of those upright ranchers with him. Virgil was right: Ike, freed from the iron fist of his old man and fearful the Earps would start talking, began ungluing so fast one could watch it day by day. Old Newman's ham fists had kept Ike humble. Now Ike was turning into a big shot and enjoying every moment.

The other thing that troubled me was that the Cowboys were flooding into Tombstone now instead of whiling away their time in Charleston or Contention or way out in the Dragoon Mountains. Virgil and I spotted boozy knots of them every night, patrolling the Alhambra, the Eagle Brewery, and Hafford's Corner. Young Billy Claiborne was hanging around town looking for ways to start a war. Even John Ringo, the politest and darkest of the lot, was suddenly drifting in and out of Tombstone.

I could put names to faces now: Billy Grounds, Zwing Hunt, Pony Deal, Hank Swilling, Pete Spence— hard men with hard purposes. It was as if they were planning to take over Tombstone, the last refuge of the law, the way they had taken over the county.

After the billiards I debated whether to head home to Mattie or to head for Josephine's cottage. I felt a twinge as I thought of Mattie; it wasn't that I cared for the sad woman who used my name and lived at my address. But I hadn't found the courage to sever the ties. We weren't married, unless you could call it a common-law arrangement. I hadn't intended to marry, not since I lost Urilla. But we had made a life, Mattie and me.

If I went there, I'd slip into a funk. I headed for Vogan's, where I knew Josie would be sipping claret under the watchful eye of my brother Jimmy, who kept predators away from her and let her enjoy her evenings when I was otherwise occupied. She couldn't stand to be alone in a dark cottage, so she sipped quietly, enjoyed company, enjoyed the starstruck miners who came to worship her, hat in hand, and to pay respects to the one and only actress they had ever talked to. She had a kind word for each.

The only problem was Behan, who discovered that she could be found there most evenings, about when Tombstone lit its coal-oil lamps and the high desert cooled swiftly and a lavender light pervaded the city. He hadn't given up on her, and sometimes when I arrived, we would sit there, a threesome: Josie sipping red claret, Behan downing amber Irish whiskey, and me sipping yellow sarsaparilla, pretending there was no tension at the table, while Behan smiled his way through the gossip.

Josie always pursed her lips, nodded, uttered very little, and gave him no encouragement. I was the one who really didn't like it. She was my girl now, and Behan was still circling her with open lust. I should have enjoyed his defeat, because Josephine had no intention of sharing her charms.

But each time Josie rebuffed him, Behan would find an excuse to leave, his genial mask would vanish, and he would stalk into the night, leaving Josie to me.

This night she sat alone, except for the pianist, Wolf Lintz, who was sharing show business gossip with her. I nodded him off. He picked up his lager and headed for the upright piano without a word, and started to hammer the ivories.

"Let's go," I said.

"And do what?" she asked. By way of an answer to her own question, she slowly slid a hand along my thigh under the table.

That was what I liked about Josephine.

Chapter 12

Ever since Doc Holliday's scrape with the law after being accused of robbing the Benson stage, he had kept to himself. He had always been the loner, but now he shrouded himself in walled silence.

The Georgian ran his own games, poker on occasion, faro, whatever suited the evening. But he was not much in evidence in Tombstone, and I knew he was gambling in Tucson, and also in Charleston and Contention and other outlying settlements, where he was often dealing at tables surrounded by Cowboys. Actually, he was gathering intelligence for me, though the world never knew it.

I had, in the middle of 1881, no status as a lawman, except when Virgil deputized me for one thing or another. But all that time I was a confidential detective and my business was to supply information to Wells Fargo, which took a deep and aggressive interest in the affairs of Cochise County and wanted tips about forthcoming banditry. I had eyes and ears in the saloons, the livery stables, the hotels, and even out among the sheiks of the desert. One of my most valuable tipsters was Sherman McMasters, who ran with the Cowboys and fed me plenty of news, and somehow avoided getting caught and executed.

"Doc, I can pay you for good information," I had said.

"Hell, Wyatt, am I a friend or not?"

"I need to know when and where they'll strike next.

Who has money and who doesn't. Who's running the show. Who's unhappy. Who shot what. Where the bodies are."

"Why, Wyatt, what makes you think these gentle Christian knights will violate any commandment?"

"I'm sure they're all saints, Doc, but listen carefully. Poker players are mouthy."

He smiled lazily, savoring the mission. For some reason, Doc liked to do things for me. He coughed delicately by way of affirmation, and washed his mouth with Pennsylvania rye, which he regarded as a prophylactic against consumption.

I have never been sure of the source of the antagonism between Ike Clanton and Doc, but I believe his sardonic remarks during one of those card games got under Ike's skin. I had watched Doc work: with the right parties at his green table, he would casually distribute the most florid compliments to everyone, always with that soft Southern gentility that stamped him. His compliments garlanded every game, and only a few grasped that he was ruthlessly making fun of those at his table.

He was fearless. In a game with McLaury or Brocius, he would deliver sweeping tributes to their honor, courage, and skill in banditry, and do it all with such crackling wit that they could summon no replies.

"Why, Ike, never has the civilized world laid eyes on a man of such finesse and guile at cards," he said to Clanton once in my presence. "Truly, sir, you are a knight errant of Camelot, and I marvel at your skills."

"What's that supposed to mean?" Ike replied.

"Why, sah, it's a compliment, the sort that ought to decorate your escutcheon ever more."

Ike had stared.

Only Ringo could grasp the half of what Doc was saying, and for that very reason, Ringo would have no commerce with Doc unless maybe to massacre him. But the rest of those bandits basked in Doc's casual tributes, wry smiles, and diffident apologies when Doc raked in a jackpot.

He was a regular at Charleston, gaming there two or three nights a week, and he took pains to avoid being seen with me in Tombstone. But we met quietly. I often slipped midday into Fly's Boardinghouse, where he kept a small, neat, barren room, like a bird of passage always ready to soar away, and shared the news with him.

His particular victim was Ike Clanton, whose bluster was meat for Doc's acid wit. Ike was just bright enough to know that Doc's compliments had an edge to them, but leery enough of Doc's nickel-plated revolver to suffer in silence as Doc sweetly lauded Ike over spades and hearts. It was no wonder that Ike Clanton had reserved a few lots in hell for Doc, and intended to send him there.

Ike was not quick, and tended to think of himself as more important among his gentlemen rancher friends than he was. Ever since Newman died, the unshackled Ike had started to bloat like a dead raccoon. He was the sort to make threats, play the bully, but back off the moment anyone called his bluff. Doc treated him as if he were an eleven-year-old boy, which, now that I think on it, maybe Ike was.

As the summer heat lifted and the cool of October drifted into Tombstone, I supposed that maybe 1881 would pass without much more trouble. The most disturbing event of that time was an Indian scare, which swiftly deflated when no bloodthirsty Apaches were to be discovered in anyone's backyard. Virgil patrolled the town, keeping a shaky peace. I focused on my faro game and the mining claims I had bought, and was spending more time with Josephine, who liked to hob-nob with the riffraff each evening.

One October day Ike waylaid me on Allen Street, and for a moment it looked like I was in trouble. I was unarmed.

"You've been talking," he said, tugging at my sleeve like a six-week-old rottweiler.

"Talking?"

"About the deal you swore on your honor you'd keep secret. Holliday knows. So does Marshall Williams. He said he knows all about the deal."

I had never said a word to Doc. And I had never told the Wells Fargo office manager a thing, and had not ex-plained my purposes when I had him wire San Fran-cisco about the reward.

"No, Ike, that's bunk. What did Williams say?" I asked.

He dodged that. "Word's out, and I'll tell you, Earp, you're a marked man."

"What does Holliday know?"

"He knows."

"What did he tell you?"

Ike glowered at me. "I warned you, Earp."

He stalked off, leaving me puzzled. I knew my brothers had said nothing. I headed for the Wells Fargo office and found Marshall Williams slouched there, studying whorehouse postcards.

"I sure love sports," he said, tucking the photos of ladies in dishabille back into a drawer.

"You been talking to Ike?"

"About what?"

"You been telling him things you don't know?"

Williams smiled at me. "Oh, Wyatt, cool off. I just had a few mescals with El Lacrimoso, and I was gloating that the company wouldn't have to fork over a nickel now that Leonard, Head, and Crane were six feet under."

"Is that all you said?"

"What is this? What am I supposed to say?"

"Watch your tongue when you drink, Marshall. You may have caused some big trouble."

"What the hell kind of trouble?"

"He took it his own way. That's all I can say."

"Well, who gives a damn?" Williams said.

I don't exactly know what happened. I think Williams' cheerful observation that the company had saved itself some reward money got puffed into an accusation by the guilt-ridden Ike Clanton. And once Ike had persuaded himself that I had blabbed about the snitch, he got frightened and maybe a little crazy and more than a little dangerous. What was that biblical verse? The guilty flee when no man pursueth. That was Ike, all right, scared of an execution by Pony Deal or Curly Bill. But I didn't know how Doc fit in, or why Ike was raring to plant Doc underground.

Then, late at night on October 25, Frank McLaury and Ike Clanton rolled into town with a wagonload of beef, which they promptly disposed of to blind and deaf and dumb butchers and settled in for a night in the saloons, their pockets full of cash.

I was immediately made aware of their presence: I paid stable boys, madams, and barkeeps coin to keep a lookout for any Clanton or McLaury. Both had threatened my life and the lives of my brothers, and I wanted to know where they were at all times. I had kept my part of our deal but apparently they didn't believe it. So it was always worth knowing when they were in Tombstone.

They downed a few mescals at the Grand Hotel, the Cowboy hangout, and then Ike bucked the tiger at the Eagle Brewery while Frank played poker. Around one in the morning, at the Alhambra, Ike ran into Doc, who was dealing. Ike was on the prod and was soon castigating Doc for one thing or another; I wasn't there at the start of it and only heard about it later. Doc is deadliest when he goes quiet, but this time Doc was simply fending off the boozy Clanton.

"Go rest your princely locks on a pillow, Ike," he said, "like a true son of Beelzebub. Next thing you know, the Baptists will have you baptized, full immersion and all, and you'll have to take up a new life."

I have to admire Doc for holding back his temper, which can erupt violently.

But Ike was cutting loose. "You start blabbing on me, Holliday, and you'll see your faro bank busted once and for all."

Doc pushed himself back from the poker table. Three other players skidded their chairs away, fearful of flying lead. "I'm afraid I don't know what you're talking about, but if you'd like to confess, I will grant absolution," Doc said. "In the name of the Father, the Son, and the Holy Ghost."

"Goddamn you, Holliday, you're asking for it and you're going to get it."

Doc's response was to sit quietly with his hand at his bosom, a signal as plain as the rattling of a rattler. He was wearing his usual Mona Lisa smile. "Ike, go heel yourself," Doc said.

I caught the last of this and went to fetch Morgan, who was sipping something at the bar. He was acting as a special deputy constable and was armed. I wasn't. "It's Doc and Ike. Break this up or there'll be blood running through the cracks in the floor," I said.

Morgan lowered his stein and moved swiftly. "Doc, lay off. Ike, get out of here."

Nothing happened. The two were at loggerheads. Then Virgil walked in, the steel badge at his breast, and with the ease of an old constable, he stopped things cold. Suddenly there were three Earps, two of them armed, surrounding the combatants.

Virgil eyed Doc and then eyed Clanton. "You are," he said quietly, "about two seconds from landing in the pokey and paying a fat fine to Judge Wallace tomorrow morning."

Doc smiled graciously, the old Southern civility surfacing at once, his even teeth gleaming in the lamplight. His smooth hand appeared once again; he had not been armed but had made it seem so.

I added my own two bits. "Go home, Ike," I said. "You talk too much for a fighting man."

Ike glowered and refused to budge, so I walked him a way, listening to his rant. Tombstone slumbered peacefully. Only a few lamps lit Allen Street. I stood in the dark, under a canopy of cold stars, and I thought that would be the last of it and Ike would sleep it off. How little I knew.

Chapter 13

I escorted Doc back to his rooms through the deep, chill dark. Hardly a lamp was lit except on Allen Street. Doc seemed pensive.

"I surely don't know what Ike was exercised about. Am I supposed to know something I shouldn't?"

"It's nothing."

"This nothing was enough to get me killed."

I accompanied Doc up the porch of his rear rooms behind Fly's Studio. He knocked. It was so dark I could barely make out the door. Kate Elder opened a moment later. I could see she wore nothing at all, her alabaster flesh vaguely visible, but it was too dark for me to enjoy it. She stared, saw me, stood taller, covered nothing, and let Doc in. She was a hell of a woman.

"I believe I will let Miss Elder take pleasure in my company," Doc said.

"Enjoy yourself," I replied as the door slid shut.

I debated heading home to Mattie, who was just two blocks away, but chose Josie instead. Mattie would be lost in booze or off on her lonely ventures to nowhere, and that always depressed me. Josie was always eager for my company, anytime, anyplace, anywhere. She wanted me to call her Sadie now, as her San Francisco family had, and I was reluctantly relearning her name. You'd think someone would stick to one name. But in my mind, she would always be Josie. I headed for the feathers.

Before walking Doc home, I had cooled down Ike

outside the Oriental. Ike was particularly rancid, mostly just fuming about Holliday, but he was itchy and crazy and at one point he announced that the next day he would meet me "man for man." I had finally told him to go to bed, Doc didn't want to fight and neither did I; there wasn't any money in it. I thought he would. He seemed tired just then. But I was wrong again.

I have heard stories over the years about an all-night poker game at the Oriental, with Tom McLaury, Ike Clanton, Virgil, John Behan, and some other unnamed gent in attendance. I have never believed it, and think it is the work of yellow journalists and sensationalists. According to the legend, Virgil dealt aces and eights, the dead-man's hand, to Tom McLaury, which makes the story even more suspect to anyone with brains. I wonder if the Earps will ever escape the bushels of printed nonsense written about us.

Virgil would have been at the end of his day, including his night rounds, and dead tired. He was not the sort to gamble all night anyway. Allie would have raised hell. He had utterly no use for these men, who had been threatening his life, and wouldn't have squandered ten minutes with them, much less the hours of two to six on the fateful morning of October 26, 1881.

It's strange what people believe: tell them that the participants in the forthcoming gunfight played poker together all night before killing each other, and they accept it with perfect credulity.

I laugh whenever I hear it. I read somewhere, maybe some pulp detective magazine, that Allie had stayed up all night waiting for Virgil. Well, the hell she did.

She wouldn't stay up all night for the Second Coming, and if it was after nine, she would demand a refund. I wonder why writers invent that stuff. There's nothing worse than a journalist, except maybe a novelist.

I never asked Virgil about it, regarding the whole story as too absurd to mention. It's too late to ask him now; he died in Goldfield, Nevada, in 1905. I might ask Allie; she's around and will outlive the rest of us by twenty years because she's too mean to die. But I am certain that if there was a poker game, it didn't have Virgil in it—only Cowboys and maybe Behan, who was a Cowboy for all practical purposes. Frankly, I doubt that Behan was there, either.

The sensationalists never did get their story straight. In some accounts Doc was there; in others, he wasn't. And if there was a game that night, it was simply a way for Ike Clanton and Tom McLaury to pass time in the small hours until the rest of the Clantons and McLaurys arrived, along with their allies, for the showdown they had in mind. How better to while away the hours while the Cowboys collected? Some were coming from great distances, making their slow way on horse. They had something going, and it would have happened no matter whether Ike was drinking heavily or not.

I think now that other things, big things, were going on. By dawn, there were more Cowboys in town, including Frank McLaury, Billy Clanton, Billy Claiborne, Wes Fuller, and a raft of sympathizers, including a few backshooters such as the bartender Billy Allen. I think maybe some of this nighttime rendezvous had been planned. Frank and Ike had persuaded themselves that unless they killed the Earps, their Judas game would surface, and they had worked themselves into a scheme to get it over with. And I think they figured that by goading Doc, they would suck the Earps into a fight.

I slept soundly, not anticipating the sort of trouble that exploded the next day. If Ike was cantankerous, so what? How wrong I was to sleep without worry. I think Virgil slept well too. But it wasn't a long rest for either of us. Ike was working himself into something resembling a fit, and that eventually tugged us out of our beds.

I woke up to trouble, and that trouble never ceased that grim day, and only grew worse and worse, taking on a life of its own that no mortal could stay, and not all the powers of heaven or hell could halt. Ike, it seemed, had been parading around town from dawn onward, a rifle in hand, threatening the lives of the Earps and Holliday. I had not even breakfasted before I was tipped off. Virgil was soon awakened by his constables and told much the same thing.

We would have to disarm the sonofabitch, throw him in the jug for a while to cool down, take him before the magistrate on any of several charges, and make sure he stayed unarmed afterward. But it wasn't really Ike I was wondering about. Blowhards don't shoot. Not if they can help it. Frank McLaury was in town and he was the one who bothered the hell out of me. He was a crack shot, well practiced with small arms, cold-spirited, and fully capable of calculated murder. Now, I heard, he was in town too. All we needed was Joe Hill, and we'd have the whole trio of betrayers on hand.

I first heard of the trouble from Ned Boyle, a bartender I knew, who slipped over to Josie's place and told me that Ike was wandering Allen Street, armed, and threatening to kill the Earps and Holliday on sight.

I stayed in bed. Next, Ike visited Junius Kelly's Saloon and began haranguing everyone present. It was the same story: he would kill the Earps and Holliday. Junius, a friend of mine, told Ike to cool down before he got himself killed.

A. G. Bronck, one of Virgil's constables, stopped at Virgil's house to let my brother know that Ike was on a rampage. Virgil yawned, did nothing, and smiled at Bronck. "Let him roar," he said. Somehow, Virg and I were on the same trajectory: let Ike wind down, and it would all go away.

Maybe, in retrospect, it wasn't the right thing to do. But Ike had been up all night, supposedly shipping alcohol into his system, and sooner or later he would sleep it off. But the situation needed watching, and all that morning, while Virg, Morgan, and I slept, or tried to, Tombstone was being treated to a strange and forbidding performance of a man bent on murder. But was it one man or men?

I look back on all that with curiosity. Where was Frank McLaury all this while? Asleep in the Grand Hotel, the great Cowboy hangout? And Tom? And where did Billy Clanton fit in? Why wasn't he with his brother? And Phineas Clanton, where was he? Somehow or other, there was more to this than Ike's demented prowling, but I've never been able to put it all together.

Was Ike some sort of stalking horse, actually sober and calculating, whose task it was to lure the quarry, the Earp brothers and Doc, out of our beds and homes? Was he really drunk at all? Was all this something of an act calculated to provoke the confrontation that he and Frank McLaury itched to start?

I entertain these thoughts even now, decades later, without being very sure of what it all means. No one saw Ike drinking much of anything that night. There's a part of me that still believes that Ike was cold sober that morning, picked his fight with Doc in a calculated manner intended to provoke the Earps, wandered Tombstone making threats with a rational and well-conceived plan in mind, and was even then engaged in premeditated murder.

But how can I prove it? We didn't bite, at least not at first, and not until we were rested. But as the clock ticked on, the time came that we would have to deal with it—deal with every Cowboy who had mysteriously gathered there, that bright October day, to settle old scores with the Earps. They never had much of a score to settle with Doc, but they saw Doc as the bait to get the Earps under their gunsights.

But I am a codger now, and spend my days in speculations, and don't expect that all of them fit the facts. That's the fascination with this thing that happened so long ago: there are always new approaches to weigh. Josephine usually won't talk about it: the subject is absolutely closed, and she veers the talk in any other direction when it turns toward the fight. Allie is worse; she thinks the fight was won singlehanded by Virgil, and the other brothers were spectators or liabilities or incompetents or traitors. Well, that's Allie. I sort of enjoy the old witch, and I hope she can stake out a pleasant corner in hell.

Josie takes a different view. She has put the whole business upon some sort of altar, and treats it as a holy relic, like the fingernail of a saint. I like that in her; she's a regular catamount when it comes to defending me against the detractors and debunkers who seem to make me a special target.

Actually, that pleasant morning of October 26, she watched me dress, fear written across her face, knowing I would have to head out into a bright morning and deal with Ike, who was on a tear. I didn't think it would amount to much: Virgil or I would haul him before the magistrate, relieve him of a few more dollars in fines, make sure he was no longer armed, and hustle him out of town until he could cool down.

I kissed her while she still lay abed, and she clasped my hand. She was a brave woman, but some intuition told her this would be a terrible day, and she clung to my hand a moment, not wanting to let go. It was a gift of love.

Chapter 14

I headed home to change clothing and collect my gun belt. If I was to be a special city constable this day, I would wear the proper dress, which would be my black broadcloth suit. Virgil and Morgan would wear the same; it was expected of city police.

"You were with her last night," Mattie said. She was sober and collected this morning.

"There was no one here," I replied, wondering if she understood my message.

"You could have come home."

She probably had been crying. Her eyes were red ruins. She was trapped in a prison of boredom as well as addiction, and my avoidance of this house was only making it worse. The Earp women had gathered around her and were all resentful of me, but I didn't see any of them trying to straighten up Mattie. They despised Josephine, and I sensed some dark undercurrents flowing through their opinion of her.

Mattie pouted and watched me snap a new celluloid collar to my white shirt and tug it on. I favored a large black silk bowtie, and noosed my neck in it. I donned my black trousers and slid a belt into them. I cinched my gun belt with its Colt revolver to my waist and felt its cold weight on my hip. I pulled the double-action revolver and rotated the cylinder, checked the five loads. They were all right. I returned it to its sheath and put on my suit coat, which bulged over the weapon. It was an awkward way to dress, but we had to deal with Ike.

Even before I reached my home, I had heard more about Ike's rampage. Harry Jones, my lawyer friend, had warned me on the boardwalk that Ike was on the prowl. Now Ike had a rifle and revolver and was wandering the streets of Tombstone, threatening to kill any Earp on sight. He had been in Hafford's and other saloons, letting the world know. Jim had sent word that Ike was scaring half the town, looking for people to kill.

I could not fathom Ike's conduct, and to this day I doubt that he was drunk at all, and even less do I wonder whether he was deranged. Apparently he had been up all night and was looking bedraggled. My instinct was and is that he was cold sober, and that he had a purpose in mind, and that his brother Billy and his Cowboy friends knew of his purpose, which was to draw all the Earp brothers into the streets for a murderous showdown. I also think that most of the Cowboys wanted no part of it, and thought Ike was crazy, and that is why, when the showdown came, they were disorganized and arguing.

Virgil met me at the door and approved my attire with a glance. "I deputize you," he said. That sufficed. He too had been warned by several concerned people. He seemed quiet enough.

He discovered Mattie hovering in the shadows behind me.

"We'll be back in a bit, Mattie," he said. "We have a dangerous fool walking the streets."

"Oh," she said. "You'll settle his hash."

I smiled. Virgil also wore a Colt revolver, the barrel

shorter than mine. We rarely did; Tombstone was a peaceful town for the most part. A billy club sufficed.

We collected Morgan, who was also attired in the regulation police dress. A revolver hung from his waist. He flashed a smile at us, injecting some of his innate cheer into the morning. He would count it an adventure. We looked like penguins, I thought. Eventually some would say we looked like morticians. Virg deputized Morgan also: we were now a police force.

"Well, let's find the sonofabitch," Virgil said.

It was afternoon on a cold, bright October day.

My first impression was that there were scores, maybe hundreds, of citizens watching the show. The Clanton-McLaury circus had arrived in Tombstone, and the spectators were waiting for the elephants. We trooped toward Allen, supposing Ike would be loitering among the saloons there, and everywhere people nodded, or gave us a smile or a salute. They had all heard Ike, or at least heard about him, and now they were ready for the show.

But then Virg turned to me. "Try Allen. We'll try Fremont."

I left them and headed toward Allen Street, wondering where and when I would jump Ike. Plenty of people were watching and ready to duck for cover, but no one was following—not with the prospect of some flying lead. I dealt methodically with the storefronts along Allen, focusing mostly on the saloons. I doubted Ike would be found in some milliner's shop.

At Hafford's I stopped conversation.

"He's been here and gone, Wyatt," said Charlie, the barkeep. "Watch out."

I nodded. "Was he drinking?"

"No, just loudmouthing."

Then I got wind of a commotion up on Fremont, and found Virg and Morg there, with Ike sprawled on the wooden walk, holding his head, which leaked blood through his fingers. I knew at once that Ike had been buffaloed.

Ike glared up at us. "If you'd been a few seconds slower, there'd be a coroner's inquest," he said.

I nodded. Another threat.

Morg was holding the Winchester rifle and Ike's revolver. I wondered where they had come from.

"Okay, Ike, get up slowly," Virg said.

Ike did, dabbing at the laceration on his head with a bandanna. He looked petulant.

We took him to the magistrate, Wallace, who had to be summoned to hear the case. We sat there in the courthouse, Ike bleeding and glaring, and the three of us keeping an eye out for trouble.

I had had it with him and told him so while we waited. "You threatened us last night and all morning, and now you're going to quit and get out of town. I don't know what's eating you, you cattle-thieving sonofabitch, but this is the end of it," I said. "You'll get out of town or you'll get your fight."

Ike actually smiled, or maybe it was a leer. I had the distinct impression that a fight was just what he wanted, what he had provoked, and what he had decoyed us into.

It took a while to formalize the complaint and put Ike before the judge, and when at last Ike had been fined twenty-five bucks plus costs for carrying weapons in town, I let him have it.

"I'll take a fight to you anywhere, anyplace, even in

your hangouts, among your crowd, you thieving bastard. If that's what you want, you can have it. I'm tired of this, and it's going to stop."

I hadn't really expected that the challenge would shortly become reality.

Ike pulled some bills out of his pockets, paid the clerk of court, and got a receipt. "Where do I pick up my guns?" Ike asked.

"Grand Hotel, and only when you're ready to pull out," Virg said.

Wallace glared at me, but said nothing.

We watched Ike shuffle away, still dabbing his head with the bloody bandanna.

"What do you think?" Virg asked.

"He's done for," Morg said. "He'll quit."

"I can't figure out what's eating him," I said.

"Your deal with him," Virg said. "It's like a noose around his neck, and any talk by us would spring the trap."

It still didn't make sense to me. If they were serious about killing us, some rifles from ambush would do it.

"It's all wind," I said. "But if they want a fight, I'll give it to them."

Outside of the courthouse I ran into Tom McLaury, and tore into him.

"If you want to make a fight, then let's fight right now," I said.

Tom raised an arm, but it was too late. I buffaloed him with the barrel of my revolver, and he tumbled to the ground, shocked at me. I saw his pupils widen and then his eyes glazed over. He shook his head, stared up at me in amazement.

"Go ahead, fight," I snapped.

"Wyatt," Virg said. It was a rebuke.

There was something in that thief's face I didn't like and should have worried more about than I did. I don't remember whether he was armed, probably not, but he probably had a revolver stashed somewhere. McLaury was rubbing his head, dabbing blood. I had not hit him as hard as I had dropped Ike.

"I'm tired of having my life threatened," I said to Tom.

He stared up at me darkly, through a veil of pain.

"You can go," I told him. "Get up and get out of town."

Virgil shook his head and walked off.

I thought it was over. We had disarmed Ike, let Tom know we were ready for anything, and told them to get out. It would be a quiet day after all.

Not ten minutes later, when I was buying a cigar at Hafford's, Billy Clanton and Frank McLaury walked by, glared at me, and headed for Spangenberg's gun shop. A crowd edged along, expecting trouble. So the others were in town now, not just Ike and Tom. And I would find most of them in the gun shop. That didn't bode well.

One of their horses had clambered onto the boardwalk and pushed its nose into the doorway. I decided to move it back to the street, and maybe get a glimpse of what was going on in there. So I did; they all stopped their bargaining and stared as I backed the horse off those planks. No one said anything. Ike was in there. The blood on his head had congealed brown. They were buying cartridges. Frank bolted out the door, yanked the reins from me, and backed the horse off the sidewalk himself. I let him.

Inside, the Cowboys were jamming cartridges into weapons. They could legally do that inside the shop, but not out in the street. A small crowd had gathered and was watching and waiting. Watching and waiting. Looking for blood. I would gladly have taken a bullwhip to all of them.

I retreated, having learned what I needed to know. These men were arming for war, arming themselves within the city limits of Tombstone, not caring whether we knew it. They were intent upon whatever they were going to do, and we had to stop them.

Then, amazingly, Doc wandered by, politely shook hands with those threatening to kill him, all the while surveying the Cowboys and their weapons.

"Why, if it isn't the Clantons and McLaurys," he said. "Looking after your black powder, I see. It's good for piles, I'm told. I also hear a good dose gets rid of tapeworms."

I marvel at Doc sometimes.

I found Virgil and told him.

"That's it, then," he said.

"Guess so."

"See anyone else?"

"There's some Cowboys around. Claiborne is one."

"This town's police force is under attack," Virgil said, "and we're going to do something about it."

"Well, that's how it was in Dodge," I replied, "every time the Texans rode in."

Virgil shook his head, saying without words that this was different, and these criminals calling themselves Cowboys weren't some wild but more or less honorable drovers who had driven beef north for Texas cattlemen.

"We'll disarm them and send them on their way," he said. "I think I can talk them into it."

Morgan laughed.

I gazed at the growing crowd, which was following us around as if we were a circus parade. For all those spectators, this was even better than a public hanging.

"No choice now," Virgil said, and indeed, there wasn't.

Chapter 15

I wish I could say we knew what we were going to do and started doing it, but in truth, we didn't. We drifted back to Hafford's Corner to await events. This was Virgil's decision. It's my nature to go after a threat before it builds into something too big to handle, but we didn't do that. Virgil thought maybe the Cowboys would pull out and that would end it.

The Cowboys emerged from Spangenberg's gun shop, no doubt well armed, and stared at us. We stared back.

"Arrest 'em for carrying in the city?" I asked.

"No, not if they're heading out. They can do that if they're heading for a livery barn," he replied. Virgil was hoping the whole thing would dissolve peaceably.

We watched the Clantons and McLaurys and a couple of others head for Dunbar's Corral, which was Behan's place, where they always kept their horses.

"I think they're leaving," Virgil said.

"I hate to let them go," I said. "They're asking for it, and we should give it to them."

He turned to me, granite-faced. "If it is necessary, we will. If it is not, we won't."

I wanted it over with. For weeks, months, our lives had been at peril. But this was Virgil's call; he was the chief of Tombstone's police.

There was not a cloud marring the bright blue sky. Except for all the gawkers, this could have been a normal fall day in the mining town. But it wasn't a regular day; something bad was building up, electrifying people, inciting whispers and gossip. I did not like all the sightseers everywhere; I nodded my brothers into Hafford's for a drink. Maybe we could talk without a dozen people straining to overhear us.

Within it was quieter. I nodded to the barkeep, and he poured me a sarsaparilla, and two more for my brothers. I paid. My brothers didn't sip that day; they would imbibe nothing that might dull their senses.

We did not need to follow the progress of the Cowboys. A few tattlers made it their business to inform us exactly where they were and what they were doing. For the moment they were at Dunbar's livery stable, and they were arguing. Virgil took it for a good sign.

Two businessmen offered us armed men: a dozen merchants ready to slay outlaws—the Citizens' Safety Committee, as they had styled themselves. Virgil firmly turned them down. We did not want citizens getting themselves killed, and that was exactly what could have happened if they had gone against the likes of Frank McLaury or Billy Clanton. At least that seemed right back then. I have changed my opinion since then.

A Mr. Sills found us. He was a Southern Pacific Railroad man in town to convalesce from an injury, and he had overheard four or five Cowboys threatening to kill Virgil and all the Earps if necessary. He did not know the names of these rough-talking men. The engineer thought to pass on the information to Virgil, chief of Tombstone's police.

I thanked him. He did not know us, took no sides, but acted as a good citizen must to warn those who were in harm's way. I remember him still: a keen-eyed man who didn't hesitate to act to preserve the public safety. He had, he said, heard these threats as the Cowboys, dressed in the manner of stockmen, made their way from Dunbar's livery barn to the OK Corral, leading horses, and passing him.

"I think they may be leaving town, then," Virgil said.

But in fact the warning from Mr. Sills crystallized our resolve. We would have to deal with the McLaurys and Clantons if they were talking of murder.

Virgil nodded to me, agreeing that the time had come. No words were necessary. Morgan understood that too.

Behan found us at Hafford's, driven by the rumors and tensions rife in Tombstone. Virgil bought him a beer.

"You can't go down there," he said. "There'd be blood."

"We're going," Virgil said.

"I can't allow that."

"This is a job for my city police. They're armed, threatening me and my brothers, and scheming to draw us into a place of their choosing."

Behan weighed that. "I'm told they're arguing among themselves. Maybe they'll quit town."

"They're arguing about how and when, not whether," I said.

"You going to call on your vigilance committee?"

"Hell no," I said. "They'd get themselves hurt. This is a matter for sworn lawmen. You want to join us, John?"

Now, at last, the chips were down. Those were his friends out there, threatening the Earps. He glanced swiftly at Virgil, and his gaze slid past me to Morgan. "I'll go talk to them," he said.

"What'll you say, John?"

"I'll say there is going to be no trouble here, I won't allow it, and they should disarm if they're staying or leave if they insist on wearing sidearms."

We listened carefully. Behan was not siding with us, and we didn't miss that.

"All right," Virgil said. "Go disarm them if you can. We'll wait, but only a minute. The longer the wait, the bigger the trouble."

Behan abandoned his lager. "You can't just go down there."

"We will keep the peace. We will disarm them," Virgil said.

I listened closely. Virgil was very much in command and calling the shots.

"You could join us, John," I said.

Behan's swift, sharp gaze did not conceal his fear or his loathing. He was caught where he did not want to be. He whirled away from the bar rail. Bright light momentarily pierced Hafford's as the doors swung open and he vanished into sunlight. Then the doors swung shut upon our gloom.

"Sills thought there were five," I said. "Who are they?"

"Maybe more," Morgan thought. "We can deal with that."

"Two Clantons, two McLaurys, Claiborne, who else?"

"A backshooter or two," Virgil said, "if assassination is what they're up to."

"Watch the windows," I said. "Wherever this ends up, watch open windows."

I sipped. My throat was dry. I didn't like this waiting. It is not my way to wait and let danger build.

We didn't talk at all after that. The barkeep hovered as far from us as he could, fearing us, or perhaps thinking he might catch some lead. The few patrons had slithered away like lizards, leaving us to our devices in there. We were free to talk, but the conversation had ended. I thought of Mattie, sipping red-eye, and Allie, and Louisa. I didn't think of Josephine. She wasn't an Earp. I thought of Jim, tensely serving drinks at Vogan's, and Warren, around town somewhere, told to stay out of police business, and I thought of Colton, out there in California paradise, where my parents occupied a comfortable cottage.

Virgil straightened suddenly, set down his glass.

"All right," he said.

We filed out into the blinding sun, our eyes slowly adjusting. There were silent crowds, as if time had stopped. No one moved. People stood, making shadows across the boardwalks.

That was when Doc found us. He looked as natty as ever, dressed impeccably, his lean body upright. He wore his long gray coat against the chill. His consumption had so weakened him that he took cold easily. He was carrying his gold-knobbed ebony walking stick, which he didn't need because he didn't limp. It was his ace in the hole. Since he could not carry, he used a stick with a spring-loaded dagger in it, an old and effective gambler's device, available from certain New Orleans dealers.

But now he was carrying; I had no doubt about it.

His life had been threatened this day and on previous days, and if anything, Ike Clanton seemed to be more intent upon slaughtering Doc than on murdering us. I soon found out I was not mistaken. Doc had his nickel-plated Colt's revolver at his breast.

"You gentlemen going somewhere?" Doc asked.

"Down the street. Disarm them if we can. We're going to make a fight, if it comes to that," I said.

"You could use some company then."

"It's our fight. No need for you to mix in."

"That's a hell of a thing to say!"

He was talking about an old and treasured friendship, about mutual loyalties that stretched back several years, and something more. He believed in us and what we had to do.

Virgil nodded. "All right. There's something you can do," he said.

We followed him over to the Wells Fargo office, and he motioned Doc inside. When they stepped out, Virgil carried Doc's walking stick, and Doc had snugged a standard short-barreled Wells Fargo scattergun under that gray coat.

"Some insurance," Virgil said.

It made sense. Now we were four. Against . . . four, five, six? We didn't really know.

"Doc, don't use that thing unless we mix it up. My purpose is to disarm them. I'm a peace officer, and we're going to act as peace officers."

Doc nodded, absorbing Virgil's clear command.

We started west on Fremont. The Cowboys were along there somewhere. People watched us as if it were a parade.

"I'm going to wave this stick to show them we're not

starting a fight," Virgil said. "I want to talk. I want to get to the heart of this. But if they draw, let 'em have it."

That seemed clear enough.

Someone in a doorway ducked inside as we passed.

For some reason, I didn't think much would come of all this. Confronted by lawmen in force, the Cowboys would hustle themselves into their saddles and ride away. I don't know why I kept thinking that, when the other half of me was icing up for a fight. That's what I do: I ice up.

We saw the OK ahead, but the bunch had congregated behind the pen, in a vacant lot on Fremont, for some reason. It dawned on me that they were a stone's throw from Doc's rooms, at Fly's.

Doc saw them there. "The bastards are looking for me," he said. "And here I am."

There were no disagreements to that.

Chapter 16

We saw them in there, off Fremont, crowded together on a narrow lot between the frame buildings, along with a couple of horses, a few smashed tin cans, some broken brown bottles, and a sun-faded issue of the *Nugget*. I spotted skinny Billy Claiborne, and maybe Wes Fuller, one of their bunch, his slab of a back to me. But John Behan was there too, and we could only wait.

I was all iced up now, cold, as if my body didn't exist, as if I had no nerves. Behan was talking, pointing. They spotted us, shifted around back there, eyeing us as if they couldn't make out who we were or what our purposes were. Tom McLaury put his horse between him and us and I made note of it.

There was division among them, which boded well.

Virgil waited, waving that black baton like the switching tail of a cat.

Behan finally headed our way, on Fremont. We met on the boardwalk, under a gallery.

"They won't lay up their arms until you do," he said. "Then they'll decide."

There it was again: outlaws telling peace officers to disarm before they'd disarm. The *attitude*.

"What? What?" Virgil was incredulous.

"I'm stopping this. I'm sheriff here and I won't allow it," he said.

"We're going to disarm them," Virgil said.

"I've been down there to disarm them."

"They're disarmed?" I asked.

"Yes, I told them to consider themselves under arrest."

"All right, we'll go in," Virgil said.

"No, don't do that," Behan said.

"Out of the way, John," I said.

"You told them they're under arrest. Then we'll go in. This is a city matter," Virgil said. "They're disturbing the peace and threatening us."

He brushed past Behan and we started toward them again, intuitively spread wide, the space between us crucially important. The Clantons and McLaurys and Billy Claiborne were milling around in there. Behan trotted toward the door of Fly's Photo Gallery and slid inside, out of harm's way.

Virgil began waving that black baton overhead, making it plain we were not shooting. But he had his other hand on the revolver in his pocket.

"Throw up your hands, boys," he yelled. "We're going to disarm you."

Someone else slid off toward Fly's Boardinghouse. Maybe that weasel Billy Allen or Wes Fuller. I could hardly tell, with the faces shadowed by those big hats. I made note of it and glanced at windows.

I wanted one thing, to pinpoint Frank McLaury, and if there was resistance, he would be my first shot; he was far and away the most dangerous. Those big hats shadowed faces, and I wasn't sure who was who. Tom McLaury stood behind a saddled horse with a rifle sheathed on it, a safe rampart protecting him. I recognized Ike. He had a chipmunk face, chipmunk teeth, and a scraggle of beard. And there was Frank McLaury, his lips parted. And Claiborne, twitching. And Billy Clanton, the lids of his eyes half closed.

We were close now.

"Hands up, boys," Virgil demanded.

Billy Clanton did not buy it. I saw him thumb back the hammer on his Colt. Frank did too, snaking that black sidearm up and out. Tom was doing something behind the cover of his horse. I saw fire in Frank's eyes.

"Hold up. We don't want that," Virgil said.

Claiborne ran.

I had never been in a gun war, not like this one anyway, but I knew what I was going to do: shoot Frank McLaury. I yanked the piece out from my suit coat, leveled, and shot. Billy Clanton shot at me the same moment and missed.

My shot threw Frank backward in a haze of acrid smoke. He grunted. He wobbled, his arms flying, and sagged.

Virgil's effort at disarming the Cowboys failed; he drew his revolver, pitched away the baton. It had come to that.

There was a pause. I followed Billy Clanton as he aimed. I saw Tom McLaury reach for something. He looked surprised, as if he didn't want to be there. Ike was bobbing around, looking scared.

Ike bolted my way.

"Don't shoot," he screamed. "I'm not heeled."

He was heeled, waving his revolver. "Then get out," I said.

Ike grabbed at me, ran past me; I couldn't turn to see whether he would backshoot me; Billy was aiming at me. A crackle of bullets then. Frank was still up and shooting. Virgil and Morgan fired. Doc leveled the shotgun and I heard it boom. Tom McLaury screamed; his horse screeched and bucked. I shot Billy Clanton, driving him back. Smoke boiled through that lot. I heard someone shoot from off to one side, Claiborne, maybe, or someone else, someone not close in.

Billy crumpled, fell in a heap, pulled himself up, and shot at me from the ground.

Virgil howled; he had taken a bullet in the calf and tumbled to earth. Frank's shot, I thought. I glanced, helpless. Virgil sat up, found targets, shot.

Doc's shotgun found Tom McLaury and riddled him, wounding the horse.

Doc yelled, "I'm hit." A bullet had seared his hip. He did a small dance, dropped the shotgun, extracted his nickel-plated revolver.

A shot staggered Morgan; bright blood bloomed at his shoulder. He fell.

"Oh, hit," he yelled. I saw fear in his eyes as he fell. He was very young and bullet wounds are a strange thing in a young body.

"Get down," I yelled.

I stood in front of him. A shot seared where I had been a second before.

My brothers were down, but both were game. They kept on shooting. There were shots coming from somewhere else. Fly's, maybe. Ike, maybe. Fuller, maybe. Claiborne, maybe.

"I've got you," Frank said to Doc, the revolver wavering.

"You're a daisy if you do," Doc replied and shot. Frank flopped onto his back, perpetually surprised.

Tom was dying; Frank groaned, hate boiling out of him, along with his blood. Billy was game, but sinking fast.

"I am dead," he said.

There was an awful silence.

The horse screeched again. Blood ran from a dozen holes in it.

I saw the people now—people everywhere: standing in the shade, in doorways, on the street in the sun. It had lasted a few seconds. I was standing. Doc was standing, a hand jammed to his hip. I saw some pink there, on his trousers.

Morgan was plenty hurt. His shirt and suit coat ran red.

Virgil's leg was blood-soaked. He lay flat on his back, staring.

I didn't trust those sonsofbitches around there, and squinted at the windows, the shadows, the doors, and saw one or two men duck into corners. Some backshooters maybe. I reloaded.

My brothers were hurt.

I heard a mine whistle. It was the Vizina.

Armed men, merchants mostly, came running, white shirts and sleeve garters. They gathered around Morgan, hurt worst, cut away his shirt and bound his wounds tightly. He was game, but pale.

"Oh, God," he said.

Virgil was hurting more, and groaning. That wound through the calf tormented him almost beyond bearing. Some of the businessmen wrapped sheeting around it, and the sheet turned red. I squinted at dark windows, at shadowy men standing at the corners of buildings, at people in doorways, my revolver in hand. The spectators thickened. But hardly anyone came close.

Doc, cussing softly, pulled off his coat, examined his

severed trousers, found that the bullet had burned him, lacerated skin but nothing more.

"Drinks are on me," he said. "I'll die with my boots off." No one helped him. He doctored himself, with a strange, lonely dignity. It occurred to me that I might be wounded and not know it. I studied my suit, my limbs, and found nothing. Not even a hole in my suit.

John Behan emerged from Fly's. He had seen some of it, stayed out of harm's way. He studied the dead and dying. Billy Clanton was slow about it, gulping air and spasming. Frank was stone-cold dead. I wondered where Ike was, and whether Ike might shoot me from some shady corner.

Behan studied the dead, examined Virgil and Morgan, and approached.

"I want to see you," he said.

"I won't be arrested now."

"It shouldn't have happened."

"You told us they were disarmed."

"I didn't say that."

"Three Earps heard you."

I turned away, looking after my brothers.

Moments later I saw Behan huddled with Richard Rule, reporter for the *Nugget*, pointing, talking. Rule was scribbling notes. I didn't see Mayor Clum, editor of the *Epitaph*, around. Rule would have the scoop and the chance to twist the story the way he wanted.

I didn't think it was over, and stared bleakly into the crowd, my revolver in hand, looking for Wes Fuller or any of the Cowboy bastards who might be waiting for the last laugh. Josephine stood half a block away, on Fremont, a handkerchief pressed to her mouth. She did not approach, but when she saw me standing and alive, she started to capsize, but righted herself, stared again. There was a strange invisible wall between us: she could walk no farther, and I could not walk toward her. She sobbed, wheeled, and ran off.

The women came; they had been only two blocks away in our homes. Allie first, a fiery little bundle wailing as she fell beside Virgil. Louisa, crying as she beheld pale and groaning Morgan. And Mattie . . . standing stiffly, staring at me, no tears in her eyes. The Earp women stood by their men. Morgan looked the worst, but Virgil was in the most pain. Allie plucked up his revolver, still hot from the shooting. Morgan's had vanished somewhere.

"You never get hurt, do you?" Mattie said.

I had no time for her.

Allie glared up at me. "Now see what you've done."

"I did not shoot Virgil."

"Because of you . . ." She comforted her man, held his hand, wiped his face with her apron.

• "Billy Clanton shot him," I said. "Virgil killed him."

I studied Virgil, who writhed in pain. Morgan's whole back was red, but he looked like he would make it. I walked over to Doc, who was dabbing at his hip.

"Why in hell did you let Ike get away?" he asked.

"He didn't lift his gun."

"You should have drilled him. Tom shot me with something, and it wasn't that rifle," he said.

"You sure?"

"Frank was down and firing at you. Tom shot me. Where's his revolver?"

"You all right, Doc?"

"Give or take two lungs, I suppose so."

"Behan will be coming around."

"I'll talk when I'm ready."

Doc stuffed his revolver into his bosom, picked up the walking stick. I saw Kate hurry from the boarding-house, beelining for Doc.

"Now you've gone and got yourself shot," she said.

"I tried, Kate, but they didn't get me. I turned this way and that to give them the chance. I painted a bull's-eye on my chest. They're just bad shots, the whole lot."

"They were here waiting for you," she said. "I watched them here, waiting, looking for you."

"That seems to be the sum of it," he said.

She was helping him along. I saw something in his face that I will never forget: tears in his eyes. It was a torment for him to walk but maybe the tears weren't for that. I watched as he hobbled to their rooms. She would patch him and cuss him, even as he wept.

A cart and dray arrived at last as more and more people boiled onto Fremont Street to see the latest sensation, better than the circus, better than a hanging.

As I moved up Fremont, Behan tried again.

"Wyatt, I'm arresting you."

"For what?"

"For murder."

"Goddamn you. You almost got us killed. Why didn't you arrest them? They were threatening the lives of peace officers. Carrying weapons. You'll answer for what you didn't do. Right now, I'm taking care of my brothers. I'll answer for what I've done. I'm not leaving town," I said.

Behan didn't blink.

It was time to get Morg and Virg to safety. Now armed men crowded around. At last I put away my revolver, which I had in hand all the while, my fingers glued to the grip. They loaded my brothers onto that hack and hauled them off, to live or die. I followed along, Mattie beside me, the Earp women flooding their handkerchiefs.

I looked back on that empty lot, and knew that my life and my fate had changed right there, amid the broken glass.

Chapter 17

I cleaned my Colt revolver, running an oily rag through the barrel and each cylinder, while the women bustled around me. I was sitting at Virgil's kitchen table that fateful evening, thinking about what was to come. Five brass shells lay on the tabletop. After I had wiped the barrel and cylinders and firing pin with solvent, I reloaded.

The revolver felt light and strong in my hand. It stayed with me now; I would not be without it. Two or three hours earlier it had been used with good effect against persons.

Virgil and Morgan were both lying in the bedroom. George Goodfellow had seen to them, washing and binding the wounds. Morgan had taken a bullet across the back muscles, tearing up tendons and chipping bone, and his was the more dangerous wound. He had lost more blood than I wanted to think about. Virgil had been plugged through the calf, and his wound was so painful that Virgil could barely endure. Goodfellow, an expert with bullet wounds, sounded optimistic.

"They'll recover if the wounds don't mortify," he said on his way out. "I'll leave the bill on the kitchen table. It's itemized by the patient. Eight fifty for Morgan, six for Virgil. A simple perforation costs less. Some bone chips to pull out of Morgan, you know. If the bullet hadn't exited Virgil's calf, you might have some expense there. Pulling a bullet can be costly. They flatten if they hit bone, and it's hard to get at them. Takes some morphine and muscle. Some shot-up men would rather die than pay the bill."

It was plain that Dr. Goodfellow wanted to talk. I set down my revolver and waited him out.

"The cheapest I ever charged for a gunshot was one dollar. A gambler named Jasper, Jeptha Jasper, I believe, got shot in the bosom by a rancher over a small dispute at cards, where the ball struck a silk handkerchief and carried it in about an inch. Right between the eighth and ninth rib. When I saw the little round hole, clean as could be, and the green silk handkerchief neatly poking out, I just gave a little tug and brought the ball right up and slapped a plaster over the hole. One dollar, I said, dropped the ball in his hand, and he was off my examination table and out the door."

He didn't want to leave, and lingered there. I knew that nothing was zestier for him than a good bullet hole or two.

"Widows rarely pay, you know. If the patient dies, the doctor's services weren't worth a plugged nickel. I'm sorry I have no bullet for you. Some men turn them into lucky charms." He eyed me. "Not that you need a charm. You mind if I look at your suit of clothes? There's got to be some holes somewhere."

"There's not a hole," I said.

Outside, several of the town's businessmen, six men from the public safety committee, stood armed and ready to defend the Earp houses. I was grateful for their presence. Who the hell knew what the Cowboys would do next? There might well have been fifty in town.

But my worries were misplaced. It was not lead bullets that would shower us, but word bullets. As I look back upon a long life, I realize I have always underestimated the malignity of harsh words, and what happens when words are fashioned into lies, or into legal documents. Just then, the danger lay in paper bullets, not lead ones.

Allie, Bessie, and Louisa cooked a skillet or two of johnnycakes, looked after the wounded brothers, and glared at me. Allie blamed me, and her gaze was enough to put frost on boiling water. She had it in her head that I had opened the ball, and that if I had not shot at Frank McLaury, none of the blood and death would have happened. Let her think it. I had shot only when I saw McLaury slide the hammer back on his revolver, intending to drill me.

Mattie was not there; she was at my house, next door, finding ways to obliterate the moment. I was glad of it. Her Chinaman sometimes spared me her complaints.

Bessie and Jim hovered over all of us; two strong people comforting us in tough times. I worried about a potshot through the sheet-covered windows to the lamplit people within, but I needn't have: no one could get close to our houses save for those who were welcome there.

I did not respond to Allie. I was thinking about Virg, lying in pain, his leg elevated and wrapped tightly in bandaging, a little morphia quieting him for the moment. And about Morg, who lay on his stomach on a cot beside Virg, the bandaging across his back soaked with brown blood, and stared at the dark floor of the sole bedroom in that little house. And about the men I had killed or helped to kill.

Some people, I don't know who, had carried the

dying off the streets and indoors. Billy Clanton had died slowly, in gasping pain. Tom had died faster, a dozen shotgun balls and some bullet wounds in him. Frank had perished fast. Behan had caught Ike on Toughnut Street and arrested him. He was in jail now, along with his brother Phineas, which was probably the safest place for Ike to be. I heard that the photographer, Camillus Fly, had taken some photographs of those who croaked, and that the coroner, Henry Matthews, had taken elaborate notes. He had found nearly three thousand dollars on Tom McLaury, the proceeds from another sale of stolen beef. The bodies were in the window of Ritter and Ream, City Undertakers, for all the world to see.

I learned from George Parsons, who paid a visit, that people were still standing around that vacant lot, and they had been there through the afternoon and evening, studying blood in the clay, finding auguries in it. I suppose it was better than some show at Shieffelin Hall, and would get more encores.

There would be a hell of a funeral, and I would get to see who was on what side. I thought to get a room at the Cosmopolitan Hotel where I could watch, but then I thought better of it. I knew who was on what side. And the hotel would be a dangerous place to be during that hour.

"Eat or not," Allie snapped.

I wasn't hungry. She yanked the half-eaten johnny-cakes from me. Louisa glared at her. She had wept, but now she was supportive, ducking into the dark bedroom every couple of minutes, smiling at me a little, brightness in a gloomy little cottage.

"Wyatt!"

It was a voice at the front door I thought I recognized.

I went there but did not open.

"John Behan's here," the voice said.

"All right," I said. I picked up my revolver and eased the door open a crack. Behan stood back from the porch. I surveyed the Citizens' Safety people, and opened wider.

"See you," Behan said. He had Winfield Scott Williams with him, a county attorney.

I nodded and let them in and steered them into the kitchen.

"Virgil fit to talk?" Behan asked.

I nodded.

"For one minute, just one minute," Allie said.

We all crowded into the bedroom. Morgan lay face-down and ignored us, or was asleep. Virgil stared up at the faces above him.

"You doing all right?" Behan asked.

Virgil didn't reply. He wasn't doing all right.

"A few questions," Behan said.

"They're both alive. If you've satisfied your curiosity, you can leave," I said.

"Official business, Wyatt. I'm not here to argue. I have my duty."

"You saw the fight. What more is there?" Virgil said.

"They weren't expecting a fight, you know. Holliday started it. Was he deputized?"

"Billy Clanton and I started it together," I said.

"Was Holliday deputized?"

"No," Virgil said. "But I made him one of my posse."

"Holliday's going to face a murder charge. Maybe others."

"Is anyone protecting him?" I asked. "Is there a guard at the boardinghouse?"

"No."

"Why aren't you protecting him? He could be dragged from his rooms and butchered. Is that your duty or not?"

Behan shrugged. "He can take care of himself. And he has help," he said, referring to Kate. "There'll be some actions filed—against all of you and Holliday. A coroner's inquest and then a preliminary hearing."

"I'm prepared for that. This was done in the line of duty," Virgil said. "And for your information, my brothers were all deputized and acting as city police. We had dangerous men threatening us, and we responded with force when we had to. That's all there is to it."

Williams was taking notes. I guessed he would be the prosecuting attorney if it came to that.

"You had your vigilance committee out," Behan said.

"It's not our committee and I told them to keep out of it," Virgil said. "We didn't want them meddling."

"But they're meddling right now. When the Vizina mine whistle went off, there they were, armed and organized."

"There they were," I said. "And so what?"

"They're your men."

"No. Get that through your head, John: they aren't ours and we didn't want them in this. They volunteered before, and we said no."

"Clanton's going to file murder charges. You stay in town. And I'm disarming you."

"The hell you are," I said.

He didn't press the issue.

Then he got to whatever was working inside of him. "If the vigilance committee tries to take over this town, or lynch Ike or Fin Clanton, or any other of the Cowboys, like Wes Fuller or Bill Claiborne, I'm holding you responsible—you personally."

I grinned at him. What else was there to do? He knew damned well what the score was. This whole thing was for Williams' benefit.

"You done here?" I asked.

He softened a little. "Looks like Virg and Morg will be all right," he said.

I bit back the reply forming in my head: *no thanks to you.*

I saw them to the door, the revolver cold and strong in my hand. Jim and Bessie left next, escorted through darkness to their adjacent house. I didn't want to go to mine, but had no choice. Tonight the Earp houses would be well guarded. But citizens' safety committees never could hold together for more than a few hours. Tomorrow or the next day we'd be on our own again.

I slipped to my porch, holding my revolver.

"Good night, Wyatt," said a soft voice in the darkness near my house. "We're here and you'll be safe. No one can get within fifty yards."

"Thanks," I said, and slipped through the dark doorway.

I didn't light a coal-oil lamp. I could see enough. Mattie was sprawled in a Morris chair in the front room, her legs spread wide, her skirts half up, an empty glass in hand, as near as I could tell.

"Why did you come here? You could be with her," she said. "You can be the big hero."

"Mattie—"

"You want to have a guard around tonight, so you came here."

"I'm going to bed."

"Is she good? Does she know all the tricks?"

I didn't reply. I hoped Mattie would stay in her chair all night. I didn't want her boozy breath fouling the air.

"All I ever wanted from you was a smile," she said, and sniffled. "You never smiled."

I found my way to my room and began unbuttoning in the dark, not wanting to light a lamp and make myself a target.

"No picnic," she said. "Never a picnic. We never went on a holiday together. When I pickled the cucumbers, you never noticed."

I set my revolver on the nightstand, and readied myself for bed. But when I finally drew up the covers, I didn't sleep. This day I had killed. I had avoided that before. All the years of lawing, and I had gone out of my way to avoid it. I had used my revolver in the line of duty, but never had gotten into a gunfight. Now three lives had stopped suddenly. A man is given a name, and has that name until his body quits, and then the name fades away until only a few relatives know it. Soon enough, no one would remember Clanton and the McLaurys. When my body quit, no one would remember Wyatt Earp for long, not even the drugged woman in the parlor.

Trouble hung over me. I was not at all confident that the Earp brothers would escape murder charges and, if we did, whether we could escape assassination. I knew only that it had not ended; it had barely begun.

Chapter 18

Doc and I sat in that stinking jail feeling helpless. My attorney, silver-maned Tom Fitch, was arranging bail and I knew he would have no trouble getting it. We each needed ten thousand dollars, an enormous sum. I threw seven thousand into the pot, all the cash that I had, most of it from my faro bank. But I didn't like sitting in John Behan's jail, unarmed, surrounded by cutthroats. The consolation was that several members of the Citizens' Safety Committee patrolled outside, well-armed, ready to fight off a lynch mob.

There had been a hell of a funeral parade, blocks long, and more Cowboy allies crawled out of the woodwork than I had ever imagined lived in Tombstone. A brass band playing dirges oompahed down the street. All three of the dead were dressed nattily in dark suits and laid in silver-mounted caskets with their names and birth dates engraved on them. Billy Clanton was carried in one ebony hearse; the McLaury brothers together in the second hearse. Ike and Phineas Clanton rode in a wagon just behind. I didn't see the event, but I learned it was the largest in Tombstone's brief history, some three hundred mourners on foot behind the cortege, plus carriages, horsemen, and a four-horse stagecoach, the whole of it stretching two blocks. I could scarcely imagine such an outpouring of sympathy for three outlaws, but I understood exactly what it meant for the Earps and Holliday.

That boded ill. And so did that sign in the undertaker's window next to the three deceased: MURDERED IN THE STREETS OF TOMBSTONE, it read. The prospect of a lynch mob outside my jail cell was so real I sometimes thought I heard it collecting there.

Always my thoughts returned to John Behan, friend of the Cowboys, who could have prevented all this. Behan lay at the root of everything wrong in Cochise County. Behan had let the outlaw element do what it would in exchange for political support for his Ten Percent Ring, and probably for some bribes, doled out as taxes. Behan could have told Ike to vamoose and not show up in Tombstone until he had cooled down. Behan had told us he had arrested the Clantons and McLaurys, and had done nothing of the sort, endangering our lives.

When my thoughts probed at all the ways things went wrong in that place, they focused on Behan. Now, decades later, they still do. With any honest, law-enforcing sheriff in office, Democrat or Republican, the whole tragedy would not have unfolded.

But over the years I've wondered if Virgil might have handled it differently. Oddly enough, I believe he might have prevented the trouble by doing exactly the thing he rejected. A group of armed citizens, determined to end the outlawry and threat of violence, might have confronted the Clantons and the McLaurys in a way that left them no choice but to leave, and to respect the peace there. If those Cowboys saw that it wasn't just the Earps, but an armed community solidly insisting on law and order, things would have ended differently.

Probably even the calculating John Behan would have concluded it was unwise to side with the lawless.

That was what made him so anxious about the vigilance committee, why he kept asking us about it, why he kept thinking the Earps led it and it was our creature.

But we were proud people, professional peace officers, we Earps, and we would accept no help and would do our duty as we saw fit. It is a weakness in me more than in my brothers. Often in these intervening years I have considered where my pride led me, to my sorrow. I blame myself. If Virgil had accepted such help from those citizens I would have raised hob with him. So Virgil said no, and minutes later he lay in a pool of his own blood, Morgan suffered a lengthy bullet wound that tore up flesh and bone along his back, and we all faced grave charges.

There was a coroner's inquest starting October 28 to which we Earps and Holliday were not invited, so we gave no testimony and could refute nothing that was being inked into the record. Where was the justice in that? I could see the way things were going when I read the testimony, avidly published by both papers.

Behan, it seemed, had changed his tune. The story he originally gave the *Nugget* as to who fired when and who said what had suddenly vanished, and now he was calculating ways to take advantage of the fight, drive the Earps into prison or to the gallows, and reign triumphant. I never gave John Behan high marks for truthfulness, and even less do I do so now, after decades of reviewing that chapter in our lives.

No longer was he saying that Billy Clanton and I both fired at the same moment, after I had seen Frank McLaury start to draw; now it was reported that the Earps were bent on murder, that we had butchered largely unarmed men who were surrendering with their hands in the air.

I was amazed, as these things drifted back to me, how swiftly the story had changed, and how damaging it was to the Earps.

Now Behan was saying that he heard Billy Clanton yell, "Don't shoot me. I don't want to fight." He then testified that the Earp party began shooting, and Tom McLaury pulled open his coat to show that he had no weapon, and screamed, "I have nothing."

Just how Behan heard all that from inside Fly's doorway I don't know. He had marvelous ears that could catch conversations on the other side of doors and windows.

Ike Clanton testified that they were all leaving town and, he said, when the Earp party arrived, "Frank McLaury and Billy Clanton threw up their hands; Tom McLaury threw open his coat and said he had nothing; they said you sons of bitches have come here to make a fight. At the same instant, Doc Holliday and Morgan Earp shot."

The testimony went along pretty much like that. They were making a case for murder and it was obvious that they had met beforehand to unify their stories. Some onlookers testified, and what they said didn't help us much. In the end, I thought, the bystanders weren't important; the altered testimony of the sheriff and his Cowboy cronies was profoundly important.

Next thing I knew, the coroner, Henry Matthews, was officially concluding that the McLaurys and Billy Clanton had been shot to death by Wyatt, Virgil, and Morgan Earp, plus Doc Holliday.

The papers made fun of the obvious verdict. But already, the mood had changed. Now the Tucson papers began editorializing against us. We were no longer lawmen tackling dangerous criminals; we were a gang of cutthroats bent on destroying law-abiding citizens such as those fine ranchers, the Clantons and McLaurys.

I didn't like the swift and fickle shift of loyalties, but thought that would pass when the facts came out. How little I understood the power of words used as bullets, lies that cut like knives, insults that stabbed like lances.

Immediately after that, Ike filed murder charges. Justice Wells Spicer set bail at a stiff ten thousand for each of us, including Virgil and Morgan, who were in bed, and Doc and I found ourselves unarmed, defenseless, in Behan's jail, and awaiting the efforts of friends to spring us on bail. Those were slow and sweaty hours.

Doc sat fatalistically on the foul bunk. A man who had staved off death from consumption for years was better equipped than I to contemplate his own demise, and so he sat quietly. What annoyed him most was the lack of cleanliness. Doc scrupled to wash and dress as a gentleman always, and there he was, in soiled clothing, blond stubble on his jaw, feeling himself less than presentable. There we had a stinking pail to answer our bodily needs, and nothing resembling a bowl and pitcher and towel to attend to our toilet. I was used to it. Doc never quite managed.

We spoke little; there were funneling ears everywhere. Breakenridge kept peering in at us, as if we were objects of personal fascination.

"Mr. Breakenridge," Doc said one time when Billy hovered around, studying his prisoners with moon eyes, "you're sublimely fit for your position. I've never known a man so well suited to look in on prisoners and keep a sage and knowing eye on them."

"That's what I'm paid for," the deputy said cheerfully. "It takes experience."

"I'm sure you'll make a career of it," Doc said. "You have the ambition to carry it off."

Billy blushed.

But at last Behan himself unlocked the barred door. "Fitch has made bail for you," he said. "Don't leave town."

"Mr. Behan," Doc said, "your accommodations are sublime. The cuisine is memorable, better than Delmonico's. The fragrance sweeter than orange blossoms. The beds offer divine rest. I shall recommend your hostelry to various people."

"Doc, your humor kills me," Behan said.

Doc smiled.

I walked past Behan, the author of our troubles, and I was free, more or less. The town's safety committee escorted me home and kept me under guard there while I washed, shaved, and dressed. I had urgent business with Fitch. All of the Earps in that fight faced murder charges, and maybe the gallows.

Mattie appeared in the doorway of my home, looking disordered. She had been sampling again, but just what had enlarged her pupils I did not know.

"You smell," she said.

I ignored her, tumbled water from a pitcher into a vitreous white bowl, and scrubbed myself.

"Out on bail," she said.

"Yes, and it was a lot of money friends put up for me," I said. I wiped my face and wrestled my way into a shirt.

"I need money," she said.

"I don't have any."

"You spent it all on her."

I buttoned my sleeves, slipped into my black suit coat, slid a revolver into my coat pocket, and headed toward the door.

"I don't know why I'm here," she said.

"You're not. That's the trouble."

She stared at me, her eyes black pits.

I felt a moment of pity, as I often did, and then stiffened against it, and left. Armed friends swiftly surrounded me. But I felt naked. An assassin would find an easy mark and I didn't doubt there would be men like that looking for ways.

I hadn't seen Josephine, and knew I wouldn't soon. My life had become public and I walked nowhere without security. Others of these stout friends, businessmen, shopkeepers, barkeeps, and mining executives guarded Virgil's house, and also Morgan's and Jim's.

I wondered what Josie might do, whether we still would be lovers, whether all this might frighten her away. I thought it would. She was simultaneously bold and adventuresome, timid and eager for the respectable home she fled. I could only wait and see. It would not be easy to be the lover of a man charged with multiple murders, and I knew she would be arguing that very thing inside of herself as the daily headlines screamed. And it would get worse before it improved.

Tombstone rested peacefully in the morning sun. The November days were short and the buildings cast long shadows. I headed for the office of Tom Fitch, off Fremont Street, knowing how much my life and those of my brothers would depend on his skills. He knew mining towns, having practiced in Virginia City, Nevada, where he had acquired a reputation for winning.

But he was also too smooth for my taste, too courtly. I would have chosen a bulldog if I could have. He had started as a newsman, been elected to the California legislature, and practiced law in Nevada and California and Utah. He was a friend of Mark Twain, had been a delegate to the Nevada statehood convention, and was once elected to Congress. In Utah he had handled litigation for the Latter-Day Saints. I did not know whether he was a Mormon. He had another attorney, T. J. Drum, as part of the defense team. Drum was defending Doc. Maybe Drum should have been my man too. But with all those moneybags putting up bail and arranging counsel, I had little choice. The silver-voiced orator would defend me.

I knew something else about Fitch: in Virginia City he had become an editorial target of the powerful *Territorial Enterprise*, which raked him for abandoning the Union Party at the Nevada statehood convention. Fitch replied, in print, that the editorial policies of that paper reminded him of the love of God, and it didn't take long for the *Enterprise* publisher, Joe Goodman, to add the tail to that biblical verse: "which passeth all understanding."

That led to editorial barbs about their manhood, which led to the code duello. The gents met on the field of honor near Virginia City one September day in 1863, the weapons Colt Dragoon revolvers. Upon taking the appropriate steps away from each other, Goodman fired, shattering Fitch's kneecap. Fitch walked with a limp the rest of his life, including those moments he defended me.

I supposed that a man who had survived a duel might keep my neck out of a noose, though I wasn't sure of the logic of all that. For better or worse, Tom Fitch was my man and my brothers' man, and our fate rested on him and his ability to pick apart the lies.

Chapter 19

I look back upon that preliminary hearing before Justice Wells Spicer as a postgraduate course in lying under oath. But I also look back upon it as proof of the vulnerability of liars, who can't quite get their stories right and consistent and true, and get tied into knots by their own words.

I am thinking of the ways that Ike Clanton lied himself into defeat when it became plain to every person in Spicer's courtroom that the whole fabric of his story was unraveling. It was Ike who provoked the gunfight—Ike whose ramblings led to our salvation.

The hearing began November 1 and lasted a month, and if we had lost, my brothers and I would have faced a murder trial. It was a bad month, and for a while, I despaired of ever seeing blue sky again, except through iron bars. We had money enough because a number of citizens gave or lent it to us and we added all that we had.

But the other side had ample funds too. For one thing, Will McLaury arrived. He was a Texas lawyer bent on avenging the death of his brothers, and he set out to do it not only in court but in the public prints, and by every other means he could devise, making particular use of the *Nugget*.

Guilt or innocence didn't matter to him. He wasn't there as the blindfolded goddess of justice. No evidence could dissuade him from his belief that his brothers were innocent ranchers, engaged in ordinary stock raising, who were murdered by outlaws wearing badges.

I don't suppose that if his brothers had ascended from hell long enough to tell him the truth of it, Will would have altered his opinion one iota. He was going to hang the Earps and Holliday, who were guilty as sin, and that was the whole of what absorbed his energies.

But there were other formidable men on that prosecution team. First, the new county prosecutor, Lyttleton Price, and then there was Ben Goodrich, a former Confederate officer, bulldog lawyer, teetotaler, and veteran attorney for the Cowboy element. These substantial men had additional support from several other firms, paid to abet the prosecution. I feared them. There were more lawyers seeking to string a noose around my neck than I cared to see across those tables in the temporary county courthouse. The brick one that stands in Tombstone now had not yet been finished.

Doc and I were alone in the dock; Virgil and Morgan lay abed, gravely injured. Doc's attorney, Drum, and Fitch, had correctly surmised that the prosecution would go after Doc, whose reputation made him vulnerable, all the more because it was mostly legend.

Doc knew it too, and listened bleakly in that chill and dark courtroom. Will McLaury, dressed in fine checked suits, surveyed us with hooded eyes, as if the only thing that would satisfy him was the sight of us hanging from nooses.

"Yon Cassius has a mean and hungry look," Doc said, amused.

"All the better," Fitch said, a remark that puzzled me.

Spicer was a balding, fleshy man with a way of listening intently to everything said. I knew that nothing would escape him. I have never supposed he was in our camp though I soon heard rumors of it. His loyalty was simple: to justice. He would have lowered the whole justice system upon the Earps if the evidence had led him to.

I don't suppose he was any friend of the Cowboys, either. He was well acquainted with the stagecoach robberies and rustling in the area and the lists of suspects. I found myself paying close attention to him, to that slightly jowly face with the thinning hair above, to the calf-eyed gaze that read deeply into the witnesses. To the respect he paid to the attorneys on both sides. I could find no bias in him one way or another. Indeed, the ten-thousand-dollar bail he set for us was evidence of how seriously he took the matter.

Much had obviously happened in those few days between the fight and the inquest, and now the witnesses for the prosecution had a coherent story put together. There had plainly been some coaching. The oddity was that this new version of the street fight starkly contradicted the first accounts published by both papers, which I thought had covered the fight fairly accurately.

Over these decades, the exact words spoken by all those people have frayed in my head but not the general tone of the testimony. They started off with Billy Allen, saloon man, friend of the Cowboys, alleged witness. John Behan came next, and by the time those two were done, it was plain to all of us what the story would be: Doc started it, and it was all premeditated mass murder by a mob with badges.

"When the order was given, 'Throw up your hands,'

I heard Billy Clanton say, 'Don't shoot me. I don't want to fight.' Tom McLaury at the same time threw open his coat and said, 'I have nothing,' or 'I am not armed.'" Behan continued smoothly, "I can't tell the position of Billy Clanton's hands at the time he said, 'I don't want to fight.' My attention was directed just at that moment to the nickel-plated pistol, the nickel-plated pistol was the first to fire, and another followed instantly. These two shots were not from the same pistol. The nickel-plated pistol was fired by the second man from the right. The second shot came from the third man from the right. The fight became general." He added that the first two shots were fired by the Earp party.

That was some testimony, coming from a man who had hidden from flying lead within a vestibule.

They knew that Doc was our vulnerable spot; they knew that the Earp brothers had a fine record as lawmen, so they dug at the weak point. Doc, they claimed, had pulled his nickel-plated revolver and opened the ball. Just how he did that while he was carrying the Wells Fargo shotgun is beyond me, and has intrigued assorted people ever since.

I like to think he did it juggler style, tossing it up, blasting off six shots with his revolver, then catching the shotgun midair and finishing off Tom McLaury with it. But Doc was more modest, and claimed simply to have employed the revolver with his right hand, and the shotgun with his left, while reserving his feet for stiletto work and his teeth to hold spare ammunition. I suppose learned professors will be debating his skills for years to come.

Behan, of course, proceeded along the lines that the Cowboys were leaving town, politely showed the constabulary that they were unarmed and pleaded for their lives before the Earps executed them. He added that he heard us announce beforehand that we were going to descend on them and make a fight, something very different from disarming them. He was a man with amazing ears, hearing conversations from half a block away, and from behind walls and doors.

I sat there in that stuffy room, the windows closed against the November chill, watching Smiling John Behan spin these stories and stick with them under cross-examination. I have to give him credit; he made a credible and earnest liar. From him the court learned that he had disarmed the Cowboys, that he had warned the Earps against confronting the Cowboys, and that the Earps had slaughtered unarmed men engaged in nothing illegal.

I think John had it in for me. I hadn't really taken Josephine Marcus from him; she had already left his too-public bed. But he liked to think it, believing that all the world was his private property, including her, and therefore he was the aggrieved party in the matter. And I confess I took some pleasure in aggrieving him, which now I regret.

I did not see her during the entire proceeding. She neither came to the courtroom nor attempted to rendezvous in any fashion, but was forced to rely on the papers. The Earp women were sometimes present, even Mattie. But Big-Nosed Kate Elder was not, preferring discretion. That was wise. Her presence would have been noted and would have turned the court further against Doc, given her obvious vocation. Mattie watched me from fevered and bright eyes, somehow never crossing a certain line between coherence and incoherence.

There was a look in her face, those evenings at home after each day's ordeal in the court, which suggested pity and fear. She wanted me freed. She stayed fairly sober or sensate, and quietly made me comfortable, touching my cheek with her hands, straightening my collar, placing perfectly broiled steaks and mashed potatoes and gravy before me. I saw it, and we had moments of peace in my household. She perhaps enjoyed the reality of being welcome among the spectators with the other Earp women, while Josephine's presence would have embarrassed me. For once she possessed something denied to Josephine. I was glad Mattie was there.

She was calling herself Mattie when I met her in Bessie's parlor house, and only later did I learn that her real name was Celia Ann Blaylock, and she was not yet twenty. She was tender and sarcastic then, the boldest girl in the place, and I snatched her away. Not many men find a willing wife in such a place. I wish I had looked closer at her pillboxes.

The prosecution was too smart to blame much on Virgil; it was well known he had only a baton in hand, Doc's walking stick. So they went after Doc.

It was effective. Across the West, and in Tucson especially, the tide turned against us, and now the daily papers were editorializing against the Earp Gang, who wore badges and terrorized honest citizens and were worse than the Cowboys. We were losing the war of words. And it was at last beginning to dawn on me that those words could wrap our skinny necks in hemp, kill us just as effectively as bullets. The gunfight that Behan had painted in sworn testimony was not the gunfight I knew had happened, not even the one he had described to the reporter from the *Nugget* minutes after it had happened.

Try as he might, Fitch made no headway against the testimony, and Behan insisted under cross-examination that the nickel-plated revolver started the fight, no matter that Doc was carrying a shotgun.

"For a man hiding from bullets in Fly's photo studio, he sure saw and heard everything," I whispered to Fitch.

Fitch nodded, but never made anything of it, never asked Behan where he had been during the fight. I wish he had taken the whole court to the site of the street fight and showed where Behan had hidden when lead was flying.

Spicer rapped his gavel and stared at me. He brooked no breach of decorum in that court.

I remember Fitch asking whether Behan and Allen had met beforehand to compare testimony, and whether Behan had offered to contribute to the fund to pay the prosecution attorneys. Lying John Behan said in both cases that he had not. Behan said that the McLaurys and Billy Clanton had not caused trouble— not even Ike was causing serious trouble or disturbing the peace of Tombstone in the hours before the street fight.

Fitch asked about the deal between Behan and me that Behan had reneged on, and Behan weaseled his way from that one, until the unanswered question was lost in a mountain of words.

Fitch and Drum seemed inept to me, unable to deal with the testimony, and I grew impatient with them and wanted them to cut through the lies. All I knew just then was that we were losing, and should have been winning; we were deputized peace officers disarming dangerous criminals who had publicly said they would kill us, and now we were being cast as a gang of murderers. Even in the San Francisco papers, which were closely following the hearing, the tide was turning. Each night we met with our attorneys to plan the next day's strategy, but each day we fell further into the pit.

The testimony was slowly tightening a noose around my neck. I heard the bells toll, and they tolled for me.

Chapter 20

Virgil lay on his bed, his calf bandaged and elevated. He looked ill, I thought, as I studied him in the buttery light of a coal-oil lamp. Morgan lay on his stomach, beside him. He had walked from his house next door with Louisa's help. He looked all right, though his wound was debilitating him. Neither had shaved, and both looked ragged.

Several of us crowded into that small parlor. Doc was there, in a mint green shirt, natty gray cutaway suit, and bowtie. The lawyers, Drum and Fitch, occupied creaking chairs that Allie had dragged from the kitchen. Allie and Bessie and Louisa watched from the doorway.

Fitch opened the ball. "They're working on you, Mr. Holliday. We'll deal with that now. What about the second shotgun charge? It was a double-barreled gun, wasn't it? Where was it directed?"

Doc pondered it. "I don't rightly remember. One caught Tom McLaury when his horse sidestepped. I'm not sure I fired the other. I pitched it and drew my handgun, which was at my bosom."

"According to the coroner's report, Tom was the only one who took a load of buckshot," Drum said, studying some documents through his wire-rimmed spectacles.

"Maybe I got him twice," Doc said.

"Did you shoot first, as alleged?" Fitch wanted to know.

"No. I didn't even have the shotgun out of my coat."

Drum scribbled something and looked up. "Now who of our party shot first?"

"I did," I said. "I saw Billy thumb the hammer of his revolver, and Frank did too. But I shot at Frank."

"Are you all agreed?"

Virgil and Morgan nodded.

"Who of the Cowboys shot first?"

"Billy Clanton pulled and shot at me. He was the most excitable," I said.

"Are you all agreed?"

No one disputed it.

He turned to Doc. "When did you start?"

"When I saw that Tom, behind that nag, was not covered by the others, and was reaching for something."

We hashed out that moment for several minutes. None of us could remember Doc firing first; and all of us remembered he had used the shotgun, not the revolver.

"No handgun was found near Tom afterward," Fitch said.

"I think I saw someone, maybe Wes Fuller, around there after he fell," Virgil said. "I think Tom had one."

"You're implying someone picked up a revolver?"

Virgil shrugged. "I can't say."

"They're working toward a scenario in which you Earps fired on men who were either unarmed or saying they didn't wish to fight. That's their case. And their target is you, Mr. Holliday."

"I'm the old bull's-eye," Doc said, oddly nonchalant.

As I remember that evening so long ago, every one of us agreed about what had happened. The Cowboys and Behan were building a case on lies again, but none of us could come up with anything that would punch a few holes in their story.

As the witnesses paraded past Judge Spicer over the next few days, it only grew worse. Will McLaury was grinning wolfishly as the evidence, such as it was, piled up against the Earp brothers. I sat there, wondering at last whether maybe I would be the only law officer in history strung from a noose for trying to enforce the law of a city. They wouldn't touch Virgil, who approached while waving that walking stick. Nor Morgan, who had fallen early in the fray. Just Doc and me.

The same papers that had applauded us a few days earlier now were talking about innocent men gunned down by thugs with badges. I knew that Allie and Louisa were scared, but Mattie kept to herself, except to weep now and then.

Afterward, back in my house, she slipped up to me. I could smell whiskey on her breath.

"It's bad, isn't it, Wyatt?"

"It's bad."

"I pray you'll get through."

"Mattie . . ."

She clutched me to herself, her thin arms clasping me close, and then she sobbed against my chest, great convulsions of tears, as if she were crying not just for me, but for herself, for her world, for all that had gone sour in our lives. I had hoped to wear that shirt another day, but now it was headed for the Chinaman.

She made me uncomfortable, and I slowly extricated myself from those desperate arms and went to bed. Her face was wet and radiating pain. I could not look at her, and slid under the blanket facing toward the rose-colored wallpaper.

I wondered how Josephine was bearing it. I hadn't seen her, couldn't keep her, couldn't even send messages to her. Then I heard from Marshall Williams that she had given up her cottage and skipped town. Not a word to me. I didn't know where she had gone. Back to San Francisco, probably, where it was safer in her parents' nest. She was still a girl in some ways.

I supposed I'd never see her again. I was notorious, and things looked bad, and she decided suddenly she had no future in Tombstone. I wondered whether I did. She was gone, she who could melt me with the touch of her hand, who could be companionable without saying a thing.

I didn't say a word to Mattie or give her the pleasure of her victory.

Then, late in the hearing, Ike was sworn in and suddenly everything changed. I stared at that droop-eyed bastard as he swore to tell the whole truth, and I was ready to leap up there and strangle him before the bailiffs pulled me off of him. I know now that he was a strange amalgam of conceit and mental slowness. Slow Ike is what I call him now, King of the Outlaws. He lasted until 1887, when a range detective shot and killed him. He was dodging the law at the time and had some felony warrants outstanding. So he learned nothing from the trial; he was incorrigible and got himself improved by a range detective.

Now, as he sprawled on the witness stand, he was dressed in a new checked suit, had managed to bathe, and had visited a tonsorial parlor that had trimmed his scruffy beard and unkempt brown hair, and he had all the outward marks of respectability. But almost from the first, he dug a hole that he and the whole prosecution team could never climb out of.

He told the standard story that he had rehearsed along with the rest, including Claiborne, Billy Allen, Wes Fuller, and John Behan. That made five witnesses all saying the same thing: Ike and his bunch were heading out, they weren't interested in a fight, they raised their hands or opened their coats to show they weren't heeled, and then the murder began. The prosecution had found a few bystanders to support the story and make it all credible.

If he had quit there, I might not be here now, decades later, to remember it. But it pays to recollect that Ike was both vain and slow, and that turned out to be a fateful pair of deuces.

It began with a simple question asked at the end of a long day.

"Did you threaten the Earps before the fight?" Tom Fitch asked.

"No, sir," Ike said.

That certainly won some attention in court.

Ike pleaded a headache the next day, but the following day he took the stand again. I remember it well. One after another of Ike's threats made in the hours before the fight were read back to him from the testimony of others, and Ike was forced to acknowledge that indeed he had made the threats.

Then the whole deal between Ike and me to lure Leonard, Head, and Crane into my hands came up. Now Ike took the tack that the Earps and Holliday were scheming to pipe the stolen money from the stagecoach into their hands; that Doc had killed Philpott, the stagecoach jehu, and now the Earp boys wanted to kill Ike to silence him. The Earps and Doc, it seemed, had taken Ike into their confidence and admitted the robbery while parleying behind the Eagle Brewery.

"Doc Holliday told me he was there at the killing of Bud Philpott. He told me that he shot Bud Philpott through the heart," Ike proclaimed.

Indeed, Ike said, he had heard all of this from Virgil and from me. "Before they told me, I made a sacred promise not to tell it and never would," he said. But now, on the witness stand, he was revealing the dark secret for the first time, for the sake of truth.

I remember sitting there, listening to that stuff, thinking that I had just walked off the gallows. It didn't matter to Ike that no money had been taken from that stage and there was none to split up; Bob Paul had driven the coach to safety.

Ike had prepared his little yarn, reversing the reality, making it seem that the robbery was an Earp gambit, and the street fight was an effort to silence those who knew about it, especially Ike, even though Ike survived when a bullet from me could indeed have silenced him. Ike's logic, or the lack of it, stunned the court, and his attorneys could not shut him down. I saw Spicer blotting up Ike's every word.

Our man Fitch hardly needed to drive home the point, but he did anyway. I remember silver-haired Fitch, pacing before the witness, his lips forming the question he was about to spring, a certain delicious glint in his eye.

"Didn't Marshall Williams, the Wells Fargo agent, state to you he was personally concerned in the attempted stage robbery and killing of Philpott?"

Ike considered craftily whether to agree, and then Fitch lobbed another.

"Didn't James Earp also confess to you that he was personally concerned in the attempted stagecoach robbery and the murder of Philpott?"

Ike, seeing the chance to implicate a few more of his enemies, would have agreed but for the sudden noisy objection of the prosecution attorneys, who at last were able to shut up their star witness.

I felt a tidal shift of feeling in that hearing room. That damn fool Ike had blabbed himself into defeat.

Then it was my turn. I started to read a carefully prepared statement, to which the prosecution instantly objected, but eventually Spicer admitted it, pointing out that nothing in the Arizona code prohibited it.

We prepared it because I don't have the gift of words, and it was plain to Fitch and Drum that I would muddle things up. I would need to read something if I hoped to make my case. So I simply told what happened in my own way, with the sentences polished up a little. I made my whole case too, going back to the time when Virgil as federal marshal attempted to recover army mules from these Cowboys and the McLaurys actually threatened his life for doing it. I detailed all the affronts to the law, the threats, the warnings, and finally, the need to disarm these dangerous men.

Virgil, up and about now in late November, followed me on the stand, and his testimony supported my own. And even as he talked, the Cowboy house of cards built of lies tumbled down. There were a few more witnesses, and a few more disputes, but that was it: we could only wait for Wells Spicer's decision.

Chapter 21

I remember that solemn afternoon of November 30, 1881, less for Spicer's verdict that set us free than for the murderous glare radiating from Will McLaury as Spicer quietly read it. McLaury may have worn the tweeds of a civilized lawyer but he was a barbarian within, and I had the chilling apprehension just then that he would be the instigator of terrible things, and that the peril we had faced would be nothing compared to the afflictions that this man would place upon us.

My apprehension proved to be correct.

The Honorable Wells Spicer convened the hearing at two o'clock, and after we had quietly assembled, he began reading. As he read, thunderclouds of rage swept that courtroom. His decision became one of the most quoted and fabled conclusions in the history of the West, so I won't go into it here, at least not in any great detail.

It started badly for us when he read that Virgil's handling of the Cowboys was unwise and censurable, but he added that he could attach no criminality to the attempt to disarm and arrest the lawbreakers, nor in Virgil's gathering of staunch and true friends—that is, Doc—to assist in the hard and necessary task.

"Was it for Virgil Earp as chief of police to abandon his clear duty as an officer because its performance was likely to be fraught with danger? Or was it not his duty that as such an officer he owed to the peaceable and law-abiding citizens of the city . . . to at once call to his aid sufficient assistance and persons to arrest and disarm these men?

"There can be but one answer to these questions, and that answer is such as will divest the subsequent approach of the defendants toward the deceased of all presumption of malice or of illegality."

I heard that with blooming relief and barely listened to the rest. Spicer was by no means done, and in his own way gently made mincemeat of the opposition. Spicer knew how to spot a fraud when he heard one, and even though he clothed his decision in the dispassionate language of the law court, he was, in my estimation, calling the Cowboys a bunch of damned liars.

I can thank the coroner, Dr. Matthews, for some of the evidence that freed us. Matthews had made a thorough examination of each body, recording the exact trajectory of each bullet, and all this was duly brought out in court. Spicer shredded the testimony that Billy Clanton was shot with his hands up. The angle of the wrist wound, the judge noted, was "such as could not have been received with his hands up." Likewise: "The wound received by Thomas McLaury was such as could not have been received with his hands on his coat lapels. These circumstances, being indubitable facts, throw great doubt upon the correctness of the statement of witnesses to the contrary."

And as for Ike's contention that the Earps were scheming to assassinate him, Spicer noted that Ike didn't make sense. "The testimony of Isaac Clanton, that this tragedy was the result of a scheme on the part of the Earps to assassinate him and thereby bury in oblivion the confessions the Earps had made to him about 'piping' away the shipment of coin by Wells Fargo and Company falls short of being sound theory, on account of the great fact, most prominent in this matter, to wit: that Isaac Clanton was not injured at all, and could have been killed first and easiest, if it was the object of the attack to kill him. He would have been the first to fall. . . ."

In short, the Cowboy case was bull.

I saw Tom Fitch smile.

"There being no sufficient cause to believe that the within named Wyatt S. Earp and John H. Holliday guilty of the offense mentioned within, I order them to be released."

I remember that moment. Dead silence at first, then a rush of air, and then hubbub. I stood, a free man, and shook Doc's hand and the hands of Fitch and Drum, but even as I did, I felt that gaze across the room burning into me like bullets. Virgil and Morgan had come to this session even though they remained weak. They shook my hand heartily. We were brothers, and always would be brothers, and that was the most important thing in my young life.

Will McLaury stood, isolated, a strange aura about him.

He had never come to grips with the reality that his brothers were criminals, were murderous, or had violated any law of the territory or of the city, or any moral law. He saw only that his brothers had died at our hands and the slaying must be avenged, no matter that the court had just concluded that what happened had the sanction of legal law enforcement. His only law was an eye for an eye, a tooth for a tooth.

So terrible was his gaze that people shied from him,

and there were stark spaces around him as he slowly made his way into the cold afternoon. I feared him and watched as he silently stalked by, and knew in my bones he would be the author of darkness.

"Look at that," said Virgil.

"Like someone walked over my grave," Morgan said.

I wished he hadn't said that.

From the back of the room, Jim, Bessie, Allie, Louisa, and Mattie smiled at me. We Earps had gathered for this.

I walked outside, into cold sunlight, a free man. Doc patted me on the shoulder and headed home, a solitary man with no one but Kate to welcome him or cheer his victory. No one slapped his back or celebrated his release. No woman hugged him. No reporter sought to interview him. He stood erect, in the pale winter sun, blinked, and walked quietly through the whispering spectators. I suddenly wished his mother and father could have been with him at that moment. Then he was gone from sight, around the corner, and I knew the next time I saw him, he would be sitting at a green baize table, with cards and chips lying on it.

Both Virgil and Morgan were up and about now. We celebrated with a feast at the Cosmopolitan Hotel, and relaxed a little. But the public safety committee had not relaxed its vigilance, and the shadow of assassination hung over us all. Virgil talked of getting out of Tombstone. I wanted to stay.

"I'm going to register to vote in this county," I said, and the next day I did. That act was a shot across the bow of John Behan and his political machine, whose approach to law and order had wounded my brothers and put us in the shadow of the gallows. It was part and parcel of my plan to win that office and wear that star.

"Maybe we should move on," Virgil said. "Tombstone's not the same and never will be."

"Better than ever," I replied. My stubborn streak was showing.

Clum approached me. "Our men can't guard you at your houses night and day," he said. "I don't even know about tonight. They want to quit now that it's over."

I couldn't expect them to stand guard anymore. "We'll make arrangements," I replied. "You've kept us safe for over a month, and the Earps will never forget your sacrifices, the sleep lost, the time devoted to us."

"I'll tell them that," Clum said.

We moved into the Cosmopolitan Hotel, where we could sleep secure. We did not at first know that the vengeful Cowboys had rented a room in the Grand Hotel across the street, and were keeping an eye on us through the blinds.

Tombstone had changed. I thought we'd be celebrated for restoring the peace, but instead, much of that town hated that decision to free us and made us unwelcome. Men spit when I walked by. Others turned away.

How strange it was. From the moment Judge Spicer had read his decision, we had no real home in Tombstone. I saw it in the *Nugget*, which redoubled its malice, but I also saw it in every saloon, in the merchants, in the hostlers in the livery stables, and even in the Wells Fargo office, where Marshall Williams dealt peculiarly with me. Well, we would show them a thing or two. Virgil was the chief of police and there would be peace in this city.

Even though Marshall Williams had already informed me that Josie had skipped town, that first night of liberty I quietly slid over to her cottage when I had darkness to shield me. She had indeed vacated it, leaving no word of her whereabouts. It was a cold and cloudless night when I knocked on her dark door, and I was on the watch for trouble. As the knocks echoed hollowly, and no one answered, I realized that she was really gone, that I wouldn't see her again, that it was over.

I felt bad. I liked her because she liked me as I was, and never pestered me or wanted to know what I was thinking, or how I felt about her. But she made herself a companion, sharing life and love with me. She was the first woman since Urilla I was comfortable with mostly because she didn't butt into a man's business. As for Mattie, she was always digging into me one way or another, wanting something I couldn't give. It was little things. How did I like that dress? What was Urilla like? Why didn't I like to go on picnics? Who were my friends?

I'd get so I just shut up, and then she would wheel away with a whirl of skirts and next thing I knew she was blotting out her mind with something or other. It made me mad.

Now I had the task of living with Mattie in one small hotel room about big enough for us to turn around in, and I knew before a week was out that I'd haul her back to Fremont Street and be done with the hotel. At least I could keep out of that room, and that needful clawing at me for company. She was the loneliest woman I ever met, and it was all her doing. Josie would have just minded her own business, welcomed me in her arms, and kept to herself.

We held a council of war at Campbell and Hatch's Saloon and Billiard Parlor, where we could occupy that back room and talk privately. Morgan still hurt every time he reached over the table and stretched those torn-up muscles but Virgil was the same as ever, and had gotten his police chief job back after his suspension by the city.

"Who's threatening us, if anyone, and what do we do about it?" Virg asked, lining up his cue to pop the eight ball into a pocket.

"So far it's all threats. They've threatened Spicer's life, and John Clum, and us," I said.

Virgil made his shot, eyed the table, and puzzled over the next one. Nothing looked easy. He chalked his cue and lined up shots, and rejected them one by one.

"It's all talk," Morg said. "They got licked in court and now they'll just bluster and blow until they wind down."

"No, not just talk. Will McLaury's still here, still pulling strings, still talking to all those people, from Behan and Woods to some of those with trigger fingers, like Wes Fuller," I said.

"The point is, what do we do?" Virgil asked.

It was a good question. And I had an answer I was thinking about. "Go after them, Virg. You've got the badges. We know who they are. We know that if we do nothing, we're sitting ducks. But if we get up a federal posse and clean out this county, we'll preserve the safety of everyone, including ourselves. Behan won't do it, but there's enough federal laws that've been busted to let us do it. Mail robbery, stealing government property . . ."

Virgil waved his cue as if it were a baton. "Wyatt, we can't do that."

"Why not? This is our one chance. Strike hard, break up that bunch before they hurt us again."

"He's right, Virg. What we need is to round up the whole Cowboy bunch and ship them out of the county, once and for all," Morgan said. He popped his cue, attempting to drive all the balls on the table out of the county, and put two into pockets. He chortled.

Virgil stood there. I'll never forget it, because what he said was so fateful. "No, Wyatt. We're professional lawmen. We can't go out on a snipe hunt, looking for whatever we can find, targets of opportunity. It's not right and not legal. We'll stay right here, keep our guard up, and behave like the peace officers we are."

I knew better than to argue with him. When Virgil talked that way, with a sober finality in his words, all one could do was back off. I didn't like it. My whole instinct was to strike hard, then and there, out in the arroyos and canyons, and scatter the Cowboy crowd for good.

"We'll return to the way we were, Wyatt," he said. "You've already started your game at the Oriental. Doc's dealing again as if nothing happened."

"The women want to go home," Morgan said.

"That's true. Allie's about ready to go home, no matter what we say," Virg said. "She's fed up with hotel life."

"All the women want to," I said. "Mattie wants to."

They glanced at me a moment, their thoughts suddenly private.

"I'm not ready for that," Virg said quietly. "The first thing to do is show them we're not going to be pushed around. We'll pick up where we left off. As soon as Morg's healed up, he can ride shotgun again. But we'll be ready for trouble, and if it comes, we'll meet it and strike back."

"We're broke, Virgil. I've bled myself dry to pay Fitch. My mining claims and a few lots are all that's left. Morg's broke. You're broke. How are we going to pay for these hotel rooms?"

"It won't be for long," Virgil said.

I didn't like it, but I wasn't wearing two badges, and in the end, what happened would depend on Virgil's judgment, his decisions, and his courage.

Chapter 22

One way or another, we received death threats. And we weren't alone. Mayor John Clum, our staunch friend and editor of the *Epitaph*, received one. Judge Spicer received one and bravely brushed it off. Our attorney, silver-tongued Tom Fitch, probably did. He denied it publicly but hastily decamped to Tucson. Doc Holliday was a target but he simply kept his game going and stayed wary.

Rumors whirled. Supposedly there was a blood list, a vengeance list, and those of us who had resisted the outlaws were on it. I didn't doubt that somewhere there was a bullet intended for me. It would only be a matter of time.

The threat made to Spicer came in the form of an anonymous letter to the *Epitaph*:

Sir, if you take my advice, you will take your departure for a more genial clime, as I don't think this one healthy for you much longer. As you are liable to get a hole through your coat at any moment. If such sons of bitches as you are allowed to dispense justice in this territory, the sooner you depart from us the better.

Judge Wells Spicer made the effort of a reply, which also took the form of a letter to the *Epitaph*:

I am well aware that all this hostility to me is on account of my decision, in the Earp case, and for that decision, I have been reviled and slandered beyond measure, and that every vile epithet that a foul mouth could utter has been spoken of me, principal among which has been that of corruption and bribery. It is but just to myself that I should here assert that neither directly nor indirectly was I ever approached in the interest of the defendants, nor have I ever received a favor of any kind from them. Not so the prosecution—in the interest of that side even my friends have been interviewed in the hope of influencing me with money, hence all this talk by them and those who echo their slanders about corruption. . . .

In conclusion I will say that I will be here just where they can find me should they want me, and that myself and others who have been threatened will be here long after the foul and cowardly liars and slanderers have ceased to infest our city.

That was a brave response from a brave man and I admired it. The threatening letter sounded like the work of Will McLaury to me. I first thought it might be Ike's work, but Ike's vocabulary did not include a phrase such as "genial clime." Will McLaury, who was still in Tombstone stirring up trouble, probably authored the threat.

Being a bull's-eye is a hard thing to live with. It made us edgy. We started at shadows, looked a long time at passersby, studied men standing at bar rails. The citizens' committee guarded us each night at the Cosmopolitan Hotel, but that island of safety sat in the middle of an ocean of danger.

Then it was discovered that the Cowboys had rented a room in the Grand Hotel opposite our hotel, with a window overlooking Allen Street, where observers could keep tabs on us through a slit in the blind. A clerk at the Grand, Jack Altman, noticed that the room was constantly being visited by men such as John Ringo, Bill Brocius, Ike Clanton, Pony Deal, Milt Hicks, and others of that dubious crowd. He slipped across the street to warn us, and after that, we kept a sharp eye on that shutter, which had one slat missing, knowing that eyes followed us and a rifle barrel easily could, at any time.

"Jack," I said, "you've done us a hell of a favor."

"I don't like that crowd. I'll let you know if I see anything more."

"Be careful," I said. "If you're caught, you'll be on their list too."

Altman stared at me, smiled, and nodded.

That room was always occupied and no lamp was ever lit in it. So the threats were real, not simply some sort of intimidation. Watchful men were stalking the Earps and their friends, and we felt it in our bones. Tombstone was not a good place to be now.

Still, Virgil insisted on normalcy as much as possible, so he patrolled the streets as soon as his wounded calf permitted it, staying armed and wary. I ran my faro game and tried to rebuild my fortunes. My funds were badly depleted by hotel living and legal fees, and a good run with my faro bank might help.

I wanted to strike them, strike hard, but Virgil's reminder that we were professional peace officers and could not start fights stayed me. I also stayed armed; so did Morgan and Doc, no matter what the ordinance said. Virgil was a stickler for enforcing the law but this time I didn't see him growling at Doc or the Earp brothers.

The *Nugget*, with Undersheriff Harry Woods editing, and Richard Rule pumping out copy, never let up on us, and successfully agitated the town against us until I felt isolated. The *Epitaph* railed against the outlaw element and Behan, but with less effect. Woods and Rule waltzed around the ponderous Clum. I was learning about the lethal power of words, but it was a lesson poorly learned.

Once again, my thoughts turn to John Behan, who spent those days scheming against us rather than cooperating to enforce the law. Had there been cooperation, each lawman staunchly siding the others, the terrible things that descended on the Earps would never have happened. Behan was not there upholding law and order when we needed him, and his defection from duty will long be remembered.

Then, in mid-December, John Clum quietly started on a business trip that would take him out of town. He and four others boarded a night coach headed for Benson and the railroad, a coach without a guard because it carried no bullion, no mail. Clum took the jump seat, which offered a fast exit.

Just a few miles north of town, at Malcolm Station, the coach was ambushed. Robbers materialized out of the darkness and called for it to halt, but the driver, Jimmy Harrington, whipped the team onward as a barrage of gunfire penetrated the coach. The passengers dropped to the floor, but Clum stepped out the opposite door, ready to drop off the speeding coach. When at last the coach halted and the driver cut out a wounded horse, Clum quietly vanished into the darkness and set foot for Benson. He didn't doubt that the bandits had attempted to assassinate him.

I supposed he was right when I later heard of it. Clum walked all the way to Benson and wired Behan, who set out to search for the bandits, of course finding nothing. The *Nugget* laughed it off. Their weapon was ridicule now, as if all that had happened was a joke. I don't recollect that they condemned the robbery or called for the robbers to be brought to justice. They were having too much fun with poor Clum, a decent and thoughtful man, but one ponderous with words and ideas.

My holiday season wasn't improved by Mattie's funk, either. She hated the hotel but dreaded to leave it, and managed to drink herself into oblivion each day. There was little for the women to do there, where they had few womanly chores to occupy them. Allie's main occupation was nagging Virgil. Only Louisa kept her grace and good humor about her, and I came to believe that Morg was the luckiest of the Earp boys in that department. The hotel had become a prison for us all.

Then, one cold night after Christmas, while Virgil was leaving the Oriental, our world flew apart. Near midnight, on Allen Street, four shotgun blasts tore into Virgil, the buckshot shattering his arm and striking the small of his back. The assassins had struck at last, this time from a building under construction, from which they could easily escape. The blasts tore up the front of the Eagle Brewery, and the damage drew spectators for weeks. Three men were seen racing into the dark and were swiftly lost from sight, even though pursuers took after them.

I remember hearing those blasts, coming so fast I wasn't sure how many there were. Then Virgil staggered into the Oriental, his heavy buffalo coat soaked in blood. Only the thickness of that massive coat spared his life.

I saw him stagger toward me, and knew that grief had found us again. I caught him as he stumbled into my arms, and swiftly carried him across to the Cosmopolitan.

"Wyatt," he said. "Help me. I don't know . . ."

Whether he would live, I thought.

Lou Rickabaugh or someone sent for a doc, and by the time I carried Virgil to his room and got his blood-soaked coat off, Drs. Matthews and Goodfellow hurried in, began to stop the blood, and to see what might be done.

Allie was sobbing. Virgil hadn't lost consciousness and stared up at me while the doctors cut away his clothing. But he had slid into shock and said nothing, his eyes funny-looking. His left arm was a ruin. His back had absorbed shot but somehow none had struck his spinal column or a vital organ.

Virgil looked as if he might fail at any moment. There was more bright blood there on that bed than I could endure.

"I'll get them, Virg, and that's a promise."

He didn't blink, but stared at me.

I laid my revolver on the nightstand.

Our Citizens' Safety men sealed us in there, and for the moment, we were secure.

That arm was red pulp and only a tourniquet kept Virgil's blood inside of him.

"Amputate," said Matthews.

"Well, let's see," Goodfellow said.

Sopping away blood, they bared the broken humerus. I peered over their shoulders. It was yellow, splinters in a sea of red.

"Can't save that," Matthews said.

"We'll cut it out, save the arm," Goodfellow said, reaching into his Gladstone for a set of shining surgical tools, including a variety of small, sharp saws.

Goodfellow turned at last to Allie. "We're going to try to save his arm, but it'll be useless when we're done. We'll cut out five inches of bone and sew him up. It's better for him to have a bad arm than have none. And safer. I don't think he could stand an amputation."

"Oh, save him, save him," she cried.

Virgil spoke up at last. "Go ahead. My law days are over."

They wasted not a second. Goodfellow had all the skills of a butcher, and with blinding speed, he cut through bone, extracted the shattered portions, and then both doctors began suturing that ruined arm. Virgil was still bleeding, and the morbid certainty that he would die in a few minutes filled me. The room reeked of sweat and fear and bad breath.

They finally finished and bound the arm while Virgil groaned softly. So close was he to closing his eyes forever that they gave him no morphine, afraid it would finish him. But they were not done. They rolled him over gently, and started in on his back, where several balls had pierced his left side. One by one they plucked those that remained in him—flattened or twisted lead they lifted gently out with forceps and dropped onto the bedside table. After that, there was only the sterilizing, the washing with a mild carbolic, and then the long wait.

Virgil had slid into a comatose state, his white pallor the precursor of his doom. I did not know what was happening outside the small sanctuary of his room, but George Parsons had won admission, and he had some news.

"Ike Clanton's hat! It was found in that building, right there, Wyatt," George said. "The idiot. And someone saw Frank Stilwell there just before. And there was someone else, maybe a half-breed. Some people saw him. And get this," Parsons added pregnantly. "It just happens that Will McLaury conveniently left town two days ago."

Familiar names, obvious motives, a hat as physical evidence. I thought maybe I could make a case. I wanted to tell Virgil, but he was in his own world, barely hanging on.

After a long vigil through that night, in which we sat beside Virgil while life and death wrestled within him, I headed into a gray dawn to the telegraph, and wired U.S. marshal Crawley Dake:

VIRGIL WAS SHOT BY ASSASSINS LAST NIGHT. HIS WOUNDS ARE FATAL. TELEGRAPH ME APPOINTMENT WITH POWER TO APPOINT DEPUTIES. LOCAL AUTHORITIES ARE DOING NOTHING. THE LIVES OF OTHER CITIZENS ARE THREATENED.

—WYATT EARP

Chapter 23

Virgil lay abed, fevered and comatose, while Allie applied cold compresses to check the heat raging through him. I sat beside him as much as I could, feeling helpless. Morgan was far from recovered. I was the only Earp fit to ride.

Crawley Dake had immediately appointed me a deputy U.S. marshal with the power to appoint deputies, but for the moment there was little to do except see Virgil past the worst of it. As December faded into a new year, the *Nugget*'s Democrat candidates swept into office, and we had a new mayor, John Carr, a new city marshal, Dave Neagle, who also wore Behan's badge, and new county officials, including Milt Joyce, none of whom supported us. Harry Woods and Richard Rule had won the war of words, and day after day, their sheet ridiculed and condemned us. I was too worried about Virgil to pay much attention.

A new rash of stagecoach robberies afflicted Cochise County that January. The Bisbee stage was hit near Hereford, not far from the Clantons' ranch. After an ambush and chase, masked bandits stopped the coach and took $6,500 from the strongbox. Wells Fargo, responsible for the money, would have to make it up. I knew at once who had led that bunch: John Ringo. The robbers had threatened the driver and shotgun messenger, W. S. Waite and Charlie Bartholomew, with death if they revealed who they were. But those two didn't have to tell me. My informants supplied the names.

Wells Fargo decided to do something about it. The company sent its top detective, Jim Hume, to look things over and put a halt to the robberies if possible, but his own coach from Benson was stopped by masked men and robbed on January 7, with the bandits collecting about fifteen hundred dollars from the passengers, along with Hume's two revolvers and every cent he had.

He reported the affair to the *Epitaph*. The *Nugget* thought it was pretty comic. That was the trouble with that paper and the lawmen it endorsed. They thought it was all comedy. Men were robbed at gunpoint, and that was supposedly funny. Hume checked into the Grand Hotel and lost no time finding me for a private talk.

He was excited. "Wyatt, I had a good look at that bunch," he said. "Not only that, I talked with them steadily and got a sense of how they spoke. I think maybe I could identify some of them just by listening. What's their watering hole?"

"A saloon in Charleston run by a man named Ayers," I said. "It's a private matter, but Ayers is on my payroll. He's passed along some good tips."

Hume's eyebrows rose. "You have some good information, then."

He was right. "I've put men in their gangs, paid men in the livery stables, men in the saloons. I could name most of the robbers for any holdup within hours," I said. "The problem is proving it. Getting the goods on them in a way that will stick in the courts."

"Go get them, then. You've got the badge now. We'll

pound it out of them. I'm tired of this and so is the company. Get them, and we'll use some persuasion."

I smiled. Hume was a man I could work with.

I put a small posse together the next day and rode for Charleston and Ayers' watering hole, but no sooner did we wander in than we found Hume bellied up to the bar between a pair of Cowboys well known to me.

Hume eyed us suavely. "We were just about to have a drink when you gents arrived," he said. "Will you join us?"

"I could wet my whistle," I said. "We're just passing through and took on a thirst. I don't believe we've met."

"Barcelona Gates," he said. "Out of California."

So we drank.

Hume never let slip that he knew us, and only later did he tell me that the pair he was with were two of the bandits. He knew their voices and their mannerisms, but he had no hard evidence and could do nothing. We rode back empty-handed, as usual.

Late in January, I put together another posse, employing some federal and Wells Fargo funds, and attempted to round up those who tried to murder Virgil. I had warrants for Ike and Fin Clanton among others. That time I had Doc and Morgan with me; each man was heavily armed with a shotgun, a rifle, and revolvers.

"You up to it, Morg?" I asked.

"Wyatt, it's been three months."

"Louisa didn't want you to go. She said you can't lift your left arm right."

"A little exercise will improve that, Wyatt. I can lift it enough to shoot."

He did look better but there were still black hollows under his eyes, and he still slept on his stomach, which told me something.

Doc was grinning. "You sure you want a certified double-distilled stagecoach robber along?"

"Cut it out," I said.

No sooner had we ridden out of Tombstone than we found we were being shadowed by a gang of Cowboys. They never engaged us, stayed a few miles back, but kept us under observation. That was a hell of a thing: the posse was being watched, and we couldn't shake our pursuers. We stormed Charleston one night, knocked on every door, woke irate citizens, but we didn't find a single Cowboy in town.

"Wyatt, the only thing left for us is to rob a few coaches," Doc said. "I'll make sure all the passengers see me. I'll pass out some business cards."

Only Fred Dodge laughed.

After a lot of hard riding across that bleak chunk of high and naked desert, we again came back empty-handed, riding quietly into Tombstone one cold night. I had spent a chunk of Wells Fargo money on nothing.

The Cowboys obviously had as many informants as I did, maybe more, and our every move was noted. I remember riding back to Tombstone in a sour mood. I felt frustrated as hell: we couldn't even move, couldn't plan, couldn't strike because they were always a jump ahead of us.

Hume and I were getting nowhere. But intelligence was a two-way street, and one of these moments we would have some advance knowledge of an impending strike, and then we could do something about the mob riding freely through John Behan's county.

The sheriff, of course, did nothing but lament the presence of robbers in the county, and shed a few crocodile tears. At least it was being noticed around the territory that Behan had yet to bring a stagecoach robber or rustler or bandit to justice. Sometimes facts spoke for themselves, and Behan's record was speaking loudly in Prescott. Someday the world would understand how it was with him, and the direction the backslapping politician and his machine were taking Arizona.

Will McLaury had left town two days before Virgil was shot, and I still turn over in my mind what his role had been. There were those, like Ike Clanton, who needed no encouragement to shoot Virgil, and no doubt they did so, with or without McLaury's assistance.

I am sure of this much: he knew about the forthcoming assassination, left a convenient two days ahead of it, and did nothing to prevent it. He may have been a lawyer, a civilized man, and all of that, but in his failure to report what he knew was coming, or prevent it, he shared in the guilt. To this day, I believe Will knew and kept silent, and thus was an accessory before the fact.

In all the months he was in town, we never spoke, but through all the years that followed, he has never been far from my mind. I would bet my last nickel that he rejoiced upon the news of Virgil's wounding.

That was a somber winter. In Tombstone the daytime temperatures are mild in January and February, but the nights are chill and even frosty. Tombstone is an oasis in an anonymous and drab land, and some would say there is not a decent scenic view in any direction from that town. A man can stand on any prominence

around Tombstone, and see nothing to delight the eye
or balm the spirit. Just greasewood and naked rock.

Cochise County was now solidly governed by Democrats, and Clum and his paper and partisans were out
in the cold. The air was crisp, the sun low and cold, and
the town was quiet. Jim Hume was hinting publicly
that unless matters improved, Wells Fargo would quit
doing business in that area. That meant that the mines
would have to ship bullion out and payroll money in
on their own. And that meant that Tombstone's econ-
omy might tumble. But nothing happened. The hinter-
lands were still ruled by bandits.

But Hume's warnings were enough to prompt the
new Democrat mayor, John Carr, to ask citizens to co-
operate with the posses. That didn't slow down the
Nugget, which ignored the pleading of the new mayor,
and assailed my law enforcement almost daily.

I laid a few traps, tried to snare some of the Cowboys, but they were so well organized that we didn't
collar any of them. I had a sense that we were facing
two or three hundred well-informed guerrillas who always knew when we were coming. Maybe someone in
our number was tipping them off—the thought made
me wary.

Virgil had tiptoed past the gates of hell, and now
rested weakly at the hotel, his arm useless, his law career over, his badge lost to Dave Neagle, who was at
least genuinely trying to enforce Tombstone's ordinances.

"You got plans, Virgil?" I asked one bleak afternoon.

He stared up at me from the armchair next to his
bed. "California," he said. "I don't know what a one-
armed man can do there, but it beats Tombstone."

"I thought it might be that."

"San Bernardino, maybe. Nice country. Close to the folks."

"Oh, Virg, you've got a whole future of lawing ahead. I need you."

"Can't help you anymore."

"You'll always help me, Virg."

"Leave him alone, Wyatt," said Allie. "Can't you see he's hurting?"

"Allie, Wyatt and me, we're talking," Virgil said. It was a command, and she wrapped a shawl over her bony shoulders and fled the dreary room, slamming the door.

"I've a good arm," he said. "I just need to get my strength back and I'll help you any way you want."

"Mattie's ready to get out of this hotel," I said.

Virgil grinned at me. "You accommodating her?"

I stiffened and let some time pass. "Jim Hume and I are baiting some traps," I said. "If we can't catch them out in the county, maybe we can lure them in."

"Mattie and Allie are thick," Virgil said. "I think maybe she's turning over a new leaf. Maybe that's the thing: turn over some new leaves."

He was talking about Josephine, but I paid no attention. I hadn't seen her since November and hadn't heard from her, either, not even a postcard. And Mattie wasn't turning over any leaves. She was making daily visits to the Chinaman, and half the time I looked at her, her pupils were as big as half-dollars. It wasn't good, but it was no time to be riding other horses.

Chapter 24

I thought Virgil had quickened. His eyes were still hollow and his flesh looked sallow in the window light, but actually he was stronger, and for the first time, I thought he might see a Christmas again. I had been out with a posse, and hadn't visited him for a few days.

Morgan and I had pulled up chairs to talk with him, having shooed Allie off. I didn't like her hovering around. This was between brothers. Virgil was propped up on some pillows. He was following events now, and not just staring at the ceiling.

I had a lot of bad news. "We failed again," I said. "We raided Charleston a few times and didn't find a Cowboy in the whole town. They were tipped off. No sign of Ike or Fin either. Or Pony Deal. My posse couldn't take a leak without the Cowboys knowing it. Damn it, Virg, how can I enforce the law when someone close to me is talking?"

Virgil nodded.

"All we did was rile up half of that mill town, and now the press is making fun of it."

"What's the *Nugget* saying?" Virg asked.

"The usual."

"Leave it to Behan," Morgan said.

Virgil grunted. The bandaged arm hung heavily.

Another jurist in Tombstone, William Stilwell, no relation to the outlaw, had become interested in the crime problem and chose a new approach, one that didn't involve me or my brothers. "Judge Stilwell sent out a party of citizens," I continued. "Not a badge in the bunch but it was a posse, and damned if they didn't bring in the Clantons. Imagine how I feel about that."

"Why did Stilwell do that?"

"Behan won't try. And we're being watched."

Virgil nodded. "Behan won't send a posse out?"

"He's had posses out, but they're not catching anyone. So the judge appointed his own posse and sent twenty men out with John Henry Jackson, and they rounded up the Clantons and some others, including Ringo, who made bail."

"You're leading up to something," Virgil said.

"Yes, I'm tired. Let's get out of here."

"What do you mean?"

"Let's turn in our badges, Virgil."

He was waiting for me to unburden myself, and I took my sweet time about it.

"Just don't take me for a quitter. This new posse, sent out by a district judge because Behan won't act and we can't, means that the town's given up on us. We're washed-up here. The citizens of this town, the ones we've tried to protect, voted for the *Nugget*'s candidates.

"Milt Joyce, who'd like to shove us out of town, is now a county commissioner, elected by all those butchers who thrive on stolen meat, along with the miners and businessmen who want cheap meat, and booze flowing into Cowboy bellies. It was us, the Earps, they were voting against. That was what lay behind that election.

"It comes down to Behan and the ring. They've got the county and city offices. It's worse than that. The

Cowboys control every road in southeast Arizona. They've got their safe places. They have their spies and allies. There's no chance of enforcing federal law if the sheriff is on the wrong side. If there was any chance of federal intervention, we'd stand a chance, but Washington won't intervene.

"Virg, we're sealed up here in this hotel because we face a bullet if we walk the streets. They're watching us through the blinds in the Grand Hotel right now, every minute, even as I speak. They know where we are. We've done what we could, but this town laughs it off, or worse, they call us the crooks. I'm tired of the goddamned *Nugget*. For them it's a game: pour the coals on us and laugh. For us it's no game—it's death and injury. You'll need time to recover, a year maybe, and California's a good place, Virgil."

Virgil stared at the grimy window, and then at his useless arm. He could do nothing with it, not even pluck a piece of paper. "It's your decision, Wyatt," he said. I'd never heard a sadder word from him.

"All right. It's mine. We'll get out."

"Wyatt, damn it," Morgan said. He was going to fight me, but I cut him off.

"It's the lies, the words that grind me down," I said. "I'll write a letter to Dake. He's here, trying to drum up some support, and now's the time."

"Let me see it before you send it," Virgil said. "Maybe you should get some help with it."

I had that in mind. No one I knew had even imagined I could write a letter. With Fitch in Tucson, I decided to find someone local, and who better than Doc? I left at once, and found him at his rooms sewing a button onto his fly.

"Write me a resignation. Virgil and I are quitting," I said.

"Wyatt, you really mean it?" he asked. "Might I ask why?"

"We can't even go to an outhouse without it being known to them. So we can't act. And now Judge Stilwell's working around us, and working around Behan, sending out that Jackson posse on his own authority. Jackson had no trouble picking up the Clantons and Ringo on old warrants. The Cowboys were watching out for us, not Jackson's outfit, so he surprised them. You know what that means? Our allies have given up on us. We're stuck. There's no future here."

"I've lost a war or two myself, Wyatt."

"Help me write it, Doc. I'm no good with this stuff. This is more for the public than for Dake. You get what I want?"

"I imagine," he said, dipped a nib into ink and began drafting the letter, sometimes eyeing me, sometimes staring out the window. I didn't see Kate in his rooms and didn't care to see her.

Major C. P. Dake, United States Marshal, Grand Hotel, Tombstone—Dear Sir: In exercising our official functions as deputy United States marshals in this territory, we have endeavored always unflinchingly to perform the duties entrusted to us. These duties have been exacting and perilous in their character, having to be performed in a community where turbulence and violence could almost any moment be organized to thwart and resist the enforcement of the processes of the court issued to bring criminals to justice. And while we have a deep sense of obligation to many of the citizens for their hearty cooperation in aiding us to suppress lawlessness, and their faith in our honesty of purpose, we realize that notwithstanding our best efforts and judgment in everything which we have been required to perform, there has arisen so much harsh criticism in relation to our operations, as such a persistent effort having been made to misrepresent and misinterpret our acts, we are led to the conclusion that, in order to convince the public that it is our sincere purpose to promote the public welfare, independent of any personal emolument or advantages to ourselves, it is our duty to place our resignations as deputy United States marshals in your hands, which we now do, thanking you for your continued courtesy and confidence in our integrity, and shall remain subject to your orders in the performance of any duties which may be assigned to us, only until our successors are appointed.

Doc blotted the letter and handed it over. I read it carefully. "It sure don't sound like me, Doc," I said.

"Hell, no," he said. "You couldn't write that letter if you tried. Your syntax is much too elegant."

I glared at him. What did that mean? He was always saying things like that.

"Behan finally got to you?" he asked.

"Maybe Harry Woods got to me. I can deal with bullets. It's the lies that kill me."

Doc stood and I found a rare earnestness in his face. "Long after Behan's gone and his ring has collapsed, long after his name is disgraced, Wyatt, you and your brave brothers will be remembered and honored."

"That's a hell of a thing to say," I said.

Doc laughed, and we shook hands on it.

I took the letter back to Virgil and read it.

"Sure sounds like some lawyer wrote it," he said.

"Doc did."

"Doc did? I don't talk that flowery."

"Just sign it, Virgil."

"I can manage that," he said. "What are you going to do with it?"

"Have a copy made. I'll give it to the *Epitaph*."

"You know what's going to happen? The whole territory's going to cheer!" he said.

"Not all. We have friends in our corner, Virgil. One or two."

"I was just trying to lighten things around here," he said, as he signed. He looked tired.

I dropped the copy off at the *Epitaph*, which was smack across the street from its rival. Clum's bald assistant read it and whistled. Then I took the original to the front desk of the Grand, the Cowboys' own hotel, where Crawley amused himself watching the suspects. His presence in the hotel no doubt cooled off some of those schemers in that front room upstairs.

Tombstone seemed quiet that wintry afternoon. There had been a little snow, which vanished, but icy winds were cutting through town, and a cold wind was cutting through me.

Maybe in California I could get Josie back and find some way to unload Mattie. I drifted toward Josie's cottage, close to the sporting district, and found it occupied. I knocked, thinking just maybe, maybe . . .

"Come on in, hon," said a blond woman with a cast in her left eye.

"Sorry, wrong address."

"I'll make it the right address, hon."

I walked off, headed for Fremont, and braved wind and cold. It felt good to get out of that hotel. No one followed; no long blue barrels poked from upstairs windows. I found my house abandoned. The Citizens' Committee was no longer guarding it. I twisted the skeleton key in the lock, entered cautiously, found nothing amiss. It wasn't much of a place, and once I had to fight the town lot company to keep it, but it had been a home and we had put down roots, bought mining claims, started a business or two, nurtured our dreams. I stared at the nightstand, where I had placed my badge each night, where I had hung my gun belt on the rare occasions I felt I needed it close by.

The armoire was empty. Mattie had all her clothing at the hotel. I stared at the bed, where for years she had lain beside me in a white cotton nightdress that covered all of her, except for the times she wore a smile and something silky and plunging. It had been a long time since I'd touched her. What good was it to make love to a doped-up woman who didn't know or care?

I studied the kitchen, where my brothers and I had sat for hours. Everything was neat, every dish in its place. That was one thing about Mattie: no matter what she was pickling herself with, she kept a neat, house. There were thirteen brown bottles on a high shelf, redeye whiskey I had not noticed before. She was afraid to be without it.

I checked the other houses too, claptrap houses that were cold and dark and hollow and without promise. Once they had been filled with hope and dreams. Now they were bare structures, and I hastened away, feeling forlorn, knowing that California would be better.

Maybe Josephine would be there, and I would be forced to do something about Mattie. I had no feelings at all for her, nothing, but that wouldn't make it any easier.

I walked past the back of the OK Corral, past the place where our lives had changed so swiftly and brutally. There was nothing there, either. Just an empty lot full of dry weeds and shattered glass, a dead place, with nothing in it. There was nothing in John Behan's Tombstone for the Earps.

Chapter 25

U.S. marshal Crawley Dake, sporting a black pin-striped suit, bowler, and handlebar mustache, indented one side of Virgil's bed. Morgan and I sat on the other.

"What's this about?" Dake said, waving the letter between two beefy fingers.

"It's just what it says," I replied. "We're out. We're going to California before my brothers and I are butchered. There are fifty Cowboys for each Earp. I don't like the odds."

Dake pondered that. "Don't know that that's necessary, Wyatt. Hell, man, things are better than they look. Behan won't last longer than a fruit fly in a blizzard. Why do you think Judge Stilwell put together that citizen posse? Why is Behan in trouble now? He's about to face a corruption charge."

"Crawley, you're whistling past a graveyard. We can't get justice. The Clanton trial was a farce. Ike got off because he had a parade of alibi witnesses lying through their teeth."

Dake disagreed. "A man's hat isn't evidence, Wyatt. You didn't have a case against the Clantons."

I was annoyed. "One thing I know, Crawley: we can't get a conviction for any of that Cowboy bunch, not now, not ever. We've never put one behind bars for more than a few hours. Not one! Think of that: not one damned conviction after all these coach robberies, all this rustling, all the banditry and murder, after riding hundreds of miles tracking them down. They'll alibi out of anything, line up twenty friends to lie to the courts. There isn't a thing we can do. We can hunt them down, gather evidence, round them up, and the result will always be the same: alibis will put them somewhere else, or Behan's jail doors will accidentally be left open. You want to know why we're quitting? That's why."

Morgan started to protest but I glared at him.

"And I'm tired of it," I added. "I tried. I even sent a message to Ike when he was in Behan's lockup. Let's talk, maybe bury the hatchet, I said. Ike laughed it off, handed my message to the *Nugget*, and never replied. They're riding high. The Cowboys own the sheriff, the Tombstone coppers, the courthouse ring, the whole city of Charleston, and every square foot of the county outside of this town, and peace is the last thing they want.

"I saw the newpapers this morning, Crawley. Damned near every sheet in the territory is telling you to accept. Let the Earp Gang—we're a gang now—go."

Dake stood suddenly, began pacing that tiny, hot upstairs hotel room. "That's why I'm not going to do it. I'm not going to let you turn in your badge. I'm not going to let some howling newspapers push a U.S. marshal around. You keep your badges. I'll tell the *Epitaph* that I'm not accepting your resignations. The other thing I'm going to do is deputize Bill Jackson. That'll quiet the critics. We need another deputy U.S. marshal here, one not connected with you, the Earps. You get the idea? He did a good job with that posse of his, bringing in the Clantons. But Wyatt, the job's not done, and I'm counting on you to finish it up."

"With what?"

"With yourselves. You're the best I've got. You have the power to deputize, and you know where to get good men. You have the best informers, like Sherman McMasters. By the way, we're throwing him in jail as a horse thief, Wyatt, but nothing will come of it. The Cowboys trust a man who's faced rustling charges, and that'll help.

"Sherm's got ears, and you've got a man where you need one. You've been working on this for a year, and we're closer to breaking up the outlaws than you realize. I'll tell you who's going to be in hot water next: Smiling Johnny, the sheriff. I'm working on that."

He studied me. "There's something else I know. The *Nugget* was sold today. It'll be announced tomorrow. And Harry Woods will no longer edit that rag. They'll stay Democrat and support Behan, but all this abuse of the Earp brothers is coming to an end. That's how the new owner wants it."

"Woods? Out?"

"Richard Rule's going to edit it."

Maybe there was some hope. Harry Woods spent a large part of his days writing splenetic attacks on me as a sort of sport. If there ever was a man I wanted to thrash, it was Woods.

I remembered when Behan welshed on our deal and appointed Woods as his undersheriff. Woods was a bright young politician of the Southern Democrat stripe, blond and blue-eyed, with an obsession to make as much grief as he could for those he opposed, including me.

From the moment he snared the job promised me, he set out to make sure I never got a crack at it. He didn't know a thing about law enforcement, but he knew how to whittle a man down. All those months he had set his pen against us, turning lawmen into criminals and criminals into innocent citizens. I never once replied; I treated his stories with the silence they deserved.

I remembered that first *Nugget* story about the Fremont Street fight behind the OK Corral, as written by Richard Rule, their reporter. That first story was just about right, and didn't vary materially from the one in the *Epitaph*. Then Woods took over, and next I knew, the *Nugget* was saying the Earps were bent on murder and shot some largely unarmed Cowboys who had their hands in the air and were in the act of surrendering. That was Undersheriff Harry Woods' work, no doubt with a little encouragement from Behan.

Now this lousy lizard was leaving the paper. It could only get better.

"How'll the change of ownership affect Behan?" I asked.

"The *Nugget* is going to be quiet about you. It'll still be a Democrat and Behan rag."

"Crawley, how do you know this?"

"Prescott connections. Wyatt, I have a few aces up my sleeve, and I played them. Trust me."

It was that, rather than any sense of duty, that persuaded me to stay on, keep the badge. Just like that. It was that news about Woods that did it. I would do anything that was required of me, go anywhere, track down anyone, take any risk, if the *Nugget* would just leave me alone.

"Are we staying, Wyatt?" Morg asked.

He seemed so eager to get on with life that I smiled. I shouldn't have.

Dake stood.

"Virgil, you get yourself out of bed. You're still a deputy United States marshal," he said.

He reached over and shook Virg's one good hand.

"I've still got a trigger finger and most of the rest of me works," Virgil said. "Allie was happy to know."

Dake laughed. "I've a few more cards to play in Tombstone, and then I'm heading back to Prescott," he said.

The cards turned out to be valuable. Next thing I knew, the new Democrat mayor, Carr, was telling the citizens of Tombstone it was time to support the fight against crime in Cochise County and the way to do it was to support the efforts of the federal government to wipe out crime in the territory.

I wondered what John Behan thought of that, coming from one of his cronies. Maybe Dake was right: Behan had dealt himself out of office.

But nothing changed across the street, where the Cowboys still rented that room and still studied us through a gap in the blinds. Now, decades later, I should have seen it coming, should have understood that the rented room, with the silent Cowboys within keeping an eye on the comings and goings of my family, told me all there was to know.

But in fact I relaxed a little. Virgil was healing. We were talking of moving back into our houses. The *Nugget* appeared day after day without mentioning the Earps, something that I put too much stock in. Allie, Mattie, and Louisa were restless, sick of hotel life, wanting to return to normalcy. Morg finally sent Louisa to California, out of harm's way.

Maybe Dake had pulled the mining city back from the brink of street war. But even so, we decided to stay entrenched a while more in the Cosmopolitan Hotel, where armed members of the Citizens' Committee could watch over us while we slept.

Ike, freed now, had one more game to play. I was startled to discover that he had filed murder charges against my brothers and me and Doc in the little justice court in Contention on February 9. That meant placing ourselves in the custody of Sheriff John Behan and his friends, something I was not willing to do if I could help it.

I engaged William Herring and mortgaged my house, not having much money left to pay a lawyer. Behan, armed with warrants, collected Doc, Morgan, and me and hauled us off to the lockup, but at least I had the comfort of knowing that the Citizens' Safety Committee ringed the jail.

Herring, one of the committee, thought that Ike would not get far. "There's no new evidence, Wyatt. Without something new, it'll be thrown out."

But those were hard hours in which I paced the cell, studied porky Breakenridge on the other side of the bars, heard Behan laughing, while I felt utterly helpless to defend myself or my brother or Doc. Herring finally got us out on bond.

We faced a hearing in the court of Contention's justice of the peace, J. B. Smith, on February 14, and to a man we believed the purpose was to ambush us en route. There was only one solution and my friends acted on it, to my everlasting gratitude. They formed a posse, and off we went.

Behan asked me to surrender my sidearms and I refused.

"Not until I walk into that courtroom," I told him. "And then I'll turn them over to Herring."

He backed off. We traveled to Contention for that hearing, my stouthearted business friends armed to the teeth, and the Cowboys left us alone. Even my lawyer, Bill Herring, and his daughter carried arms. When we arrived in Contention, we walked into Smith's little courtroom fully armed and not intending to surrender our weapons.

Herring demanded that the trial be moved to Tombstone and be heard by Judge Lucas in the absence of Judge Stilwell. Smith agreed, and we all trooped back to the county seat. It took two days to clear us. Ike's attorneys failed to produce any new evidence that had not been heard by Spicer, and Lucas concluded that there were no grounds to prosecute.

We were freed. But we were even more broke than before. Lawyers cost money. The Cowboys were enraged and tensions were high once again. I decided to strike hard, while the heat ran high in me, and took a posse with Morgan and Doc in it toward the border, hunting down Pony Deal, Al Thibolet, and Charles Haws, who were suspected of stagecoach robbery. But the outlaw telegraph preceded us, and we rode back to Tombstone frustrated once again.

Ike's effort to bring us to trial was all it took: I was hot. I was going to run them all down and bring them to trial one way or another. I didn't care about the odds. I didn't care how I got it done, but I was by God going to do it.

Chapter 26

I look back upon that fatal Saturday, March 18, as the bleakest hour of my life. For years I faulted myself about Morg's assassination, because I knew something was afoot and did little about it.

But I no longer blame myself. There is still a hollowness in my bones, and the years have not made it any better. Yet I don't know how I could have made things turn out differently. I don't know, even after thinking on it for decades, how I might have saved my brother's life.

Things had been quiet in Tombstone for a while. Wells Fargo had not pulled out as it had threatened. My federal posses were patrolling the border, hunting down wanted men. Sometime during that period Wells Fargo agent Marshall Williams had absconded, leaving a pile of debt, some of it owed to the company. His sudden exit with a whore on his arm had started me to wondering what game he was playing. I still have dark suspicions about him, and the way our operations were known to the outlaws almost before we could throw saddles over horses.

On that innocent Friday, March 17, my friend Briggs Goodrich, brother and law partner of Ben, whose firm had often defended the Cowboys, confided to me on the street that something was up and we Earps had better watch out. Briggs had always been cordial, somehow staying above the partisanship that racked Tombstone, and I counted him an honorable man.

I too had heard rumors floating softly on the spring breeze and asked him about them. Briggs surprised me: he said that he had a message for me from John Ringo. The outlaw would play no part in *what was coming*, and wanted me to know it. That was warning enough that something was afoot.

"Thanks, Briggs. I'll watch my back," I said.

Goodrich delivered yet another warning, this time spoken to Doc and Morgan. The lawyer had seen armed men in town and informed Doc that he and the Earps had better watch out.

Morg, temporarily a bachelor with Louisa in California, brushed it off. There was a theater company in town doing a one-night stand of a play called *Stolen Kisses* and he was determined to see it. He was tired of hiding, starting at shadows, studying open windows and dark corners. He wanted some amusement and the Lingard Theatre Company could provide it.

I went to bed, or started to anyway. I had quietly scouted Tombstone that stormy night and had spotted the shadowy figures of Florentino Cruz and Hank Swilling loitering in the darker corners of the saloons, the pair of them certain trouble. Something was going to happen, but it is always the privilege of assassins to choose the time and place of the execution. I thought better of going to bed, pulled my boots on, and headed for Shieffelin Hall to waylay Morgan. This was no night to be out, not with men like that lurking in the shadows, the wind whipping, the dark alleys alive with death. I'd tell him to get to the hotel, and be quick about it.

I've thought a thousand times since then that I should simply have marched Morgan back to the Cosmopolitan, big brother style, out of harm's way, but I finally realized that if something is going to happen, it's going to happen. And Morg had his own life to live and his own judgment to follow. I've been fatalistic about it in recent years. If they didn't kill Morgan in Bob Hatch's pool room, they would have killed him, and maybe me, somewhere else, maybe the very next day.

I do not fault myself anymore. Morgan was warned. I was warned. We took our chances. My only regret is that I did not think about that double glass door, frosted on the bottom where anyone could hide, clear glass above, so people in the dark of the night could see our every move.

I can see my stupidity in retrospect. At the time, I was too dumb to sense the danger. We grow inured to warnings and discard them when nothing happens. Morg and I both had heard a thousand of them over the past few months, so Fate dealt the fatal card when our guard was down.

I found Morgan in the happy crowd after the show, intending to steer him to the hotel and safety, but it was not to be.

"Wyatt, I'm not ready for bed. How about a game or two at Hatch's?" he said.

I watched the theatergoers disappear into the spring evening and stroll away into shadows, and I thought maybe a game or two wouldn't hurt. We would be among friends at Hatch and Campbell's Saloon. Bob Hatch was one of our stoutest allies.

And so we were indeed among friends. Bob Hatch joined us, along with Sherm McMasters. We played under the coal-oil lamps, whiling away a peaceful Saturday eve. The click of cue against ball, the thump of ball into leather pocket, the angle of bank shots, the scrape of chalk on the cue tip occupied us until the night exploded.

Morg had lined up his shot, leaning far over the table, when shots shattered glass, a bullet whipped past my head and another caught Morg in the back, traveled upward through him, exited and hit a bystander.

Two seconds.

My younger brother shuddered, rolled onto the table and slid off, and I knew in a glance he was dying. Footsteps echoed down the alley. Hatch and McMasters raced after the assassins but failed to find them. Cold winds blew through the shattered doors. Gunsmoke boiled into the billiard room. The lamps swung on their hooks; blood gouted from Morg. We got him into the cardroom, where life slipped out of him.

He stared up at me, his eyes seas of pain, and beckoned me. "I've played my last game of pool," he whispered.

Morg's hound, lying at the door, sat up and howled. The sound sent chills through me.

"Who was it, Wyatt?" he whispered.

"I'll get them, Morg," I said. "I think I know who. That's a promise."

He nodded and closed his eyes. His pale face was twisted in pain. Blood oozed from the wound in his loins, but blood was also filling the longitudinal hole through his body. Goodfellow and Matthews arrived, Gladstone bags in hand, but this time Goodfellow, the gunshot expert, was helpless. The bullet had traversed much of Morgan's torso. The docs could do nothing.

Morg's dog whined and buried its face between its paws.

Once again, a bullet aimed for me had missed and hit the wall an inch from my face. I wondered why. Maybe it would be my destiny to track down those who had killed Morgan and wounded Virgil.

I've had that fatalistic sense in me all these years: I was spared so that I might bring those killers to justice. I knew from that moment on that no bullet would ever touch me, and none has, though I sometimes stood in a rain of bullets. It was an eerie feeling, this mystical knowledge, something I could never share with any other mortal, a sense of predestination, as if my life had been determined long before, at the foundation of the world.

Even as I knelt beside Morgan's pale face in the card room, scarcely aware of the crowd of silent onlookers behind me, I knew what I was destined to do next, and I would not hesitate to do it. I would learn who they were, hunt them down one by one, and execute them. A badge I might have, but I no longer needed one or cared to own one. From that moment on, my life had been transformed. Tombstone, Cochise County, the laws of Arizona—none of that mattered.

Morg slipped away, and I watched him go, wanting to say goodbye, and not able to.

Someone had gotten Jim and Bessie, Virgil and Allie. Virg came, weak on his pins, supported by Allie. Mattie came because they fetched her, but I knew she would not remember any of it, and stared blankly at quiet, lifeless Morgan, her mouth half open. So I was spared the burden of telling Virgil and Jim. But I knew that in a while I would have to telegraph Louisa at my father's house in Colton, and even across six hundred miles I would hear her screams. Doc Goodfellow knelt and closed Morgan's eyes, a gentle pressure on the lid of each one. Then Morgan was gone from us.

Bob Hatch's card room was utterly quiet.

Neagle, I think, and another city cop arrived, and asked questions but left me alone until the last. Hatch and McMasters told them what they needed to know. Then Neagle approached me.

"Who?" he asked.

"I don't know," I replied. "I didn't see them." But I did perhaps know. I put Cruz and Swilling at the top of the list and knew there would be more. This had been no secret; we had been warned. There had to be two or three shooters and some lookouts. Even Ringo had sent word he wasn't in on it. There were Cruz and Swilling and some others who I would spend my every waking minute ferreting out.

Ritter, from City Mortuary, rolled in with his meat wagon, and I watched while my friends gently lifted Morg up and carried him into the alley and the waiting black wagon.

I caught the mortician by the black lapel of his black coat. "If you put Morgan in your window, I'll kill you," I said. "Put him in the best you have and close the lid."

Ritter seemed frightened, as if his own life was endangered by being in such proximity to an Earp.

"Yes, just as you say, sir," he said and sidestepped into the gloom. I watched him bound onto the wagon seat and whip the dray horse into a startled trot, while Morgan flopped around behind.

"How could you?" Allie shot at me, and I have never fathomed what she meant.

I steered Mattie into the night and she took my arm dumbly, having barely spoken a word. She had been to the Chinaman that day, and would not comprehend Morgan's death for many hours. But there was a dignity in Mattie, even if she had vanished into another world. I was glad to take her arm. She was an Earp. Allie helped Virgil walk to the hotel, the four of us negotiating the half block of Allen Street that brought us to our rooms.

A crowd followed us back to the Cosmopolitan. Unlike so many Tombstone crowds, this one wept with us and our grief was theirs, and our danger was theirs to share. I saw Virgil to his room. We had barely spoken a word.

"You wire her?" he said at the door.

"I will."

"It'll be hell on her."

I nodded. Allie slammed the door shut, and I stood in the hallway feeling cut off from Virg, from Morg, from Mattie, from Allie, from Jim and Bessie and, in an hour or so, from Louisa. For the first time since I was born, I felt alone.

I walked into the night, unguarded, and made my way to the telegraph office. I addressed the message to my father, Nicholas Porter Earp, in Colton, California. Let Nicholas tell Louisa. I printed out what I wanted and handed it to Waverley, the night man:

MORGAN KILLED BY UNKNOWN PARTIES ELEVEN TONIGHT.   —WYATT

That was enough. That was too much said.

He read it, and reached across the counter, placing

his hand over mine, and held my hand, and I thought about telegraph men, and the hard things they must do.

"Oh, Wyatt, not Morg," he said. "Not Morg."

"Send it to James Hume at Wells Fargo, San Francisco," I said. "And to Crawley Dake, Prescott."

I paid thirty cents a word and he pulled change out of his cash drawer. The wire ran to the railroad tracks at Benson, and across to Tucson, and west along the SP route. I watched Waverley settle himself at the brass key, push his gold-rimmed spectacles down, and begin tapping the mechanism. Soon others, newsmen especially, would come to him with urgent messages about this night, and that brass key would tap the story through most of that night, and out into the dark world.

I hiked back to the hotel in safety. No Cowboy was fool enough to spend that night in Tombstone. But soon, one way or another, I would have names: one, two, three, ten names. And maybe the names of a hundred accessories who knew what was coming and did not report it. And I swore I would get them all.

Years later I remembered what I had so casually said to Briggs Goodrich after he had warned me something was up. I said I would watch my back. It must have been intuition. Virgil had been shot in the back from ambush. And Morgan had been shot in the back. And the bullet of an ambusher out in a dark alley had barely missed me. That said everything that needed to be said about the men we were facing.

Chapter 27

I've spent a good share of my life trying to bury what came next, and finally gave up a few years ago. It was mostly for Josie's sake. She is more respectable than I'll ever be, and she worries about what people think of us.

As I saw it then, I had a federal badge and that was enough for what I had in mind. Ike Clanton had asked for it; now he would get it, along with every one of Morgan's murderers.

I had little doubt who was behind the murder of Morgan and the attempt upon me while we were playing billiards. Ike had always been a loudmouth and had boasted of what he had in mind, or recruited his thugs openly. I have always wondered what he paid them. Maybe Will McLaury, still pulling strings from the safety of Texas, offered the blood money, but that is guesswork.

Whoever planned the Earp murders made no secret of what he was intending. The result was that the forthcoming assassination was known to most every Cowboy in Arizona, known to Briggs Goodrich, their lawyer, who made it known to us.

I had always been a dutiful peace officer, following those forms and protocols of the justice system that I had learned ever since I pinned on a badge in Wichita. But Morgan's murder trumped all that, unhinged me from all restraint.

I remember it clearly, and just as clearly I remember

my response, which was cold and blunt: I would hunt them down. The papers called it a vendetta, but they didn't get it entirely right. Yes, I had made that promise to Morgan as life ebbed from him. But two other things drove me. One was that if I didn't get them first, they would finish me and my brothers. The other was simply that justice was not possible in Cochise County. In spite of all our efforts, we had yet to send a man off to prison. I often wonder whether my critics really understood the enormity of that. *There was no justice.*

First I had to deal with the obvious. Ike and his outlaws intended to murder me and Virgil, and maybe my other brothers. I was alone. Warren was young and not an experienced fighter; Jim was a crippled Civil War veteran who could help only in a pinch; Virgil lay abed with a destroyed arm, pitifully weak after a brush with death.

It was up to me, which is why I have always had that sense of fate that no bullet would ever touch me because I had a preordained task to perform, and I intended to do it. I had friends like Doc and Sherm, and I would recruit them, but it was up to me to hunt down the killers and their friends.

That Sunday morning, my thirty-fourth birthday, I got Jim and Warren and headed for City Mortuary and insisted that Ritter open the lid of the casket. Ritter unscrewed some bolts and lifted the lid. Morgan lay there, oh, so still and bloodless. He looked about ten years old. I could hear Louisa's screams in my ears, though she was hundreds of miles distant. Jim and Warren stared solemnly at their dead brother.

"All right," I said. "Seal it, and we'll carry it to Benson."

"Yes, Mr. Earp. How much we share your bereavement."

I watched him bolt the lid tight. Outside, an escort of friends waited for me, among them Doc, solemn in a black cutaway and boiled white shirt and bowtie. They were all heeled; Dave Neagle and his city police didn't interfere.

A church bell tolled as we left the Cosmopolitan Hotel. People stared. A few men lifted their hats. We rode silently to Benson beside Ritter's black hearse and put the casket aboard the next Southern Pacific westbound, with Jim in the express car as escort. Bessie would follow sometime in the future. We were well armed, it being our opinion that more assassinations were possible, even during a funeral journey. My friends were looking after me.

We did not hold funeral services in Tombstone, nor did we intend to bury Morgan in that rocky plot north of town where the corpses of outlaws fouled sacred ground. There were no grand parade, no ebony hearse with its glass windows permitting a public view of the nickel-plated coffin, no crowd walking behind, no line of carriages, no weeping people, no spectators lining the streets. If one were to compare this cortege with the one for the McLaurys and Billy Clanton, one might have supposed that scarcely a soul in that mining town of four thousand cared about Morgan, while most everyone in Tombstone had grieved for the outlaws.

I wondered what would happen when Louisa saw that casket, and I didn't want to think about it. Maybe Morgan was lucky: Mattie would have stared dry-eyed at my casket.

I heard the mournful whistle and watched the

Southern Pacific local steam west, rattling down the rails, carrying Morgan to his final home in Colton. I then rode back to Tombstone without incident, well guarded by stalwart and tenderhearted friends. Ritter slipped me an itemized bill for $240, which included the casket and the hearse trip to Benson. I had no cash and told him the invoice would be met in due course.

"I'm sure it will. The Clantons and Will McLaury paid right off," Ritter said. "Substantial people, like you."

Back in Tombstone, I made plans, and they involved Virgil.

"Virg," I said, "we've got to move you and Allie to Colton. I can't be here looking after you and out with a posse at the same time. Jim's on the train, and Warren's going to be riding with me, and you'd be alone for long stretches here."

"Useless one-armed man," Virgil said.

"No, Virg, that's not it. I'm alone now except for Warren. I need to put you on a train for the sake of your safety."

"I've got a shooting arm," he said testily.

"You're not well yet. I need to move out."

He shrugged. "If that's what's needed, then we'll go."

For once Allie didn't protest or sting me with one of her barbed remarks. I left her to her packing and made other arrangements: I wanted a cadre of gifted men for my posse, not the usual sort. I wanted fearless fighters, eagle-eyed trackers, men who could stare at death and not flinch. I made my selections carefully.

"Be ready when I get back," I told them.

I didn't doubt that this war was not over. Who had

done it? Ike? Frank Stilwell? Pony Deal? Swilling or Cruz? Probably all of them. This backshooting was big enough that every Cowboy knew about it beforehand. I guessed probably four were at the heart of it: two shooters and two lookouts or horse holders.

I picked up a rumor, oddly enough from that tattler Billy Breakenridge. Marietta Spence, estranged Mexican wife of Pete Spence, was gossiping from one end of her neighborhood to the other. She was fingering Stilwell as one of the killers, along with Spence, Indian Charlie, someone unknown to her, and a man named Freis. She had risen to meet them in Spence's house late Saturday night, found them all armed with rifles, and her husband looking pale, with chattering teeth. Spence warned her that now she knew something and he would kill her if she talked. Next morning, upon hearing of Morgan's death, she knew at once who had shot him, and began talking. Maybe Morgan's murderer had lived across the street from us all that while.

"Thanks, Billy," I said, absorbing all that.

"Right across the street from the Earps," he said. "Ain't that something?"

"Where's Spence now?"

"Gone. That's why she's talking. He's mean to her, in case you didn't know."

I had my list, and I added Ike to it, who was probably the man Marietta did not know. Only hours after the murder, I knew who had done it and who to go after, or I thought I did.

I knew who I wanted to help me get Virg and Allie safely to Tucson, and I recruited Warren, Doc, Sherm McMasters, and Turkey Creek Jack Johnson to accompany us because I was fearful that we would be ambushed en route. We made it to Benson without trouble, put Virgil and Allie and Mattie in a coach, and boarded a night train for Tucson. In Benson I got a tip: a stationmaster warned me that Frank Stilwell and Ike Clanton had come through, headed for Tucson, and had openly talked about searching all the train cars passing through . . . for someone.

I thanked him. I was now forewarned.

As the four-car train slowed to a crawl at the Tucson station, Doc and I, in the dark vestibule of the front coach, spotted someone lying on a baggage cart holding something that might have been a rifle. So they were waiting. It was true. They were searching the well-lit cars to kill any Earp they could find sitting behind the plate-glass windows.

Doc and I slipped into the night, landing on roadbed while the train was stopping, and he worked one side while I worked the other. We found nothing just then.

I left Warren and the rest to defend Virgil and the women during the dinner stop. My brothers, well guarded, headed for Porter's Hotel for supper. I joined them and said hello to J. W. Evans, a deputy federal marshal standing there. But later, after we had supped and Virgil and Allie had boarded, we spotted the backshooter stalking us. Stilwell was studying lit windows; Ike stood at a distance, ever the coward, letting braver men do his dirty work.

We had the advantage of darkness and the additional advantage of sawed-off shotguns. I crept close.

"Frank," I said.

He whirled. "Morgan!" he said.

I shot him point-blank with the scattergun. Ike ran. Doc trotted up and added a couple of shots. *Morgan*. I wondered what Stilwell had meant. He lay in a red pool, twitching his last, and I would never know. We left him there but Ike had vanished into the gloom. Scores of people at the station had heard the shots, and I supposed Stilwell's body would be found in minutes. I only wished I might have added Ike to the death toll.

"Strange you should be here, Frank," I said, and walked away into the night.

I had not ever killed a man outside of professional duty, but there at the station I didn't take the time to consider what my duty had been. I raced along the lamp-lit cars until I found Virg and Allie in the sleeper, and rapped on the window as the train huffed to life. Virg saw me; I raised a thumb. He nodded. He had heard the shots. Frank Stilwell, the man who had pulled the trigger against Morgan, lay dead or dying. And I didn't doubt I would soon be a fugitive.

I watched the West Coast train chuff out of the dark station carrying my brother and Allie and Mattie, and then I was alone. My brothers were dead, wounded, or fleeing Arizona.

"Ike sure is a model of manhood," Doc said, shoving cartridges into his nickel-plated revolver.

"Doc, you're just envious of him," I replied.

We walked out of town, and then hooked a ride in the caboose of a passing freight. I used my badge to gain admittance, and in a while, we reached Contention City, and then Tombstone. I was in my room at the hotel before dinner the next night.

And I had information: my friend Waverley, the telegraph man, had received a wire from Bob Paul, Pima County sheriff, for Behan to arrest us for the murder of Stilwell. He showed it to me first and agreed to delay giving it to Behan, to allow us time to organize.

I alerted my posse. We moved swiftly, gathered our gear, and were leaving the hotel when Behan arrived.

"Wyatt, I want to see you," he said.

"Not now," I replied.

Behan simply stood there, undecided.

There was no talk of warrants or arrest, so we loaded our saddle horses and rode off. We were armed and he wasn't, and I think he wisely let us go. In any case, I was not about to be stopped. There never was an armed confrontation, but we were armed and ready.

From that point on I was a fugitive. At the same time, I was a deputy U.S. marshal leading a posse consisting of Warren, Doc, Texas Jack Vermillion, Turkey Creek Jack Johnson, and Sherm McMasters. Two of them had been my informants among the rustlers and would be invaluable to us. We knew who we were after and where they might be. We had crack shots with us, and hard men.

I didn't doubt that Behan would form a posse of his own, and that it would contain some of the county's most illustrious citizens.

The papers were howling again. They had barely reported Morgan's murder, and now Stilwell's body lying in the rail yards of Tucson was inspiring hysterical denunciation of the desperadoes known as the Earp Gang.

Maybe someday I would be able to persuade them that Stilwell was lying in wait to assassinate us, but that would come later. We had a task to do. It turned out that Alibi Ike, who knew how to exploit the press, had a story all cooked up. Frank Stilwell just happened to be in Tucson a little early, to prepare for his forthcoming robbery trial, and was lounging innocently around the train station when the Earps spotted him and pulled the trigger. That was what he told the *Star*. So once again the murderous Earps were butchering defenseless and innocent men. I had to give Ike credit for sheer inventiveness. He never did explain how Stilwell got himself in the rail yard on the dark side of that westbound train.

We rode into the night, the horsemen of the apocalypse, each of us aware that Behan's minions would soon be hounding us with warrants for our arrest. And we would be hunting down Morgan's killers. It had come to that.

Chapter 28

I have always considered myself a hard man, or at least as hard as I need to be at any given time. When I rode out of Tombstone with a posse of hard men, two of whom had lived among the outlaws as informers for Well Fargo, I was intent on one thing: bringing Morgan's killers to justice.

The romanticists and yellow journalists have all proclaimed that I sought vengeance, a life for a life. That misses the mark more than a little. What I knew then was that there could be no justice in Cochise County, where a swarm of scoundrels would alibi any rustler out of the courtroom. The only way justice could be done would be at my own hands.

I have stuck to that viewpoint all along and won't apologize for it, though most of the world thinks of my efforts to round up the criminals who murdered my brother as the darkest chapter of my life. I suffer no remorse, though I have deeply regretted the choices open to me, and wish that some other avenue of justice might have been available.

It wasn't until later that I learned that John Behan, the People's Friend, and his ambitious undersheriff, Harry Woods, had swiftly formed a twelve-man posse consisting largely of the very gang we were after, including Fin Clanton and John Ringo. Not only that, but he had deputized Curly Bill Brocius to lead yet another posse out of Contention. So there were two outlaw posses, deputized by the sheriff, hunting us down.

That, more than any other act of his, shows the low

estate of law and order in that county at that time. There Behan was, nakedly deputizing and paying such stagecoach robbers, murderers, and cattle thieves as he wanted to hunt us down, while the public watched, aghast. Behan did not imagine it, but that was the beginning of the end for him; he soon was out of office even in solidly Democratic Cochise County, and lived a squalid life after that, barely inside the law.

As Doc put it, once we learned who was tailing us, "Johnny's gotten the flower of Cochise County manhood to arrest us!"

Bob Paul, the Tucson sheriff, had come to Tombstone to join Behan's posse but was rebuffed when the posse rode off without him. Obviously, Smiling John Behan didn't want an outsider who might be a stickler for bringing in prisoners alive along. I have often wondered what Bob Paul thought as he watched Behan ride out after us with the worst men in Arizona siding him. What it must have been like to hear Fin Clanton, hand upraised, swear to support law and order or to hear Pony Deal solemnly pledge to uphold the law. Whatever Bob Paul thought of that, he kept to himself as he abandoned that nest of vipers and rode back to Tucson alone.

We headed for a certain woodcutting camp owned by Pete Spence in the Dragoons. I thought Spence might be there and was unaware that he had turned himself over to Behan and was sitting, well-armed, in the jailhouse to escape the wrath of townsmen after his estranged wife began talking. I had not alighted in Tombstone long enough to know that. I was also hunting Hank Swilling, whom I had spotted in Tombstone the night before the murder, and Indian Charlie, a horse thief known as Florentino Cruz, who had been loitering there also.

I had with me flinty men, some of whom had killed other human beings, none of them acceptable to polite society, though I keep thinking Doc would have been welcomed in any drawing room but for the false reputation enveloping him. Warren was the youngest and greenest; he had never killed anyone or been in a fight. Doc was actually a mannered sort, given to fits of anger. Sherman McMasters was an educated man fluent in Spanish whose undercover work for me had finally paid off, but like Turkey Creek Jack Johnson, another undercover man, his loyalties were now suspected by the rustler element and he could no longer operate undercover. So he was with me, and a welcome man he was too. None came harder and better.

We rode into that sunny and quiet woodlot high in the pine-clad Dragoon Mountains, scaring the woodcutters half to death, but we didn't see anyone we wanted, and a little palaver got us nowhere. We started to ride out when I noticed a Mexican or a breed scurrying away in an almighty hurry; we ran him down, firing a few shots along the way. We rode up, spread out our horses, and Cruz, our wanted Indian Charlie, knelt on the hard clay, clasping a hand over his bleeding arm.

"Who was with you when you killed my brother?" I asked.

"Senores . . ."

I shot, and the bullet seared past his ear.

"I did not shoot him, Mr. Earp."

"You were the lookout man."

Fear choked his face. "It was the Cowboy hombres: Ringo, Curly Bill Brocius, Hank Swilling, Frank Stilwell. *Sí,* it was those who did it. Now *por favor*—?"

"Why?"

"It was for twenty-five dollars that I kept watch. This they paid me to watch out for them. I am a poor hombre. . . ."

Twenty-five dollars for Morgan. I shot Cruz through the heart. He fell dead. Others fired so the death might be ascribed to several. Turkey Creek and Texas Jack emptied their revolvers. Doc didn't. He turned away. Warren looked sick.

One down for Morg and Virgil. I stared at the breed's red-soaked clothing, not liking myself. Off in the distance, woodcutters stared at us, plainly afraid they would be next. I let them think it.

I took no pride in it and tell myself I wouldn't have done it if there had been a working justice system. But sometimes in the night, I wonder.

"We are gentle Christian knights," Doc said.

"Go to hell, Doc." I was tired of him.

I stared down from the back of my horse at the warm body of a man who had played a role in a murder, and felt only coldness. His blood stained the dry grass.

I knew there would be another uproar in the press, and I knew the uproar would not stop me. My course was set and I would continue. What I had learned from Cruz was that Ringo and Brocius were there. Ringo had sent word to me beforehand, via Briggs Goodrich, that he would have no part in what was coming, and now I learned that he was red-handed. And Brocius, the blowhard, had to be right in the middle of an assassination, preferring to back-shoot a man from dark cover rather than face an armed man. Cruz's confession made it easier for me. I had a list. I would track down that entire list.

I did not then know there were two Behan posses out to kill us. We needed cash, and that meant getting help in Tombstone. We had ridden out hastily, not wanting a confrontation with John Behan, and were ill-outfitted. We slipped back toward Tombstone in the night, hunkered down on Comstock Hill northwest of town, got hold of Charlie Smith, and asked him to raise some money and deliver it to us at Iron Springs, a small trickle of bitter water in a brushy flat below a slope. Then we rode on to the springs to await the cash.

That was the damnedest thing. I didn't like the feel of the place and was moving cautiously. My instincts were right. As we rode into that watering hole, nine Cowboys sprung up and began banging at us. In the midst of them was Curly Bill Brocius, equipped, as I was, with a shotgun.

I bailed off my horse in a hurry and leveled the shotgun as bullets hissed past me. Curly Bill unloaded both barrels and balls whipped through my clothing, jerking me around, but none touched me because it was not my fate to die. I aimed coldly, fired both of my charges of buckshot at his heart, and he fell backward, his chest blooming red. I had killed him but I didn't expect to last ten seconds.

I threw away the scattergun, reached for my rifle in the scabbard on the unruly horse, and found myself in trouble. My loosened gun belt had slipped, pinning my legs so I couldn't walk. I scarcely had time to note that the rest of the posse had fled, and I was alone there, taking the entire brunt of the Cowboy artillery. I couldn't reach my rifle; the horse was rearing, half crazed, and I ended up with only my revolver. I shot into a patch of brush, heard a yell, got my gun belt up off my ass, and leapt onto my rearing horse. A bullet hit the saddle horn, knocked it off; another hit my bootheel, and I was sure I was shot. My foot went numb. I wheeled back, picked up Texas Jack, whose horse was shot, and we got out of there.

We took refuge in an arroyo with brush along it, and spread out at once into a defensive line, with the horses protected in the bottom.

Doc slid over to me.

"You're shot up," he said. He eyed the holes that riddled my coat and pants.

"My foot," I said.

He helped me pull my heelless boot. I stared, amazed, at the corrugated white flesh and varicose veins. No blood.

"Still numb," I said.

Doc suddenly sagged. After days on the trail, he had a scraggle of blond beard covering his jowls, and great black circles under his eyes. I feared the consumption would take hold of him again after a year or two of respite in the dry, clear desert. There were tears leaking down Doc's cheeks.

"You all right?" he asked me.

"I guess so. Nothing's bleeding. Not even my balls."

"Well, hell, Wyatt. I thought you were gone. Gone! This was an act of God," he said. "A damned miracle, and that's the only explanation for why you're not leaking blood from ten holes. It's God."

I nodded. "Luck, anyway. Got Brocius," I said. "Two loads of buckshot."

"Brocius?"

"I'm certain."

"Curly Bill bought it. Another for Morgan," Doc said. He ran four fingers through four ragged holes in my long coat and wiggled them. "They sure are crack shots," he said.

"I hit someone else," I said. "Someone howled."

"You're a whole cavalry troop, Wyatt."

"No, I'm a man fated to bring some outlaws to justice," I said. "Maybe it's God. I never think about him. Maybe I should. I don't know much about God."

"Let's get the rest of those bastards right now," he said.

But I had tempted fate enough. "Go ahead. I'm staying here," I replied.

We stayed there.

We learned later that the two men who were bringing cash to us, Wright and Kraker, were snared by the Cowboys, but the pair of them palavered their way out of deadly trouble, claiming they were hunting a blasted ornery lost mule. We didn't get the thousand dollars headed our way, but neither did the Cowboys. And when our messengers returned to Tombstone, they carried with them the story of my shotgun fight with Curly Bill, fresh from the mouths of that alleged posse.

But at first no one in Tombstone could imagine that Brocius had croaked and I had escaped two charges of buckshot. The *Nugget* offered two hundred of the mazuma for a look at the body, and chortled when no carcass arrived. Not even the *Epitaph*'s offer of two thousand simoleons to charity if Curly Bill would show up at the paper brought the outlaw into town, and it finally dawned on the citizens of that town that maybe Brocius would never again walk the streets of Tombstone. But that didn't prevent the damned snakey press from spotting Brocius here and there for years to come, and a dozen frauds from claiming they were Curly Bill.

Brocius never returned to Tombstone. And neither did I.

Chapter 29

Henry Clay Hooker's mighty Sierra Bonita Ranch, near Safford, afforded us refuge, and we needed it. My friend Charlie Smith had joined my little posse, bringing us to six in all, but we were facing two large sheriff's posses. Behan had deputized every hellhound who felt like forking a saddle, and given them carte blanche to hunt us down. I'm sure Smiling John and his mob, including his ambitious undersheriff, Harry Woods, thought that with that kind of manpower they would ride us to ground, kill us while "resisting arrest," and be shut of us. At least most of his cutthroats thought so.

I didn't like the odds. Sooner or later, if we lingered in southeast Arizona Territory, we would buy a one-way ticket. We were a sorry lot, half-famished, frazzled by sleepless nights, haggard from riding, our horses jaded, our hair unkempt, our duds begrimed. But at least our revolvers, shotguns, and rifles shone. It was not the furnace season, and we did not suffer from the fierce Sonoran summers that afflicted the area.

I had grave decisions to make. We may have been a posse of deputized U.S. marshals, but we were also wanted men and any Arizona officer of the law was empowered to detain us for a trial. And I was not done. I had made a promise to Morgan to bring all his murderers to justice and I would keep it if I could. I wanted Ike Clanton, John Ringo, and Pony Deal. They might not have pulled the trigger, but they were in on it.

Hooker welcomed us heartily before his massive adobe hacienda, and invited us in, though we were a sorry and bedraggled lot. He was attired in a cream linen suit. He knew Doc but not the others, so I introduced him to Sherm McMaster, Turkey Creek Jack Johnson, Texas Jack Vermillion, and Charlie Smith.

"Wyatt Earp, you're welcome here anytime. What may I do for you?" he asked.

"Mr. Hooker, if you'd provision us and grain and hay our mounts, I would ask nothing more of you. We can pay."

"Consider it done. And if you wish to borrow mounts while yours recruit, feel free to do so."

It was that sort of thoughtfulness that made me feel at home and safe, though I knew that Behan's death squad was not far behind. They had crossed the county line in pursuit of us.

Hooker's competent hands swiftly looked to our suffering horses and showed us where we might refresh ourselves before dinner. Hooker's great Sierra Bonita was largely stocked with purebred cattle, and he exercised the same care in breeding his horse stock. He shipped more beef than anyone else in Arizona, and was a favorite of the railroad. Indeed, they gave him a lifetime free pass.

He had suffered heavy losses from the rustlers, who hit his herds again and again after the Mexicans began patrolling their border, and he and his cattlemen's association had put rewards on the heads of various rustlers and outlaws, especially Curly Bill Brocius.

And that, it turned out, was his first order of business.

"You got him?" he asked me over mesquite-broiled tenderloin and potatoes.

"I did. No doubt about it."

"The *Nugget* denies it."

"That paper also said I was mortally wounded," I replied.

"I don't know how Wyatt survived," Vermillion said. "One man against nine. He just stood there, aimed at Brocius, and cut loose. I swore before God almighty, if Wyatt Earp survived, I would turn myself into a preacher."

Hooker laughed. "You get the reward then. The association will pay a thousand dollars."

"No, Mr. Hooker, you keep it. I didn't do it for money. I did it for Morgan. There's no other justice here, so I did it."

"Amen to that," Hooker said, filling my glass with good Kentucky bourbon and branch.

It was the first whiskey I had tasted in Arizona, but this time I was more than ready for a few sips. It eased the pain I was feeling in every cranny of my carcass.

"All right, then," he said. "We'll put the gold on the head of someone else and see what happens. How else may I be of service to you?"

"I expect Behan's posse, which the *Nugget* calls gentlemen ranchers and farmers, is going to show up pretty quickly. They're on our tail right now."

"We'll fight if you want us to."

I shook my head. I didn't want to suck Hooker into that. Theoretically, that mob was a legitimate body with warrants to bring us in, and Hooker could end up in grave trouble with the law.

"Mr. Hooker, no, we'll choose our own ground and

the time and place for a fight if it comes to that. What you've done, given us a chance to recruit, is all I can ask."

Hooker smiled wryly. "I think my foreman and a dozen of my hands would be disappointed."

Doc put in his two cents. "Those gentlemen farmers riding with Behan wouldn't take it kindly," he said. "I mean, solid citizens like John Ringo, Pony Deal, Ike Clanton. Most excellent frontiersmen and yeomen sons of the soil."

"Mr. Holliday, Sheriff Behan keeps excellent company," Hooker said. "I raise beef. My drovers work my cattle, and live hard but upright lives, most of the time anyway, and are often called cowboys. But that is an entirely different vocation."

Doc and Hooker hit it off right from the start. The rancher saw a patrician Southerner; Doc saw a substantial man with good manners.

"Mr. Hooker, what would you do in my shoes?" I asked.

The rancher studied on it a moment. "Have you done what you set out to do?"

"Actually, yes," I said. "Mostly, anyway."

"How so?"

"Frank Stilwell pulled the trigger on Morgan. Bill Brocius tried for me and missed. They paid. Indian Charlie served as a runner and lookout for a lousy twenty-five dollars. He paid. Ike probably planned it, maybe paid for some of it, but he didn't pull any triggers. Pete Spence . . . well, he was a part of it but he didn't pull the trigger, either. I think he was a lookout and his house was the staging area. He's still on my list. Ringo—I don't know. He sent word he wasn't going to be a part of what was coming but Indian Charlie named him. I think he was in on it, but I just don't know. But Stilwell and Brocius, who pulled the triggers—they paid."

"So you've actually fulfilled your promise to Morgan," Hooker said quietly.

With that, I knew what to do. We had to get the hell out while we could. It was over. I had focused so long and hard on riding down that bunch, I hadn't quite come to that.

"Thank you. You've steered me to a conclusion."

"The gentlemen ranchers can go back to their peaceful pursuits," Doc said, discerning the cast of my thoughts. "We will disturb their peace no longer."

I heard shouting, and the ranch's foreman, Bill Whelan, appeared in the doorway of the whitewashed room.

"Behan's two miles out," he said. "A large party."

We were a small party. I set aside my napkin and stood.

"You're welcome to fight here. These are thick walls," Hooker said, rising.

"No, not here," I said.

We abandoned our victuals and raced for the pen, where the horses stood quietly, having been watered, grained, and hayed.

"Thanks, Mr. Hooker," I said, as we boarded.

He nodded, lifted his sombrero, and watched us ride out.

I headed for a distant crest, perhaps two miles away, where we would command every approach, and waited. We put the horses in some rocky ground to protect them and set up a perimeter. There were six of us.

We knew John Behan's posse numbered more than twenty.

We sat quietly up there as the evening breezes blew through our clothing. It was neither warm nor cold. Below, in our binoculars, we could see a body of men on horse head straight for Hooker's great hacienda and spread out.

That was all we knew. I got the story of what happened down there later, and in bits and pieces.

The posse insisted on being fed and their horses cared for.

Hooker, fearless even in the face of twenty desperadoes armed to the teeth, along with a corrupt sheriff with legal powers, dealt coldly with them.

"Where's Earp?" Behan asked.

"He left," Hooker said.

It was obvious to those at the ranch that the posse knew exactly where we were. They had their own field glasses. It also became obvious that not one of that bunch wanted to tackle us, and that those questions concerning our whereabouts were all for show. As Hooker later told me, they would ride in any direction except the one that would take them to us, sitting on our hilltop, and Behan stayed out of rifle range.

Behan told Hooker he was harboring criminals, and Hooker retorted that Behan was sure one to talk, with cow thieves like that behind him.

That amused me. Henry Hooker was fearless, even in the face of an outfit like that. It almost came to a fight when Hooker's foreman, enraged by the posse's calculated insults, pulled a Winchester and said that the outfit would fight if it had to. After that, Behan backed off.

Hooker told me he fed Behan and Woods at his

table, but banished the rest of the scurvy bunch to its own table. He wouldn't have men who had stolen stock from him in his house. There they all were, he said, a bunch of bandits deputized by the most rotten sheriff in the United States, a wolfish pack if ever there was one.

They made a great show of hunting me down, and finally rode off. Hooker said that Behan had soaked Cochise County thirteen thousand for the posses, and didn't think the county could support a posse in the field much longer. At least that was Behan's excuse for heading away. The real reason was that his twenty desperadoes didn't want to tackle us.

I knew I would not be returning to Arizona, and there were things to do. In Safford I executed a deed, turning over some of my Tombstone property to my sister.

Dan Tipton rode in with the two thousand dollars we needed, half from a mining executive, E. B. Gage, a backer of mine, and half from Wells Fargo. We had enough to get by for a while.

The commander of Fort Grant, Colonel James Biddle, treated us cordially. He said that anyone recommended by Henry Clay Hooker was welcome. But he also told us he would have to hold us because there were warrants outstanding. Strange thing: when it came time to leave, we found our hayed and grained and saddled mounts waiting for us and we rode away without hindrance.

We stayed at the Sierra Bonita for several days, recovering our strength. It felt good just to be able to sleep through a night without an eye open and an ear listening.

The letter was Doc's idea.

"Back in Tombstone they think you're dead and Brocius is alive, and the *Nugget* is telling the town that intrepid Behan and his posse of gentlemen ranchers and yeoman farmers is circling in on us. I think we should improve their understanding," he said.

"It sure needs improving," Texas Jack opined.

"Good. A little missive to the *Epitaph* will remedy matters."

"Write it," I said. "Any paper that calls outlaws gentlemen ranchers is as corrupt as the sheriff is. One deals in lies. The other deals in robbery. I've had plenty to do with rotten politicians, but this is my first experience with a newspaper so rotten that it can't tell black from white," I said.

"Mr. Earp," said Hooker, waving his riding crop, "a lying newspaper is worse than a corrupt politician. Harry Woods and his successors are darker of heart than Behan could think of being. Behan is venal. The *Nugget* leads a whole community into blackness and confusion for the sake of power."

I had never thought of that. I had never worked out in my mind what newspapers are, what they do, and how they should conduct themselves. But I remembered a sermon I heard in Dodge. The Devil is a liar, was what the preacher was saying. And I had been learning through my brief period in Arizona that words count. I must not suffer abuse in silence; I could not permit a lie to go unrebutted. This was all so new to me that I left the business to those who could argue and write better than I.

Doc swiftly obtained a nib pen, ink, and paper from Hooker, and set down the truth.

He headed it IN CAMP, APRIL 4, 1882 and then proceeded with a factual account of our whereabouts, including our stop at Hooker's ranch, where we received much the same hospitality afforded to the sheriff's posse, and our departure from it when the sheriff's posse approached.

> In relation to the reward offered by the Stock Association, which the *Nugget* claims Mr. Hooker paid to Wyatt Earp for the killing of Curly Bill, it is also false, as no reward has been asked for or tendered.
> Next morning, not being in a hurry to break camp, our stay was long enough to notice the movements of Sheriff Behan and his posse of honest ranchers, with whom, had they possessed the trailing ability of the average Arizona ranchman, we might have had trouble, which we are not seeking. Neither are we avoiding these honest ranchers as we thoroughly understand their designs.

That was Doc at his best.

We learned, while resting in that haven, that a posse, if that was the word for it, consisting of John Ringo, Ike Clanton, Pete Spence, and nearly thirty hardcases, was out to polish us off, and searching hard.

There was little time.

We said goodbye to Henry Hooker, boarded our well-rested and -grained horses, and headed east. I supposed, once we crossed the New Mexico line, that my deputy federal marshal's commission was no longer valid. We had left Dake's jurisdiction. But I wasn't sure about that. Simply put, we were seven men—Dan Tipton had joined us—on the lam.

Chapter 30

We rode through an amber sunset into Silver City, New Mexico Territory, on April 15, chose a backstreet rooming house to sleep in, wolfed down pancakes at the Broadway Restaurant the next morning without being recognized, and prepared to leave incognito. But then we were found out by the suspender-snapping walleyed manager of the livery stable where we boarded our horses and tried to sell them.

"Ha! You're Wyatt Earp," he said. "I been following it. Sort of expectorated you. Guess you feel pretty sharp, getting out of Arizona."

"You buying horses?" I asked.

"You got owner papers?"

"We all do."

"Can't pay much."

"What horse trader ever does?"

We sold our nags to the leering rube for half their worth, caught a stagecoach to Deming, rode a yellow caboose to Albuquerque, and worked out what we would do, how we would split up, where we would go, how we might meet again. That was the damnedest thing, running from the law.

We were homeless. We were wanted men in the territory next door, and there was always the chance that some bravo in New Mexico would trap us and ship us back to where the writ ran against us. Doc had turned sour. His modest household was as good as lost; he couldn't go back and claim it. He eyed me testily, knowing that the two thousand would stretch very thin among us, and began downing whiskey. I didn't pity him much: I had lost far more defending myself. And all Doc needed was a deck of cards.

The street fight at the back of the Tombstone livery stable had shattered the Earp family fortunes, not just my own. I was down to nothing but some very illiquid real estate. The fight had transformed me from a respected lawman and Wells Fargo employee and gambler and mining speculator to a debt-ridden fugitive, and I was feeling as testy as Doc was.

I divvied up the cash, giving each man $250, and keeping the extra cut for myself.

"That's it? Two hundred fifty dollars for all that?" Doc asked.

"I don't know that we'll get anything out of Dake," I said.

"Your munificence is breathtaking."

"Doc, I'll be wiring the new governor, Tritle, for pardons. I'll be looking after us all."

"Yes, always looking after us. That's why you've got five hundred and we've got half that. I admire generous men."

"I've paid your way for days," I said. I'd already spent some on the rooming house rooms for us all, graining and boarding all our horses, and all our meals. They had received what I could give, and what they got for their horses.

Plenty of people in Albuquerque knew we were there and were keeping our secret for us. I had business to transact with Wells Fargo, with the Arizona governor, with my family. I never much cared for the town, but the climate was excellent and the nights cool.

I also read the headlines and knew we were losing a war that I scarcely understood. Papers across the country were calling us outlaws, a mob, a gang of cutthroats, murderers, fugitives, criminals with a federal badge. I had learned something in Tombstone, hard lessons taught me by Harry Woods and John Behan. Silence didn't work. Everything those people said about me stuck to me because I had considered it beneath my dignity to respond.

We met in the Elephant Saloon, sitting quietly at the rear.

"I'm going to talk to a paper or two," I said.

"You'd better not. We'll have a few federal marshals for this district putting irons on us," McMasters said.

"You're eloquent, Wyatt. You'll answer all our critics," Doc said. "You have a nickel-plated tongue."

"Goddamn you, Doc."

He laughed. "Beats a shotgun tongue," he said. He had downed another whiskey, and another.

I was tired of him and wished he would beat it to wherever he was going. I didn't know or care.

"Doc, you have a stake, we're done, the posse's disbanding, and I don't need you anymore," I said.

Doc stared, stood suddenly, and vanished into the soft spring night. We sat around uneasily. Dan Tipton rose. "I'll go with Doc," he said, "wherever that is. He needs looking after."

So I had blown a small, tight, loyal bunch apart. I watched Doc vanish into the dark, wondering whether I would see him again. Suddenly I felt a loss so great it drained me. Would this never end?

I tried the *Evening Review* the next morning, and found myself sitting at the desk of one Ed Chauncy.

"I have a story that'll interest you," I said. "But there's a condition."

He looked me over. "Who are you?"

"Never mind that. Do you want a story?"

"What's the condition."

"That you wait a while before publishing it."

He cocked his head, peered at me through wire-rimmed spectacles. "You're Earp," he said. "I've been hearing a few rumors."

"Then you know why I want you to delay printing it."

"I might or I might not. That's a risk you'll have to take."

He pulled a cigar out of his coat, offered another to me, which I refused, and scratched a lucifer.

"All right," he said, "what is it?"

I told him my story. I told him about Behan. I told him about the rustlers, stage robbers, and the rats who made up Behan's posses. I told him about refreshing at Hooker's great ranch, staking out a hilltop, and waiting for the posse to take us on and how they turned tail. About the street fight behind the OK Corral. About the Clantons and the McLaurys, Pony Deal, Frank Stilwell, the hearing before Spicer, the murder of Morgan, the coroner's report listing, among others, Brocius and Stilwell as the trigger men who killed my brother. Both dead.

Chauncy took notes, nodded, knew he was receiving a story straight from an Earp, even if some of it was old now.

"What are you doing here?" he asked.

"I'm awaiting a pardon from Governor Tritle of Arizona. We need to rein in Behan's posses. Until we get pardoned, we're fugitives. I think we'll have it. Behan's become so blatant that not even the county Democrats are supporting him. He stinks. Meanwhile, we're going to disappear for a while, until we can straighten things out."

"Why did you come to me?"

"I want our side told. All I see in the papers is lies about us."

"What makes you think I'll write up your story as you want it written? How do you know I'm on your side?"

He stumped me there. "I don't know. I hoped you might take the measure of me and draw your own conclusions," I said. I feared I was making a chump of myself.

"You have a notorious man, Doc Holliday, in your posse."

"Notorious only because the sensational press makes him out to be," I said.

"He's killed a few."

"Fewer than you think, a crooked gambler in Texas, and justifiably. When did he ever spend a day in prison? What's he been convicted of?"

"I don't know what's on his sheet," the reporter said.

"Have a look. Go for the police records, not what the papers say. Doc is a brave man with a hot temper, and a disease that eats at him, gives him no future. He never knows from week to week whether his candle is going to burn out. He's been pretty well here in this dry country, but he's tired, and sick, and he coughs, and when the pain in his chest gets too big, he gets a little crazy, or swallows too much sauce.

"He's my friend. He's been a loyal man, supported my brothers and me every time, without question, without conditions, putting himself in harm's way. Leave him alone, or answer to me," I said. "Doc's not happy with me now, and I can't help that. He's the best there is, and I don't listen to the ones always tearing him down."

Chauncy smiled suddenly. He was missing an incisor. "I think I might do a story," he said. "You're news. Mostly bad news. If I were to say you're in town, fathers would lock up daughters, armed citizens would patrol the avenues, and the mayor would ask the governor to call out the militia." He sucked his cheroot, and flicked ash.

"We're staying here a while, lying low, and then getting out," I said. "I won't say where. After that, print this up. I want my side told."

"I won't promise it," Chauncy said.

I stared him down. He laughed lightly, and stood. Cigar ash tumbled down his suit jacket. The gray gabardine was shiny at the elbows.

I walked out, thinking it would be all right. We were temporarily safe in Albuquerque. Doc and Dan Tipton hung around town, eyeing the ladies, wanting to know where we were heading, and eventually they rejoined us, even if Doc wasn't very friendly.

"Kate's shipping my outfit to Trinidad," he told me. "One bag of molar pullers, one faro game, and one spare suit of clothes. Goddamn, I'm back to pulling teeth. Maybe I should yank a few of yours."

"You try it and I'll empty your mouth," I said.

Doc didn't like my humor.

The next day we bought coach tickets to Trinidad on

the Atchison, Topeka and Santa Fe. I knew that Doc would stay there and gamble. He had always liked Trinidad, a mining town full of riffraff, the sort of place he enjoys. Maybe he would have the chance to shoot someone and improve his legend. I imagined he would soon have Kate Elder with him, and they could engage in domestic strife in Colorado instead of Arizona, unless Marshal Bat Masterson began cracking craniums.

I planned to head for the hills after a rest and a visit with Bat. From Pueblo, a little way north of Trinidad, I would catch the narrow-gauge Denver, Rio Grande Western Pacific Railroad to a new camp where I might survive with a faro game until the smoke cleared.

I had Gunnison in mind. I could have gone way the hell up to Montana, maybe Butte, but I decided to stick closer to Arizona, where I could keep an eye on Behan and his gentlemen ranchers. I wanted to clear my name. I wanted the _Nugget_ to swallow its teeth. I wanted to finish a housecleaning job only half done. _John Ringo. Pony Deal. Hank Swilling. Ike Clanton._

The Tombstone story wasn't over. Somewhere down there, some Cochise County thugs were still hunting me, and somewhere down there were some lizards who had vowed a blood oath to kill me and Virgil, and maybe Warren and Jim too. Until that had been dealt with, I would have to watch my back, and keep on watching.

Meanwhile, I was nearly broke. Gunnison might support a faro game. I was making plans, and those plans didn't include Mattie, but they did include a lady waiting for me in San Francisco.

Chapter 31

Bat Masterson met us in the Grand Central Bar, a joint that reminded me of a whorehouse parlor. He wore his city marshal badge under his black suit coat, as if he didn't want it displayed.

He looked like a long-lost brother to me, grinning there as he approached our table, dark and compact and lithe as a lion.

"Brother Wyatt," he said, grasping my hand, "you are looking just fine, for a man nose deep in manure."

"Brother Bat," I said, "you are an ugly but welcome sight."

Bat settled beside Warren and me. Turkey Creek had abandoned us for a safer clime, namely rural Texas, but Doc and Dan Tipton were around, having elected to board at Ritenburg House and fleece tourists. Doc's health had not been improved by weeks of hardship with my posse, and he was curing himself with drink and sleep, which meant we had to watch hawklike to keep him on the straight.

A pretty serving girl with heavy breasts like Josie's deposited a shot of rye and a glass of cold water before the town cop, and I could see that officialdom in Trinidad had its privileges. He patted her amiably on the arm, in lieu of patting her elsewhere, I imagined.

I liked Trinidad. The Santa Fe eastbound had clattered up Raton Pass and coasted down the Colorado side, and we debarked at Trinidad, a solid-brick city nestled in the crotch of the red mountains. It was a good-sized coal mining town, with plenty of action: such oases as the Tivoli, the Bank Exchange, the Boss Saloon, and the Brunswick lined its sporting district. I was tempted to stay there, set up my game, except that it was too near Arizona, and I wanted distance.

"You win your war?" Bat asked.

"Won the fight and lost the war," I said. "Morg's killers are roasting in hell. Some of those helping them are still around and hunting me. But they own the press and the law and we can't go back, at least not now. Maybe we'll get a pardon—I'm working on it. But not now."

"You got Brocius? How the hell did you do that?"

"I don't know, Bat. I aimed. That's all I know. I aimed. He never aimed. He just shot, and not a ball touched me."

"Tell me about Stilwell."

Bat was obviously well-versed.

"He and Ike Clanton were laying for us at the Tucson station, and we spotted Frank lying on a baggage cart as the train rolled in. No doubt in my mind what they had planned. Those cars were lit. It was dark out. They were going to finish Virg and me and vanish into the dark. But Doc and I—we prevented it."

I didn't much want to talk about that, not even to Bat.

Bat smiled. "Self-defense," he said. "They come shooting, and you shoot back."

"That's not how Ike Clanton's telling the story to everyone," I said. "According to Ike, he and Frank Stilwell just happened to be there in Tucson so Frank could consult a lawyer before his stagecoach robbery trial, very peaceable, and had the misfortune to run into a berserk Wyatt Earp, who gunned Frank down just for the hell of it. By the way, Ike ran. He won't fight, in spite of his big lips."

"If I could get a buck for every one of Ike's lies, I could retire," Bat said.

Holliday plowed through the batwing doors, spotted us, and came over. He looked baggy-eyed, but otherwise immaculate.

"It's Dodge City again," Bat said, making room.

"I am heeled inside your city limits," Doc said, "and plan to stay heeled."

"I didn't hear you," Bat said.

Before two drinks had been consumed, Bat had our whole story, our triumphs, misgivings, worries, and fears.

"They're still after us. I wouldn't be surprised to see men with shooters in their hand walk into any place where I am, sent by Ike, maybe by Will McLaury. And it wouldn't matter whether they have a hunting license, a warrant, or all that. There would be burned powder."

Bat nodded. "I don't doubt it."

"We had no choice, Bat. No Cowboy's ever been convicted or sent to jail or hanged for murder down there. The gang's as strong as ever, except maybe it now lacks a few triggermen. The courts can do nothing, with twenty liars to alibi them all. And Behan's on their payroll. That's where the trouble is. Behan protects them and the press, the *Nugget* and now the *Epitaph*, are both against us. I had a deputy marshal badge and I used it the only way I could."

"No trial, no jury, no sentence."

"Yes, that's it and I won't apologize."

Bat looked troubled, and I could pretty well read what was passing through his mind. There was an odd pause. Doc and I both knew that Bat was weighing it all, coming to conclusions.

"There wasn't any other way," I said.

The town cop downed a second shot of rye, and chased it with water. I finally had the sense to shut up, and Doc said nary a word.

Then, after two or three minutes, Bat had reached some place in his mind where he wanted to be. "Count on me," he said. "Not because we're old friends, or because we live in the same circles, or because we're veterans of Dodge City. No, Wyatt. It's because I believe in you. You did what you had to do, made a hard decision and stuck to it. And you too, Doc."

"I didn't know you'd consort with fiends and desperadoes," Doc said. "Personally, I prefer fiend. It's rather enchanting, don't you suppose? How many men get to be called a fiend? By newspaper count, I have sent, oh, forty, fifty innocents to paradise. Now can you beat that? How many do they claim for you, Bat?"

"Thirty, last I read it somewhere."

"And you, Wyatt?"

"Eighteen. Eight in recent weeks, and ten before that."

"There now. The gentlemen gamblers at this very table have dispatched a hundred souls to their reward," Doc said. "Maybe I should try for one-oh-one this quiet April evening."

Doc waved at the serving girl, a lush Mexican beauty with a blouse that revealed golden flesh.

"Another double whiskey sour," Doc said.

I knew I would be leading Doc Holliday back to the hotel and putting him under the covers, or he would get sprightly again, as he had in Albuquerque.

"I wish I could have helped you, Wyatt," Bat said. "But I couldn't."

"Bat, if you'd been there, we could have handled the whole thing."

"You put too much stock in me."

"You have a way with the press, Bat. I don't. They're always on my back. And you have a way with badmen. Whatever it is, they run, and keep running."

Bat smiled. He liked that. "Let me tell you something: whenever you need help, call on me. Any of you. You too, Doc. Call on me."

"I hope we won't have to," I said.

Doc shrugged. "It doesn't much matter to me whether I succumb to asphyxiation from lungs that have died before the rest of me, or from strangulation by hemp."

"I don't think that's true, Doc," Bat said.

"Maybe I'll just shoot up the town," he said.

Bat sucked on his drink. "What are your plans?"

"I'm heading for Gunnison and a faro game," I said.

"I'm going to skin tourists in Pueblo or Denver. You'll find me on Blake Street," Doc said.

"You have a bank?" Bat asked me.

"Not much of one. It took all the loose cash I had to keep out of John Behan's jail," I said. "I've some property there but I can't get to it. I deeded some lots to my sister, but I need to sell some mine claims, and I need to get back there to do it."

"Tight, then."

"Broke as I've been. And the rest are just as bad off. Our assets in Arizona are out of reach. That's why I've petitioned Tritle, the new territorial governor, for a federal pardon. But they say we won't get it. We're too hot for any politician to touch. So . . . I'm starting over."

"And you, Doc?"

"You should see my dental tools," he said. "I can crowbar a molar in three minutes and sledge out an incisor in forty-three seconds, two dollars a tooth."

"You have all that stuff here?"

"They were waiting for me here. Kate sent them."

"I'm going to Gunnison with Wyatt," said Warren.

"What do you think will happen with the outstanding warrants against all of you?"

"Well, Bat, that's going to depend on Sheriff John Behan. There's a five-hundred-dollar reward for each of us. On the other hand, he's lost support in Tombstone and his own party's fixing to throw him out of office. So I don't know."

"Wyatt, John Behan isn't going to quit, not until you're pushing up forget-me-nots," Doc said.

"It's Harry Woods who won't quit. If Harry Woods weren't undersheriff, I'd be all right. No one thinks about Harry Woods except me, and I think about him more than I want to. As long as Woods is there, we're in trouble. He's the spider in the web."

"Woods don't know the butt of a revolver from the barrel," Warren said.

I turned to my brother. "Harry Woods is the most dangerous man we face. Behan? I can deal with him. Ike? I can deal with him. The rest? Hired gunmen. But Harry Woods is the rattlesnake. His weapons are lies."

I could see that not one man agreed with me, so I let it drop.

There had been something tender in that reunion, something that transcended friendship. I have never been good with words, and I wouldn't know how to put it. But Bat and Doc and I shared a moment that would linger with us the rest of our lives. I never tried to describe it, not even to Josie.

We stayed around Trinidad a few days. I camped outside of town to save money, and also because I figured I could hotfoot it out of trouble easier. The press had caught up with us again, and the whole country knew where the Earp Gang was holed up. I decided it was time to move.

We caught the Santa Fe north to Pueblo, and there we split up. Doc decided to try his luck in the old adobe town for a spell, and Warren and I caught the Denver and Rio Grande Railroad out to a new mining camp. Maybe we could start over out there in Gunnison, maybe not. I would know after I had settled in and talked to the coppers. If they didn't want some Earps around, I'd shuffle on.

Texas Jack, Warren, and I dropped off the narrow-gauge coach onto gravel and looked around. Gunnison was young and cold, set in a wilderness just opened to mining, with long, austere slopes rising toward high horizons. I didn't know what sort of faro game I could set up, or how safe I might be, but I'd soon find out. We camped outside of town for a while, looking things over, and then I made myself known to the town constables. After a little palaver, they welcomed us, even thought of us as some sort of heroes. I set up my small-stakes game and lived quietly.

It turned out I wasn't safe at all, and Bat's pledge of help would mean more to Doc and me and Warren than I had imagined. I think maybe I owe my life to Bat. And Doc does, without a doubt.

Chapter 32

When the issue is whether you are going to hang, I do not recommend newspapers as the source of your information. Yet that was all I had, plus a couple of terse wires from Bat. Each day the narrow-gauge Denver and Rio Grande would drop a bundle of Denver papers in Gunnison, and from those lying rags I discovered Doc's fate in Denver. And mine.

In May, a bounty hunter and, it turned out, a confidence man named Perry Mallen snared Doc, employing a big revolver to do it, and turned him over to Denver lawmen for extradition to Arizona. He represented himself as a Los Angeles deputy sheriff at first and, later, as an Arizona lawman. And in due course, he was exposed as a confidence man. But that came later, and all I knew at first was that I had plenty to fear.

The capture of Doc set off a furor in the press from one end of the United States to the other. He had a few defenders, but mostly he was assailed as a fiend incarnate, killer of scores of men, who would promptly be returned to Arizona Territory, tried, and executed. All this I absorbed with mounting alarm.

Suddenly, the Earp Gang was making headlines, and every hour things looked worse.

The first wind of trouble came in the pages of the *Denver Tribune*, which had a reporter on hand when Mallen corralled Doc and accused him of killing Mallen's partner, Harry White, seven years earlier, in Park City, Utah. Doc defended himself, saying he'd

never been in Park City, Utah, and Mallen was no
Cochise County officer, no Los Angeles officer either,
and a damned fraud.

Bat leapt in, vouching for Doc, saying he was a man
of good repute and a deputy U.S. marshal. But to no
avail.

The *Denver Republican* proclaimed:

> Doc Holliday, the prisoner, is one of the most noted
> desperadoes of the West. In comparison, Billy the
> Kid or any of the most noted desperadoes who
> have recently met their fate, fade into insignifi-
> cance. The murders committed by him are counted
> by the scores and his other crimes are legion. For
> years he has roamed the West, gaining his living by
> gambling, robbery, and murder. In the Southwest
> his name is terror.

I read all that with mounting alarm. It got worse.
The *Rocky Mountain News* leapt in, vilifying Doc and
the rest of us and, at the same time, celebrating Mallen,
the brave captor of a notorious badman. I sat there in
Gunnison, feeling helpless, seeing clearly what was
coming: an attempt to extradite all of us and ship us to
our doom.

Bat wasn't taking any of this lying down. He swiftly
offered an interview to the *Republican*. "I tell you that
all this talk is wrong about Holliday. I know him well.
He is a dentist and a good one," he said. In Dodge City,
where Bat had served as a sheriff and city lawman, Doc
"was known as an enemy of the lawless element."

Bat explained that the whole purpose of this was to
snatch Doc back to Arizona, where the outlaws could
and would kill him, and no fair trial was possible, as-

suming Doc survived long enough to be brought to the bar.

Amen to that, I thought, wondering what to do, where to go, how to fight. There was no escape. My new friends in Gunnison could have tracked me down easily.

Bat was no fool. He saw how things were going and wired his acquaintance Henry Jameson, the city marshal in Pueblo, asking for a warrant charging Doc with bilking a citizen in a confidence game. Bat wanted to change the jurisdiction, fast, before even worse trouble befell Doc. I've always admired Bat for that. He understood the law and how it might be employed to help Doc.

Meanwhile, Doc was fighting for his life. I opened the *Republican* one day, over breakfast in the Good Luck Café, and found this:

> If I am taken back to Arizona, that is the last of Holliday. We hunted the rustlers, and they all hate us. John Behan, sheriff of Cochise County, is one of the gang and a deadly enemy of mine who would give any amount of money to have me killed. . . . Should he get me in his power, my life would not be worth much.

The same applied to Warren and me.

"Let's run," said Warren. "Anywhere. In Montana, we'd be safe."

"We'll ride this out right here," I said. "We have friends in Arizona, including the governor. Bob Paul knows what's what. He's not going to confuse us with Ike Clanton."

"He's the one with the warrants for you and Doc," he said.

That was true. Six-foot-four-inch Bob Paul had become sheriff of Pima County, and that was where we had shot down Frank Stilwell, and that was the county where we were wanted men. And even if he was quietly on our side, there would not be much he could do for us.

"I don't think he'll serve us if he can help it," I said. "He knows it was self-defense. Why else would Stilwell and Clanton be hanging around the Tucson station when our train pulled in? Just to pass the time of day? They were trying to kill Virgil and me, and Bob Paul knows it, and he knows that what I did was something I had to do."

But maybe I was whistling in the dark, especially after I found that Bob Paul had come to Denver and was awaiting extradition papers from Arizona, and giving interviews to the Denver papers that didn't sound a bit friendly to us.

In the *Rocky Mountain News*, Paul was quoted as saying:

The so-called Earp Gang, or faction if you please, was composed entirely of gamblers who preyed upon the Cowboys, and at the same time in order to keep up a show of having a legitimate calling was organized into a sort of vigilance committee, and some of those, including Holliday, had United States marshal's commissions.

I felt a keen disappointment. Bob Paul had been someone I was counting on to help us. Now he was against us. But maybe Paul was being cautious about siding with us in public, whatever he felt privately. He had duties to perform as sheriff. I learned later that he did favor us, though he never much cared for the way I handled the Stilwell matter. He played his cards close to his vest that whole time, and I didn't know from day to day whether he was with me or not.

But if the furor in the Denver papers was something, the furor in the Arizona papers was worse. Day by day, friends mailed the clippings to me, and I didn't much care for what I saw. It was like watching an avalanche rumble down on top of me.

Behan, I learned, was planning to come up to Denver to take Doc into captivity, no matter that the outstanding warrants rose from Pima County. But Paul had that right and duty, and Behan couldn't break away or get the funding for it.

I lived in hourly fear of a knock on the door of our rooms, but it didn't come. I kept the sheriff of that county apprised of my every move, which I knew was the safest thing to do, and it won Warren and me some respect.

Things were happening that I didn't know about then, and didn't find out about until it all blew over. Bat, one of the most loyal and sterling men in all the world, didn't rest until he had secured our safety, and somehow he did it. He obtained a midnight audience with Governor Pitkin of Colorado to apprise the man that if Doc and Warren and I were bound over to Arizona for trial, we would not survive, that being the state of affairs in southern Arizona.

The next day, at a hearing on the extradition, Bob Paul assured the Colorado governor that every effort would be made to protect the prisoners, and he had special forces ready along the way, at Willcox, Bowie, and Deming, to alert him of impending trouble from the Cowboy bunch.

Imagine it: one Arizona sheriff was stationing guards en route to prevent the murder of prisoners by another Arizona sheriff and his gang. Pitkin must have listened in amazement.

I think Bob Paul's protestations that he was taking special measures to protect us, along with Bat's reasoned argument, did the trick. Pitkin denied the requisition on two grounds: the extradition paper from Arizona was flawed, signed by the wrong man, and there was a charge outstanding against Doc in Colorado. I have always believed that Governor Frederick Pitkin had other, deeper motives for springing Doc. He was on my side.

The wrath of the Arizona press reached new heights upon hearing of our release, running furiously against me and those who had stood beside me, but at that moment I didn't care. When I received that telegram from Bat, informing me that Doc and I were off the hook, I quietly closed my faro game, headed into the spring night, stared up at the stars, and acknowledged my debt to my Creator. The fate that had kept me from harm, that had steered bullets elsewhere while I sought the justice that was denied me in Cochise County, had once again preserved me to be among the living. And Doc too. They shipped him down to Pueblo to stand trial, but the case was postponed, and it never came up again.

I heard he was drinking, and I imagined that would get him into trouble. But it would not be Behan trouble. Doc could make trouble for himself to his heart's content.

Over the years I have pondered the sensational press, and the damage it does, and its lust for power, its hunger to exert its will and impose its politics on the rest of us, and I have always felt that there is something malign in that press, something that cries for reform. Harry Woods taught me a lesson about bald lying for political gain that I have never forgotten and will take with me to the grave. I am for a free press. I am also for a responsible one, which requires a hunger for truth and withholding judgment until the facts are known.

The effect of all that was that I shied from all publicity until recent years, when I have quietly considered the prospect of telling my true story before I die. All I wanted back then was for my notoriety to slip away. It never did. I had been stamped as a villainous criminal behind a badge, or I had been stamped as a hero fighting against overwhelming odds. But either way, my name was no longer my own.

That was as close a scrape as I've ever endured, and I would be the first to acknowledge my fear. I've been in hard circumstances, danger from the elements, danger from criminals, but never was I so vulnerable as when the engines of law and order came close to burying me.

I returned to my faro game in Gunnison, but life had changed once again, and so had I. The local constables were as pleased to have me there as could be. Warren was free to go wherever he wanted to start a life. Doc dealt on Blake Street in Denver, and wrestled with his declining health.

I liked Gunnison but was restless. I had real estate and mining claims in Tombstone, and wanted to return, at least for a while. But that would require a pardon from Governor Tritle. Was that too much to ask?

Chapter 33

Years later, I was still reading lurid accounts of my days in Gunnison. One fellow claimed that I was a walking arsenal, with a pair of revolvers tucked into shoulder holsters. I was heeled, all right. I kept a revolver handy, under my suit coat, while I dealt. I knew that Ike Clanton and maybe Will McLaury were not done with me or my brothers, and I was ready to defend myself. The local constables knew it and never questioned me.

I was waiting for the Arizona pardon that never came. I was too naive about politics to grasp that I could never return to that territory; the cumulative effect of all that bad press made me a hot potato. Not even my political friends would vouch for me.

I had plans. Once cleared, I wanted to run against Behan and tell the world what sort of sheriff he had been. And I wanted to retrieve my property. I was broke in the sense of having no liquid assets. I hardly had cash enough to run a small-stakes faro game. But I had mining claims to sell if I could find buyers down there. And I wanted to finish it all up, clean up Cochise County once and for all. Boot out Behan, purge that stable, see Tombstone safe and free.

It was not a bright idea. At least that was what Doc told me when he came to visit for a couple of weeks. He rented rooms in town rather than staying with us out in our mining cabin west of Gunnison, and he tested the waters a bit. I was glad to see him.

"Wyatt, you can read, can't you?" he asked, a mocking smile on his face.

"Only after coffee," I replied.

"You and I, Wyatt, wear horns, dress in red longjohns, carry tridents, and eat little girls for breakfast."

"I don't care what people think," I replied.

Doc looked pained, as if I had not yet mastered the first grade. In fact, even as I said it, I knew I was retreating into an earlier self, one who scorned the opinion of others and wouldn't deign to respond to scurrilous attacks.

But I nodded, sourly. "My reputation's keeping me from a pardon."

"They still run things, Wyatt. The *Epitaph*'s new owner, Sam Purdy, is harder on you than the *Nugget* ever was. Those gentlemen ranchers won."

Doc shoved his glass at the barkeep, who poured a generous dollop of red-eye into it. Doc sipped, wheezed, licked his lips, and smiled. "It beats suffering," he said. "It requires one drink an hour to endure the pain in my chest. But it takes two drinks an hour to make it go away. I try not to drink two an hour when I am making my living, but then I get testy."

Testy sometimes meant that Doc's hand was nesting in the bosom of his black suit coat while he stared down a player at his table. There were players in Colorado who would never forget the way Doc watched the cards fall while his pale hand warmed itself under his lapel.

I knew his chest pain had been building ever since the hard riding we had done, and that he was numbing it in any way he could, apart from the fact that he was happiest with a half dozen shots in his belly.

"Behan didn't win," I said.

"Your enemy isn't just Behan. It's the press. It's Harry Woods. It's deliberate lying, like saying the rustler crowd is really a bunch of gentlemen ranchers. They knew exactly what they were doing when they said that. That's Harry Woods' work, and now Richard Rule's work. If there had never been a *Nugget* in Tombstone, you and I would not be sitting here, admiring our pale white necks."

He was right, and in time I came around to that view myself. There will always be violent and crooked men; it's when the press and politicians side with them that trouble blooms.

I remember one night, long after the sporting crowd had abandoned the saloon, when Doc and I sat at his faro game and waited for a last player of the night, who never walked through the double doors. Barney, who owned the place, was already extinguishing some of the coal-oil lamps in the chandeliers to save a nickel. Smoke hung in the air, irritating Doc's lungs.

He coughed softly, and I was reminded that he might have had a fine dental practice in Atlanta, might have married some Southern belle dressed in white lace and great flower-bedecked straw hats, might have attended the Presbyterian church on Sundays, listening solemnly to sermons while he sat on the varnished pews, might have lived and died in obscurity, save for a deadly disease that stopped his career and changed his life.

"What are you going to do?" I asked softly.

"Live up to my reputation," he said.

"But you're not that man."

"The press has made me a different man. Now I am what the press says I am."

I didn't follow, and must have looked puzzled.

"Wyatt, wherever I go, whatever I do, I will always be the man invented by reporters. I cannot step off a steam car into a place without being taken for that man. So why fight it? I'm inclined to make use of it. The legend amuses me. Let them come to my table and think maybe I'll shoot them if the whim rises. Let them deal a poker hand, wondering whether to cheat Doc Holliday. I find it quite useful."

He sipped cheerfully, and idly shuffled chips in his hand, the way dealers and croupiers do.

"You could go back to Atlanta."

"Last I knew, there were family back there saying they never heard of this John Henry Holliday, it must be some other Holliday, maybe one born up in Virginia or Pitcairn Island. And I don't think that swamp air would help me any. And there's the small matter of making a living."

"What about Kate?"

"She's well aware that I cannot return to Arizona, and has set herself up as a boardinghouse operator in Globe, where she lives a life virginal and devoid of any past."

"You could bring her up here."

"Wyatt, you have lost your senses."

"I still don't know what you're planning to do."

Doc smiled wryly at me. "Each day the sands run through the hourglass."

I nodded. The Mint Saloon had emptied, but a new

crowd would arrive at dawn with the end of a mining shift.

"And you?" Doc asked. "Not back to Tombstone, I trust."

"I'd like to finish it up."

Doc laughed, nastily, and swallowed more red-eye. He preferred good rye, but drank whatever would addle his mind the most if that was his only choice.

I don't know why I felt so sad that moment. Here was my closest friend, a man of vast disrepute, and I knew I would soon be losing him. Maybe that was it. Maybe it was just that a chapter in intertwined lives had ended. I wondered whether we would meet again.

"I'll tell you what I'll do," he said. "When the pain reaches a certain level, I'll return to Tombstone and shoot someone who needs shooting, preferably a truth-filled newsman at the *Nugget* who wishes to be remembered as a crusader, or a gentleman rancher near Charleston planning to will his papers to the pioneer historical society, and that will speed my passage from this life and cure my disease."

He almost amused me. I watched his waxen fingers shuffle chips, the practiced hand of a veteran gambler, while we waited for the sports who never came. Up at that altitude, the nights grew chill. Doc felt it as the chill slid along the floor of the saloon, and wrapped a black woolen shawl over his shoulders. He wasn't any better off than I, having lost most of his assets in our exile.

"Doc, here we are, a couple of saloon men, making our living at the green oilcloth tables, waiting for some miner to come in and buck the tiger so we can transfer the coin in his pockets to our own. Do you regret it?"

There was a funny look in Doc's face. "Wyatt," he

said, "but for this life, I never would have met the finest people I've ever known, such as you."

That was more answer than I could deal with.

He rescued me. "Well, I suppose I'll fold for the night, as long as no one's bursting through the doors," he said, packing chips into their pockets, emptying the case box of cards, and throwing a sheet over the layout.

He stood. "This place stinks. No play. I'll starve. I think I'll head for Blake Street."

"You'll see some play there," I said.

"It's as good as any."

Doc packed up and left the next morning, and I saw him off. The cramped Denver and Rio Grande coach would take him all the way to Denver on varnished wooden seats that would grind his ass to pulp.

"Watch your back," he said, as he shook hands and boarded.

I watched the drive wheels crank over, the pistons hiss steam, and the engine drag the three red coaches away from Gunnison and, with it, my old friend.

"I guess that means we won't be arresting him," said Roy Charlevoix, one of the town cops.

"He is my friend," I said as the train chuffed softer and softer away until I heard no sound at all.

I thought about Doc and his legend. It had been hung on him and he could never escape, not even in death.

I whiled away the fall, staying in touch with friends like Fred Dodge in Tombstone. But no pardon was coming, and at last I conceded it. Politicians were cowards. Or maybe it was that I had acquired a reputation too, and legends live their own lives. There was a Wyatt Earp out there in the press, in men's minds, whom I didn't know and hardly recognized as myself. I could not even make a statement to a reporter and get it printed as I said it. Whatever I said, it came out altered to fit the reputation, this legend that somehow pervaded people's heads.

I didn't know what to do about that. A man wants only privacy, and I had none. I could not enter a town without the cops knowing it and half the time they stopped by to warn me they were watching. It was as if they were all waiting, waiting, waiting for something bad to happen to me.

My game barely kept Warren and me in potatoes.

I heard that one of my lots had been auctioned for back taxes, and the others would go soon, unless I got down there and paid up. I saw how it would go. They would clean me out of all that was left as a last hurrah. I thought of the times I patrolled the streets of Tombstone, protecting their property and their safety. I thought of the time after the big fire when Virgil and Morg and I chased the lot jumpers off, sometimes at gunpoint, and gave the lots back to their owners. They thought we were pretty fine lawmen back then, doing that for folks.

But the lot jumpers and their pals won.

I gave up on Tombstone, which meant I also gave up on Gunnison, and looked west. Maybe I could begin all over again in California.

Chapter 34

Josephine was as stiff as parchment in the cramped parlor. I don't think her parents approved of me. We sat, sipping Earl Grey tea, her assessing gaze taking me in, from my new boots to my new black suit to my freshly shorn blond hair.

I needed air. The parlor, with all its respectability, closed in on me like a velvet noose. The conversation stuttered and died, and Josie and I stared at each other, strangers in the afternoon, and I thought that I didn't belong there. It had been a mistake. This wasn't the same Josie who arrived in Tombstone all aglow with young life, raring for adventure.

She was born into a respectable but struggling family in 1861. Her father, Hyman, was a baker. And here was Josie, Tombstone and me behind her, returned to the nest at age twenty-one, uncertain about herself and her future.

She was dressed semivirginally in gray satin, which covered everything but her hands and face, and her creamy flesh was barely a whisper of memory in me.

"Walk?" I said.

Her eyes grew bright. I've never known such an expressive face. Swiftly, she found her angora shawl and draped it over her shoulders against the chill San Francisco sea breeze. We fled the apartment.

She took my arm. I steered her toward bustling Market Street, and with each step she came alive, the Josie I had known in Tombstone. Now, in the hazy sun, her dark hair shown and a touch of rose lit each of her cheeks. I knew exactly what poured through her. In her parents' loving and respectable home, her spirit floundered. Away from it, she bloomed.

I steered her toward the Embarcadero, where we could watch the gulls float freely and listen to their unending complaints. I liked being there with Josie.

"I never dreamed it would be you at the door," she said.

"But you knew I would come."

"I waited."

"Behan came."

"My parents liked him, but didn't trust him."

"Smiling Johnny."

"Oh, Wyatt."

She snugged her arm tighter into mine, and that was answer enough.

Out in the bay, a steam ferry plied its way toward the white city from Oakland.

"I don't think your parents like me," I said.

She squeezed me. "You've been written up."

"Not much of it's true."

"I was hoping you'd say it's all true," she said, her cheeks dimpling. Her gaze was assessing me. "Are you still . . . in trouble?"

"There is a warrant outstanding in Arizona."

"And will they come for you?"

"I don't think so, Josie. For a while I thought I would turn myself in there, as soon as I could get a fair trial. What I did I had to do, and it was self-defense. Frank Stilwell was trying to kill me, and Virgil too, but no one seems to remember that. And I acted in the line of duty. I guess that's how it's stated in the lawbooks. I held a

United States badge. I was trying to arrest a stagecoach robber and assassin. But I've learned a few things about newspapers and politicians."

"Stilwell was Johnny's deputy."

"Does that say something to you?"

"Oh, Wyatt, Johnny's such a cheerful man and likable, and so rotten."

"Did he want to marry you?"

"Well, he asked if I would come live with him. And if I would, we could just walk off. He was rich and he'd buy me everything I ever needed."

I laughed.

"I'm not rich," I said. "I lost everything."

"Even the mining claims?"

"There's always miracles," I said, "but if I don't get down there fast it'll all disappear into the hands of those who set out to destroy us."

I watched a white gull skim the gray water, pluck up something, and thrash toward the heavens.

"You have any plans?" I asked.

She eyed me wryly, not daring to respond.

"Would you take up with a broke gambler and former lawman with a warrant hanging over him?"

"I thought you'd never ask."

"Josie . . . I'm not out of the woods."

"Wyatt, the best time I ever had was when we were together."

"In your little house?"

"Especially then."

We were thinking of the same thing, the velvety nights, soft caresses in the dry air of Arizona, the sweetness of passion, the comfort of each other. She was a daring woman and that made her my soul mate.

She pulled free to face me. "Are you . . . What about Mattie?"

"I stopped in Colton before I came up here. It's all settled."

"Settled, Wyatt?"

She had been a dark presence in my father's home, confining herself to a small alcove. They didn't understand at first, until it dawned on my father that those huge dark eyes and listless manner were the marks of an addict.

"We're done. You know why. I gave her fare," I said.

Josie didn't respond, and I knew I owed her more of an explanation, though I would just as soon have buried it.

"She was an addict, a prisoner of whatever powders she was taking, and sometimes she scarcely knew me. I didn't know her, either. Not that way, when she became a stranger. So I said that we would go our separate ways."

"Just like that."

"I bought her a ticket back to Tucson and gave her some spending money."

"No divorce or anything."

"No. She took up with me. I gave her something she needed after I found her, and she gave me something I wanted. That's how it was from Kansas City. It was fine at first."

Josie eyed me somberly, and I knew what she was thinking.

I turned her toward me, and watched the breezes play with her lustrous dark hair, and watched the whisps fall over her forehead.

"Josie, this is different."

She didn't reply, and I wondered what her true sentiments were. We were edging toward a union, or not a union, and I didn't know where I stood with her.

"I don't want to be stuck in a house and hidden away like she was," Josie said.

I saw at once what was impeding our progress. "I don't intend that," I said.

"I don't want to be stuck in a kitchen. No beans from Josie. No dust mop. No carpet beater. I don't want to clean the chamber pot. Not like . . . what you had. You can hire someone else to do it. Is that a deal?"

"It's a deal."

"No children, Wyatt. No nursery. No diapers. Is that a deal?"

I stared at the bay for a moment. "Yes," I said.

"What if you go to jail?"

I smiled suddenly. "You'll be a widow, because I don't intend to go to jail alive."

It became a negotiation, Josie staking out a life for herself, an escape from her stuffy and proper home, the adventurer within her seeing a bright sunrise upon my sudden and startling appearance on the Marcus family doorstep.

I remember that sweet moment clearly, even now, in my old age. I was thirty-four, she twenty-one. She had a divided soul, part bold and adventurous, part the dutiful daughter of a respectable Jewish family. She would seesaw between those poles all her life, sometimes as daring as any woman could be, sometimes worrying about reputation, or respectability, or appearances.

She mirrored me in that respect. For in me, and unspoken, were the same twin impulses. I was not born into the respectable classes but needed to be a part of them. At the same time, the frontier had stamped me, and I could not be two different people inside the same body.

She ambushed me. "Virgil was arrested here for running a faro game," she said. "I saw it in the paper."

"Yes, he was. There's not much a man with one arm in a sling can do to make a living. I'm staying with him now, on Pine Street."

"But he knew the law . . . and he's a lawman."

"Gambling's a funny thing. One moment it's legal and honorable, and the next, some city or state decides it's a vice and outlaws it. And the next moment, they secretly want you to keep your game going so they can nab you and fine you now and then and keep taxes low. Virgil ran respectable games all his life. It's the way he fleshes out a thin income. Cops don't earn much."

"What are you going to do, Wyatt?"

"Same as always, Josie. There's money to be made."

"Gambling?"

"Gambling, mining stocks, land speculation, horses—there's all sorts of ways. I thought to follow the circuit."

"The circuit?"

"Some people go to wherever life is young and exciting, and there's money to be made. But 'the circuit' is a gambler term. It means the various familiar places gamblers set up shop in different seasons."

She said nothing, but hugged me a moment while a seagull shrilled overhead. She didn't say yes or no that first afternoon. I suppose I wasn't offering her the sort of secure and prosperous life a part of her wanted. But maybe that other part of her, the seagull part, the part that loved a cliff to jump off of, and the flight of wild geese—maybe that part of her would triumph.

It took a few days more. I never proposed and she never said yes. I'm not the marrying kind, and it turned out, neither was Josie. That involved more than either of us wanted to get into. But then, one evening, at the restaurant in the St. Francis Hotel, she sipped some claret and eyed me.

"Friends and lovers?" she asked.

"Friends and lovers, Josie."

"Wherever you go, I'll go, Wyatt."

Chapter 35

Fearless Wyatt Earp's knees wobbled. I stood in that cramped parlor with Josie beside me, attempting to tell her parents I was about to hijack their daughter, roll far away from San Francisco, and all without the benefit of a rabbi, minister, or justice of the peace.

That was bad enough. What was more, I was a notorious man, with a warrant for murder outstanding in Arizona Territory, a man without wealth and only a minimal living as a gambler. I was reputed to have slaughtered multitudes.

Josephine had packed and now a dray stood in the street, ready to take her steamer trunk and suitcase to the wharf.

Hyman Marcus stood stiffly, saying nothing, his unblinking brown eyes fixed on me as if I were a barracuda.

Her mother seemed softer, and offered a tentative smile.

And then Josie helped me out.

"Mama, I've been in the theater," she said. "It's a different world, one I like. I respect your wishes, but I've made my choices and I'm of age. You've met Wyatt and you've met John Behan, and you have seen the difference, and you know why I chose Wyatt."

That somehow eased the Marcuses. I guessed that they had strongly objected to Behan, or seen straight through him. Hyman had struck me as a man who could pierce to the center of things.

Hyman turned to her. "You have chosen Mr. Earp and you are certain?"

Josie drew me to her side and took my hand. "Yes, this man."

She spoke willfully. She was twenty-one, had traveled in a theater company, and had called herself Mrs. John Behan for a while. She was an experienced woman, and her parents understood that. What she wanted was their blessing.

Then her mother softened. She drew close to me, touched my arm, and smiled. "You take good care of Sadie," she said.

She clasped my hand warmly, and within that clasp was a small wad of banknotes.

"This is a little something to bless your . . . marriage," she said.

Her father solemnly offered me his hand.

Josie hugged each of her parents, and I saw in Hyman's gentle eyes a great love for his daughter, and in her mother, a sweet acceptance of the life Josie had chosen.

I had already said goodbye to Virgil and Warren, who shared Pine Street rooms while looking for sporting opportunities in the city on the bay, and now we were off for Gunnison, where I resolved to continue my faro game, it being the safest place until matters in Arizona cooled down and the warrant was forgotten.

We caught the Oakland ferry and boarded the Central Pacific eastbound. I immediately arranged with the conductor to trade our wicker coach seats for berths in a Pullman Palace Parlor Car, employing the cash Josie's mother had given us as her blessing.

The glistening parlor car was a wonder, with black

walnut paneling, plush red upholstered seats, lush drapery, a bunk that swung down from above, immaculate linens and blankets, and a fine ventilation and heating system that pumped comfortable air into each parlor. It was two cars away from the Pullman dining car. I felt like a dopey boy in a cathouse.

Josie and I were together at last as the train topped the Sierras, rattled down the east slope, crossed the great basin, and headed for Cheyenne, where we would detrain and go to Denver. That evening, after a fine filet mignon dinner, chosen from an amazing array of meals on the menu, we retired to our parlor, which the discreet Pullman porter had made ready, pulling down the upper bunk and converting the lower seats into the other bunk.

I had no intention of retiring to that upper bunk, and when Josie returned in her white wrapper from the women's lavatory, we made good use of the cramped lower berth, laughing through the night, as the car rocked eastward. The bunk was much too small for two, but that only improved the evening.

"I love you," she whispered, half asleep, all velvet in my arms.

"That's a hell of a thing to say," I replied.

She pouted. I had to wrestle the words out of me, because I don't like to confess to that sort of thing. "What you said, it's mutual," I whispered.

"You mean we both love you," she retorted, smartly.

"Ah . . . I guess you could say I feel the same about you."

"That's as close as you'll ever come to it," she said, sighing, "as far as you'll go, Wyatt." She laughed softly, and I was spared the romantic nonsense that afflicts most women.

We took rooms in Gunnison; I announced my presence to the constables there and set up my game. Those were sweet months, with Josie often present in the saloon in the evenings, where I kept a jealous eye on her, and eager to embrace me when we opened the dark door of our flat late at night. No one broke my slender faro bank, and we squeezed enough from the sourdoughs and miners to get along in that isolated burg. Those were good times but I kept myself heeled.

In May, I received a terse wire from Bat:

MEET ME IN PUEBLO. LUKE NEEDS HELP.

I hastily packed, patted Josie's ample behind, boarded the Denver and Rio Grande, and soon found myself in a quiet corner of a saloon in Pueblo, with my old friend Masterson.

"All hell's busted loose," he began as soon as we could order a schooner of lager apiece. "Luke's been kicked out of Dodge City."

"What?"

"It's a long, mean story," Bat said. "And we'll see about ending it our own way."

After leaving Tombstone, Luke Short had returned to Dodge City, run the gambling concession at the Long Branch, and eventually purchased the saloon from Chalk Beeson. Even though the days of the cattle drives had wound down, the saloon did a lively trade, fauceting booze into glasses, and emptying the pockets of boneheaded Texans. A lot of beef and a lot of drovers still arrived in Dodge, and that meant business for Luke.

Too much business, his rivals along Front Street decided. Mayor Ab Webster, who owned the competing Alamo Saloon, didn't like it. Luke's watering hole was too popular with Texas trail hands.

The city fathers thought the forthcoming election might solve the problem. Former marshal Larry Deger, no friend of mine, ran for mayor on a reform platform and won. His city council swiftly enacted scattergun ordinances against prostitution and vagrancy, and before the ink was dry on the parchment, the town cops stormed the Long Branch, pinched three of Luke's "singers," as the ladies were called, but didn't touch the sopranos in Webster's Alamo.

Short figured out the game, which smelled like a beached catfish. He did what he had to do, strapped on his artillery, marched on the jail to pay the fine and free the girls, thinking this was another sin tax, the routine method by which frontier towns financed themselves.

"And then the damnedest thing happened, Wyatt," Bat said. "The nervous town clerk, Hartman, saw Luke coming, and shot at him. He missed and Luke returned the compliment just as Hartman tripped and fell. Luke thought he'd finished the man."

I listened to this amazed.

"Poor Luke thought he'd done murder and barricaded himself in the Long Branch. But Deger persuaded him that Hartman hadn't been touched, and if he surrendered on a disturbing-the-peace charge, all would be settled. Luke did, but the lying bastards nailed him for assault, not disturbing the peace, fined him two grand, hustled him to the station, and gave

him his choice: he could go east or west. He and a
bunch of other saloon men. Deger and Webster and the
sheriff, George Hinckle, were cleaning out all of Webster's competition.

"That's an old story," I said.

"Luke went east to Kaycee, and wired me. I rode the
rails, and we held a little council of war. First I took
Luke's case to George Glick, the governor in Topeka,
who tried to straighten it out by mail, without much
luck. Those church deacons, Deger and Webster, and
the old Dodge crowd were intent on stealing the Long
Branch from Luke, and using town ordinances and
phony charges to do it. And all of Glick's threats to
send in the militia were simply brushed off with pious
responses saying nothing was wrong—the town was
just getting rid of undesirables."

All of this struck a nerve in me. Public officials who
abuse their trust for personal gain were an old story for
me, and the more Bat told, the hotter I got. Behan,
Deger, Webster—they were all abusing their offices.

"Is Luke all right?" I asked.

"He wants his saloon back. The Long Branch is the
prize money machine of Dodge, and he won't let it go
without a fight. That's why he wired me."

I could see that this was brewing into a little war,
and Bat confirmed it. Dodge, isolated on the west side
of the state, was ignoring Glick's threats, and Luke's
old pals would have to solve the problem their own
way.

"Luke is my friend. I'll back him any way, anyplace,
anytime," I said.

And so I committed myself.

By the time I was lassoed into it, Luke's whole recovery operation was well under way. I sat listening to Field Marshal Masterson, who was planning the assault in his own wily way.

"Reputations, that's what I want," Bat explained, over a second lager. "Reputations is what I've got."

"Such as?"

Bat had a puckish smile, which grew slowly over his square face, and now as he named names, the smile bloomed.

"You have to understand, I'm an inventive man," he began. "I enlisted Black Jack Bill, Dirty Sock Jack, Dynamite Sam, and a few more."

"Never heard of 'em."

"Deger and Webster and Hinkle think they have, and they've been wetting their pants."

"Who do you have?"

"How about you, Rowdy Joe Lowe, Charlie Bassett, Neal Brown, Johnny Millsap, Shotgun Collins, Texas Jack Vermillion, Crooked-Mouth Green . . . ?"

"That's a bunch. What'll I do?"

"Run the parade if you want to. We're collecting at Kingsley, near Dodge. Would you like to meet us there?"

I would, and I did.

I met Luke Short in Kingsley. He looked tired and determined.

"Luke, just one thing. We shouldn't start this war. If there's a fight, let them pull the trigger first," I said.

"I totally agree," Luke said. "We've got the governor with us for the moment, but that could change. I want my joint back and I want fair law enforcement. If they fine me for the girls, then let them fine Webster. If they ban the girls, ban them everywhere. I want you to run this."

"I'll run it. Maybe we can get it back. Meet me at the station and bring a shotgun."

Luke and I hopped the next local to Dodge and jumped off with shotguns in hand, hoping for surprise, but no one stopped us. We stood there, stared at the empty brick platform and the sleepy town, and I thought maybe we could do all this without much trouble.

"Damn it," Luke said. "The least they could do is put up some resistance."

Bat arrived the next day hefting a scattergun of his own. If you're going to fight at close quarters, that is the weapon of choice. By then, Deger and his crew had discovered us and were collecting just beyond buckshot range.

"Lay down them guns," Deger bellowed. "I'll treat you fair."

"Sorry, Larry. We're just the advance guard. Wait until you see the army," I said. "Luke's going to run his saloon again, and the law's going to be enforced evenly."

The new mayor studied me with a hooded gaze, and wheeled away.

I was by God ready. It was time to put Luke back in the Long Branch and time for them to leave him alone. They backed off for the moment, but now old Dodge brooded, and the threat of blood hung over the town.

They didn't quite get the message at first.

"We'll give Short ten days to sell, and then get out," Deger said at a parley on Front Street.

"I'll tell him," I replied. "But you know what the answer will be."

"I don't give a damn what his answer is."

That would never do, and before long, Deger and Webster were staring at some of the finest newly employed shootists in the West.

A dandy war was brewing, but I didn't like it. There could be big trouble for all of us. I still had a live warrant hanging over me; some of the others in our party were probably in the same shape. Some of those fellows across the street had attested to my character during the Spicer hearing and were old friends from the days when Dodge was baying at the moon. I figured enough was enough, and got both sides to palaver right in the redbrick middle of Front Street.

"I don't want a fight and neither do you," I told Deger. "You'll get hurt."

He nodded.

"Let's settle this," I said. "Luke returns to the Long Branch and the laws get enforced evenly."

Grudgingly, Deger and Webster shook hands with Luke Short, and even more grudgingly, they backed down, not liking the look of some of the most formidable men in the West, all armed, staring at them. I rather liked Texas Jack's get-up, with his Sharps rifle, bandolier loaded with shiny brass shells, bowie knife, twin pearly-gripped revolvers, and a rattlesnake hatband with an eagle feather tucked into it. We outnumbered the whole Dodge City and Ford County contingent, which helped.

They caved in. The war was over.

So it all came to nothing, but Bat always said that I had kept the peace by talking both sides into an agreement. That's what I've always tried to do, all my life. Luke was permitted to return to his splendid old Long Branch Saloon, which he ran for a little while more, until the cattle trade croaked, along with the great saloons along Front Street in old Dodge City, and the place became a market center for wheat ranchers, full of churches and ashamed of its past.

Chapter 36

We watched Doc shuffle through the gilded lobby of the Windsor Hotel in Denver, and I knew at once how it went with him.

He saw us and approached, his smile wide on a gaunt face. His threadbare clothing hung loose. He had always been thin but now he was skeletal. He was only thirty-five, but looked twice that.

He was about to greet us when a paroxysm of coughing stopped him cold, and he nearly bent double until the worst of it passed. When at last he straightened, there were speckles of fresh red on his handkerchief.

"Wyatt, Josie," he said, after catching his breath. "I had to see you. I heard you were in town."

We shook hands, and I felt the tremor in his.

"You're looking fine," he said, surveying us. "And I'm not," he added, sparing me a lie.

It was hard even to look at the man, so far had he slipped toward his reward. He sucked air as if he was starved for it, and was so breathless he could barely speak. Still, he was animated by a delight to be with us, and between his constant hack, and the droplets of blood that ended up in his rag, we caught up.

I steered him to a lobby divan.

He was running a game on Blake Street; he had been to Leadville, where he had gotten into one more shooting scrape, this time with an old enemy, a bartender ally of the Cowboys named Billy Allen, who took a bullet in the arm from Doc after threatening to kill him over a five-dollar debt Doc couldn't pay. Doc had witnesses who said it was justifiable self-defense, and that had ended the trouble. But Doc was a man with a reputation, and the magistrates threw him out of town. Tombstone still haunted him, but even more was he haunted by the legend, almost entirely false.

"I just had to see you this one time," Doc said.

"We had to see you too, Doc."

"I don't expect to see you again. Not for a long, long time," he said. "It's been fated that I should go first, and that time is not far off."

I hardly knew what to say to that, but it plainly was true.

"I hurt so much I can hardly get through a day," he said. "I hoped the air at Leadville would help, but it only made it worse. I guess old Holliday is running out of time."

"Is there anything I can do?" I asked.

He probably needed cash, and maybe I could help, but he shook his head. "I keep a game going. It's enough. I don't get many players, coughing the way I do, but I get enough."

He wheezed again, his whole thin body jerking as he convulsed, and I wondered how he could endure it.

He smiled suddenly. "A little whiskey, a little morphia when I can't stand it, and I get by. Long as I can pay for some laudanum." He dabbed at his watering eyes. "Now where have my old friend and his lovely lady been?"

We had been everywhere, from Coeur d'Alene to El Paso to Aspen, where I had entered into a partnership in a saloon deal. I told him about our ventures.

"I guess I know that," he said. "I keep track. I watch out for you, Wyatt." He coughed again, and turned to Josie. "I imagine you can count yourself a lucky woman."

She seemed oddly affected, and dabbed at her eyes. But so was I.

"And Wyatt's a fortunate man," he said.

"Oh, Doc," she whispered.

"And I'm a fortunate friend," he said. "Friends like you are a great gift."

He didn't stay, but hurried off, not wanting to spray us with the pieces of his bloody lungs. But I'll never forget his last handshake, when he gripped my hand as best he could, and for a moment his blue eyes flared to life, bright and clear.

"You're a hell of a fine friend, Wyatt," he said.

That was the last time we saw Doc. He died in Glenwood Springs, less than a year later. I have been to his grave two or three times. There's a simple headstone there that records the resting place of John Henry Holliday, and the dates of his birth and death. I believe his family placed it there.

Each time I visited I discovered fresh flowers there, red roses in season, sometimes fall flowers, or a wreath in winter. But always new and bright and sweet. I am sure I know who sends them. Her love for Doc transcended the grave. I like to think that sometime, in the mysterious sunlit meadows beyond the horizon, they will be together again.

Chapter 37

I never saw Tombstone again, but the city became the elephant in my life. That attempt to disarm some dangerous outlaws somehow caught the attention of the country, and I could never escape it. People knew my name, and to this day, people say, "You're Wyatt Earp!" And I don't know what I'm supposed to say to that.

It didn't change me one iota. Novelists, preachers, and other quacks like to say that a great crisis in a man's life transforms him, or they say that a man grows from adversity, but in my case they're wrong. My feelings, attitudes, and interests are just as they were before that day. I favor the sporting life, fine horseflesh, mining claims, speculations, first-class saloons, and boxing exhibitions, just as I did before I arrived in Tombstone.

I was not soured on law enforcement by what happened in Tombstone. I pinned on the badge in Idaho years later, and all my life I've worked as a security man, guarding mining claims, throwing out claim jumpers, tracking bandits or confidence men, just as I had before Tombstone. I employ surprise and force, just as I did before Tombstone. I still hate newspapers, which transformed me into an infamous man. I made use of my notoriety; nobody messed with me after that, so there was some good in it.

If I learned anything at all from that sojourn in Cochise County, it was simply that the press is more vicious than I had imagined, and since then I've been wary about blabbing to reporters, though I've done a little of that too when I trusted one. No bullet ever touched me, but lies and innuendos pretty near did me in, and that is why I've tried to polish things up a little in the years since then. I'm not a silky talker, like Behan, who says anything and gets it across. But look where all that smooth talking got him. I'd rather be a man of my word, and seal a deal with a handshake, than tonsil my way into hell, like him.

So I have the same damned character I started with, but it was tested by the things that befell me in Arizona. Some fool biographer would probably try to make a new and chastened person out of me, or he would claim that Tombstone was my baptism and I emerged a different sonofabitch, more mature, more cautious. Well, that's bunk. One thing that never changed is my reluctance to do violence. Up until then, I had avoided killing, and tried not to give any miscreant anything worse than a headache. Since then, I've done the same thing. Who have I shot since then?

Some will argue that I changed the moment I set after Frank Stilwell in Tucson, that I abandoned my belief in the rule of law and order, but I don't see it. The man was lurking in the station along with Ike Clanton, hunting for the chance to put a .44 caliber bullet into Virgil and me, and I will defend myself and my family anytime, anyplace, before Tombstone or after it. Self-defense is a lawful act.

The yellow press called it a vendetta, but I call it justice, and you have never heard me regret a minute of it. When there is no justice to be had in courts and public places, then a man must make his own justice. I am on the side of law, have always been, and always will be.

So I will tell anyone who asks me, I am Wyatt Earp, the same as before, and the same as the future. A man gets himself fashioned by his parents and what he learns and what he respects, and that is how I got chiseled into being me. And one can hunt through my interviews, hunt through my conduct from the days I walked a beat in Wichita to the times in Alaska to the years in Nevada and California, and find the same sonofabitch wherever you look.

There's been more bunk published about me than I can keep up with. Like the accounts that say I killed John Ringo down in Arizona in 1882, when I was in Colorado. I was nowhere near him when he or someone else popped a pill through his skull. I don't know what happened to him. Outlaws come to bad ends without half trying. He was melancholic, and maybe he decided to sip the hemlock without the help of anyone. He was a man without character, as limp as a wet tortilla; I never got a handle on who or what he was. He had more schooling than usual for a man in his profession, and that's as good a reason as any for suicide. In his line, when you start asking why you do it, you're a goner. He and Doc tangled a few times, mostly because they saw the other in themselves, the pair of them taunting death.

When I finally abandoned Arizona, I did so reluctantly because there were still some rough cobs around who had a hand in Morgan's murder. But one thing about outlaws: they live short and brutal lives. Ringo lasted a few months. Ike Clanton a few years before getting himself killed by a detective. Billy Claiborne, who always toiled hard at getting himself slaughtered, soon succeeded when he provoked Buckskin Frank Leslie, the finest man with a six-gun in the West, into a shootout, and then, as Billy lay dying, he discovered that Buckskin Frank deserved his reputation. And Len Redfield, who had harbored Luther King after the Benson stage robbery, was hanged in Florence, Arizona, in 1883, by a mob who thought he was a stagecoach robber and murderer. Fin Clanton and Pete Spence wound up in that hottest of all places, the territorial prison at Yuma, convicted of assorted felonies.

As for the honorable John Behan, he didn't last, either. In the next election he was up against seven other sheriff candidates in the Democrat column and puffed in last. A Republican won. Tombstone was sick of Behan and his ring. Maybe the Earps weren't popular there, given the diatribes of the local press, but the Democrat party, and then the voters, had more than enough of the sheriff who had coddled outlaws, formed posses out of their ranks, allowed his punk friends to walk out of jail, and soaked the county. He ended up a warden at Yuma, which amused my friends. Several of Behan's old pals were frying on the other side of the bars, but it didn't matter which side one was on: Yuma was the Arizona version of hell.

So my enemies swiftly fell by the wayside. But that don't mean that I wasn't cautious. For years I stayed heeled, and still do as a matter of habit, because I expected one or another of them to show up anytime, anyplace, to finish what had been started with the murder of Morgan and the attempt on Virgil.

Now Mattie. That wasn't her real name, of course. It was the name she used in Bessie's parlor house. She was born Celia Ann Blaylock, and I guess she was sorry she ever was born, the way her life spun out. I guess I'd better say a word about her, though it isn't anything I'm keen to talk on. I pity the poor woman. I paid her freight back to Arizona and turned over some property, but she couldn't redeem it for the taxes on it. Next I knew, she was whoring in Globe, and then she took her life, having gotten tired of it, and dosed herself with laudanum.

I asked myself a few times whether there was something in me that drove her to the red-eye, to the trips to the Chinaman, to the addictions. I don't know, and would regret it. Allie, Virgil's woman, always thought so. She blamed me. I pulled Mattie out of Bessie's cathouse, but that was when she was still a girl and before she got half acclimated to that life, and if anything, I gave her a chance.

But there are some who throw chances away, some who doom themselves from the get-go, and she was one. I gave her a few extra years. That's how I look at it. If she had stayed in the life instead of hooking up with me, she would have died by her own hand that much younger. I don't know how she was brought up; she never much discussed her family, the Blaylocks, but it must have been pretty sorry.

I've never strayed from Josephine since then, though we've not had an easy time. Every once in a while she gets respectable, and I can't even crawl into her bed. That's when she's Mrs. Wyatt Earp, and tells friends I'm a banker or a stockbroker or a mining man or investor. But it never lasts. When she gets tired of being proper, or bored with it, she seduces me. That's how I know she's ready to roam again, when her kisses are sweet as honey.

She's wandered the whole West with me, but she's happiest in San Francisco, her home, where she can be close to her family. Unlike Mattie, she laughs and has a good time, and when I am occasionally blue, she perks me right up. Somewhere along the way I noticed that her family called her Sadie, and I asked her what she preferred and she said Sadie, so that's what I call her, but inside of me she's still Josie, and she still brings a smile to me every time I see her. I can't keep her home, even if I were to try. If I'm at the track running my race-horses, she packs up and comes with me, and that's the way it should be between any woman and Wyatt Earp.

I've gotten to know a few movie people, and they ask me all sorts of questions about the Old West, very respectful, so they can put it down on celluloid. But they never get it right. They all swagger too much, and play the scene for all the killing they can show on film, men walking toward each other down a dusty street, like some damned duel, one man faster than the other.

I always tried to avoid that, and so did Virgil, and just about any other frontier marshal or lawman, including my friend Bat Masterson. If the filmmakers want to know what's what about the Old West, all they have to do is remember that the Earps were shot in the back.

But I don't mind them buzzing around me in Los Angeles, and I don't mind going to their shindigs, where they show me off like some prize antique. I'm the man who survived the shootout at the OK Corral. I'm the man who killed forty, maybe fifty, outlaws. I'm the man who walked into a barrage of bullets and never was scratched. I'm the man who tamed a town or two.

That's what they say. Between trips to the bathroom, I just nod and smile. Just nod and smile.

Author's Notes

In recent years, gifted Tombstone historians have conducted a massive search for primary source material that might shed light on the events of the 1880s involving the Earp brothers and their adversaries. The result was amazing: from libraries and newspaper morgues and museum collections, there came a flood of new material in the 1990s that has clarified what we know about those legendary events.

In addition, scholars have subjected existing sources to close analysis, to ascertain how much of it is consistent and true, and these analyses have also deepened our grasp of events in Tombstone, and thrown doubt upon the validity of some sources.

The research of such people as Jeff Morey and Robert Palmquist has supported the publication of two splendid histories of that period, one by Allen Barra, the other by Casey Tefertiller. I have drawn upon this new material, some of it generously sent to me by Robert Palmquist, to draw my fictional Wyatt Earp.

I hoped that in writing a novel about Wyatt Earp, I might be able to quicken a legendary figure. While I have stayed reasonably close to historical events, I have tried to flesh out the characters and supply motivations that historians can only guess at. And I have discarded much of the stiff nineteenth-century dialogue I found in the record, in part because I don't believe people spoke to one another that way. I don't believe, for example, that in the middle of the fierce OK Corral fight,

Wyatt Earp announced to Ike Clanton, "The fight has commenced. Go to fighting or get away." I reduced that to: "Then get out."

I am particularly indebted to Tucson lawyer and scholar Robert Palmquist for his generous encouragement and assistance. He sent me the original Josephine Earp manuscript, known as the Cason typescript, along with the Forrestine Hooker manuscript, uncovered by Jeff Morey and Richard Buchen of the Southwest Museum in Los Angeles, and other vital papers.

He alerted me to other new treasures, such as the Clara Brown correspondence. All during that period in Tombstone, this gifted reporter, the wife of a mining engineer, was acting as a stringer for the *San Diego Tribune*, sending that paper balanced, penetrating, and invaluable letters about events in Tombstone. Researcher Jeff Morey finally uncovered them as well as the unpublished Hooker manuscript, which was a biography of Earp drawn from interviews with him and Hooker family sources.

For those interested in pursuing Tombstone history, I can recommend several books. One is Allen Barra's warm and beautifully wrought *Inventing Wyatt Earp: His Life and Many Legends*, published by Carroll and Graf in 1998. Another is the massive and exhaustive *Wyatt Earp: The Life Behind the Legend* by Casey Tefertiller, published in 1997 by John Wiley & Sons. Another valuable work is Paula Mitchell Marks's *And Die in the West*, published in 1989 by William Morrow. This book appeared too early to take advantage of the new source material as well as recent scholarly criticism of known sources, and now is rather dated.

—Richard S. Wheeler
September 2003